Knowing Isn't Everything

A summer of despair, love and happiness

Maggie Rogers

Published by Maggie Rogers

Copyright Maggie Rogers 2025

This is a work of fiction. Names, characters, places, and incidents are products of the author's imagination or are used fictitiously and should not be construed as real. Any resemblance to actual events, locales, organisations or persons, living or dead, is entirely coincidental.

All rights reserved. This book or any portion thereof may not be reproduced or used in any manner whatsoever without the express written permission of the publisher except for the use of brief quotations in a book review.

Thanks go to

Sue Horrocks for proofreading several draft copies. All my friends in the Nailsworth writers' group. My husband Terry for his support and encouragement. Matt Maguire from Candescent Press for typesetting and the cover design.

Chapter 1

My heart sank as I pulled into the drive. Not because Aunt Ruth's car was there. No, it was my sister Rachel's pristine Volvo that nearly made me turn round and drive back home. Why were they here? Why was I here, come to that! I didn't need to be, but there was something unusual in Mother's request. Just getting a request to see her was unusual, and discovering Ruth and Rachel were both here, I felt even more uneasy. Was it a special day? Had I missed something? I sat for a few moments wracking my brain, my hands gripped around the steering wheel. It wasn't the anniversary of Dad's death, that date was imprinted on my heart, and nothing else was as important.

I got out of the car. At least my two little nieces would be a distraction, if Rachel had brought them with her. Rachel was less acerbic when they were with her. I went to the front door and rang the bell. Going round the back and in through the kitchen door felt too informal. I didn't live here anymore, and even when I did it never felt like home.

'Anna, why do you always have to make an entrance? Couldn't you just come round the back like other people?'

'Hello Mother, sorry I thought…' but she'd already turned and marched back along the hall.

I followed, knowing I couldn't win; she would have given me one of her, how dare you be so presumptive looks, if I'd walked straight into the kitchen. Ruth jumped to her feet and gave me a hug, and, as always in her company, I relaxed a little. I could see Rachel in the garden playing swing ball with her daughters. She glanced towards the house but didn't come in. I desperately wanted to know why I and the others had been summoned, but didn't want to give mother the satisfaction of knowing I was curious, so I didn't ask.

'I'll make a pot of tea. There won't be much else. I wasn't expecting everyone.'

This surprised me, but the fact that a cake or biscuits would have been made, if she'd known it was going to be more than just me, didn't surprise me in the least. I turned to Ruth and raised a questioning eyebrow.

'It seemed Rachel and the children, and me, were all just passing and we all decided to call in.' Ruth answered my look with a raised eyebrow of her own. 'Carrie said you were coming round, so I waited to see you.'

'She said she wanted to see me,' I replied. Ruth nodded, and I had a strange feeling she knew why. Before we could talk anymore Rachel came in followed by the children, who pushed past her and ran to hug me. The children's excitement glossed over Rachel's cold hello. I didn't see them often and felt moved, and surprised, by their genuine pleasure at seeing me.

Tea, thanks to Ruth, was convivial. Mother, despite what she had said, rustled up some cupcakes and biscuits, which were demolished by the children. I couldn't bring myself to eat anything. Knowing what Mother wanted from me remained a mystery and I was thinking I might just be able to leave without hearing whatever it was, which I doubted would be anything favourable. Within minutes of putting down her cup, Rachel rounded up the children, hugged Ruth, nodded at me, reminded mum about lunch at her house the following day, and was gone. I willed Ruth not to go, but almost before the thought formed, she was on her feet.

'Let me clear these up before I go,' she said, and picked up the tray and, followed by mother, went into the kitchen.

I was alone in the sitting room. It had been painted since I moved out, but most of the furniture and the carpet were still the same. A new sofa, pale green with beige squiggles, replaced the two comfy old chairs, but that was all. The curtains weren't new, they were beige with large green flowers, which as a child always reminded me of cabbages. They still did. The fresh paint was pale green, but not quite the right shade for the curtains. Just being there made me shudder. I stood up and looked at the large array of family photos arranged on the sideboard. Rachel's wedding, the girls, one of Mum and Dad, and my all-time favourite, one of Dad laughing on a beach somewhere. None of me. There never were any of me, but somehow today it felt like a slap in the face. I picked Dad's picture up and heard movement and voices from the kitchen. I was sure I heard Ruth ask if Mother wanted her to stay. I didn't hear the reply, but seconds later they both came back into the room.

'I'm off Anna, give me a ring sometime. Take care.' She kissed me and squeezed my hand as if trying to convey a message. I looked at her, but she just smiled and turned to kiss mother. 'See you soon, Carrie. Bye.'

Chapter 2

The silence after Ruth left the room seemed almost unbearable. I turned to put Dad's photo down, when Mum said. 'That's what I wanted to talk to you about, Anna.'

'What?' I was confused. What did she want to talk to me about? It couldn't be about a photograph, could it?

She bristled at my 'what' but instead of a reprimand gave a small, confusing smile and patted my arm.

'Sit here,' she said, with an almost imperceptible inclination of her head, and a twitch of her small bird-like hand. I'd often thought of her as some sort of malevolent bird, peck, peck, pecking away at my very soul.

I sat on the new sofa, and she perched in the chair opposite. Before she sat down, she smiled again. At least her mouth formed the shape of a smile, but her eyes seemed to forget. I struggled to return any form of facial expression and shuffled on the sofa. One simple gesture couldn't wipe away so many years of ill feeling.

'I've got something I need to tell you, she said, pausing for dramatic effect and smiling again.

I waited. A knot formed in my stomach, but I stayed calm, outwardly at least. I hoped whatever it was, she would get to the point soon. Every part of me wanted to leave, but I was also curious, and a little afraid.

'You know that you're adopted?'

I nodded. Of course I knew. Why was she bringing that up now? Where was this going?

'Well, your father,' she nodded towards the photo I'd been holding. 'He was your real father,' she said this without taking her eyes away from mine. Waiting for a reaction.

I must have looked blank, so she continued.

'He wasn't your adoptive father, he was your...' she searched for the word. 'He was your *biological* father,' she said, emphasizing biological, making it sound like a dirty word, just to make sure I understood her meaning.

I understood the words, but my brain couldn't process the meaning of the information quickly enough. When I was told I was adopted, I'd just assumed that meant neither of them were my actual parents. Thoughts swirled around in a blizzard of mayhem. If dad was my real father, who was my mother, where was my mother? I was formulating questions to ask when she spoke again.

'When we adopted you, I thought I couldn't have a baby of my own.'

I knew this, of course, and like so many couples, once they adopted, a pregnancy soon followed.

'And then you had Rachel,' I said, interrupting her.

'This isn't about Rachel.' A familiar note of annoyance crept into her voice. 'It's about you,' she said in a softer tone. 'I should have told you before, but, well, it's difficult.'

'Why are you telling me now?' that was probably the least important question I wanted to ask, but something in the way she was speaking made me realise it was significant.

Frustratingly, she shrugged her shoulders, 'I thought it was about time.'

I knew there was more to it, but also knew better than to ask, instead I asked the question that was burning inside me.

'Who is my real mother?' I clenched my hand until my nails were digging into my palms.

She didn't answer. I wanted to shake her. How dare she withhold information like this, and now sit there with a smile, no, it wasn't a smile, it was an unreadable expression on her face, keeping me waiting for an answer.

'She died long ago. That's why you came to us. I thought all babies were the same, that I could love you. You were too young to know any different and your father was desperate to have you so…'

'Who is my mother?' I asked again, trying hard to suppress the tremor in my voice.

She looked at me. 'I tried to love you, I wanted to, but every time I looked at you, I saw her.'

'Saw who? Who is she?' I asked, desperate to know, but a feeling of anger bubbled up as I realised mother was enjoying the drama of the moment and wanted to string it out. I wondered how many times she'd rehearsed this conversation. She was toying with me like a cat with a mouse, provoking me to react.

Tucking my hands between my legs, I stared at her. I remembered her covert pinches and less hidden slaps when no one was around, and the outrageous favouritism towards Rachel that was apparent only to me. Did I hate her? I wasn't sure. As a young child I didn't love her, and became a sullen, deceitful teenager, at least in her presence. Now, as an adult, I spent as little time as possible alone in her company. Did I hate her? I wondered again. I thought I did, but the knowledge didn't make me feel good.

She remained quiet. I stood up. Enough was enough. She looked alarmed; this wasn't in her plan.

'I'm going.'

'Her name was Deborah.'

I stopped; I was about to sit back down. I wanted, more than anything, to know all about her, but didn't want to give Mother the satisfaction of knowing how eager I was. Before I moved towards the door, mother stood up.

'I don't like talking about her. It distresses me.'

'Why did you start then?'

She didn't answer, just stared at me for a few moments, then said,

'She was a friend of Ruth's. Ask her if you want to know more.'

'I will, without question. I want to know everything.'

With that, I left. I knew my sudden departure would antagonise her, but I couldn't stay one minute longer. By the time I reached my car, I was shaking from head to foot. She didn't appear at either the door or window as I drove away. I tortured myself with the thought I should have stayed. She was ready to talk, to tell me vital information; I just walked away. Now I might never know all the details. I just had to hope that Ruth could fill in the gaps.

All the way home, I turned her words over in my mind. Who was Deborah? Why had she told me now? That was the question I couldn't answer. She'd had my whole life to tell me, so why now? The thought that Dad was my real dad sent a warm glow through me but made his absence even more acute. I wondered why he had said nothing. As far as I could remember, he never even dropped a hint, or if he did, it went over my head.

Chapter 3

The phone rang, not my mobile, the landline; I raised myself up on my elbow, then sank back down onto the pillow. Let it ring. I had an intense feeling it would be mother, and I didn't want to answer, just in case it was her. I looked at my clock. My alarm would be going off any minute, and with that, the shrilling alarm joined in with the ringing of the phone. I reached out and turned the alarm off, but the phone kept ringing. There's something about phones that trigger an almost automatic impulse to get up and answer them, but I forced myself not to react. I pulled the duvet over my ears trying to block out the sound, but it didn't work. It still penetrated my brain, setting my nerves on edge. I couldn't understand why the answerphone hadn't clicked in, but it was unreliable.

Irritated, I threw the covers off. I needed to get up anyway or I would be late for work. I walked into the sitting room and, just as my resolve was wavering, the ringing stopped. The following silence was almost more deafening, and I tortured myself wondering who it could have been. I put on the radio and turned it up loud, mainly to drown out my thoughts. The phone sat accusingly on the shelf next to an equally accusing letter that had arrived in the post yesterday. That was an unusual event; apart from birthday and Christmas cards, I couldn't remember the last time a letter with a handwritten envelope had been delivered. I didn't want to open it, at least not yet. I turned my back on both the letter and the phone and hurriedly made myself some toast and tea and took them back into my bedroom, where I munched it as I made the bed, careless of crumbs on the sheets, which was something I hated. I showered, put on some makeup and left for work without entering the living area again and seeing the offending items.

My day at work was exceptionally busy; a nurse was off sick, making us short staffed, so there was little time for thinking about anything beyond the immediate priorities. Once we'd allocated the routine clinics, I scrubbed up to help the senior vet in the operating theatre. Here concentration was essential. I admired her skill as she carefully removed a tumour from a fourteen-year-old Labrador's leg. We knew this was the last chance to save his leg and at his age, to save his life. His owner, an older man in his own right, was sitting in the waiting room. I couldn't persuade him to go home and wait to be called after the operation. So, he sat there drinking tea, provided by the receptionist, in a cloud of tense anxiety waiting for news about his best friend.

At last, the operation was over and was successful. I slipped out of surgery to tell the owner while the vet prepared for her next patient. I sat beside him and instinctively took his hand.

'Sandy's going to be all right.' I smiled up at him as tears trickled down his life worn face.

'I know I'm being silly,' he said. 'But Sandy's my life since my wife died.'

I eventually persuaded him to go home, now that Sandy was out of danger. We would keep the old dog in for a couple of days, and the old man couldn't sit in the waiting room all that time.

'It'll be awful quiet at home without him,' he smiled as he stood up. His face wearing a sad, resigned expression.

I promised we would ring with updates and told him he could call us anytime. I wondered, as I watched him leave, how on earth he would cope when the inevitable happened. His obvious grief for his wife and love for his dog for some reason made me think of the envelope sitting next to the phone at home. I shook my head to get rid of the image; that was different I told myself, and rushed back into surgery to assist the vet with another operation.

At lunchtime, now staffed with the full afternoon shift of nurses on duty, I sat munching on a sandwich and relaxing for a few minutes, when my phone rang. It was Aunt Ruth and much as I wanted to; I knew I couldn't refuse a call from Ruth.

'Anna! Hi, sorry to call you at work. I know it's difficult, but your mum is seriously ill. I thought she was going to tell you, but I …' Ruth didn't say she knew I'd left before mother could explain everything. 'It would really help if you could come up.'

There was a pause.

'Help who?' I asked, knowing how mean and small-minded I must sound.

There was another pause.

'Everyone, but I think it would help you most, in the future, I mean. There's not much time left.'

This time, the pause was longer, while an inner battle ensued inside me.

'OK. I'll come up at the weekend.'

'That might be too late. Could you come now?'

'Now? I'm at work.'

A colleague, who couldn't help but overhear, tapped my arm and mouthed 'go', flapping her arm towards the door.

'Are you sure?' I put my hand over the phone and looked at my colleague. She nodded.

'OK. I'll be with you in a couple of hours.'

I heard Ruth let out an audible sigh of relief.

'Thank you, Anna. See you soon. Drive carefully. Come to me first.'

Ruth hugged me when I arrived at her flat, but instead of

asking me in, steered me towards her car. She seemed on edge and was in a hurry to leave.

'What's wrong with her?' I asked as we sped along the road. Was it as urgent as Ruth seemed to think? After all, it wasn't so long ago, I'd seen her, and she didn't seem too bad then. It hadn't even crossed my mind then that she might be ill.

'Ovarian cancer. Her diagnosis was about six months ago. I think she must have had it for much longer, but she kept quiet about any symptoms, and didn't go to the doctor. So, who knows for how long, and now it's too late. She didn't want anyone to know, not even Rachel.'

'How long…?' I asked and guessed her illness was the reason she'd told me about my mother now.

'They said hours, maybe a day or two, but that was yesterday. That's why I wanted you to come straight away.'

The crack in Ruth's voice as she told me, surprised me. She kept her eyes on the road, and I noticed her hands tighten on the wheel. I don't know why I felt surprised. They were sisters, and I knew they were close. I said nothing. I couldn't think of anything reasonable to say. There was only one thing I wanted to ask Ruth about, but I knew now was not the right time.

Chapter 4

When we arrived at the hospice, Ruth was out of the car and moving towards the door almost before I put my feet on the ground. She looked round urging me to hurry, and I hastened to catch her up. A lady sitting at a small desk in the bright, pretty reception area greeted Ruth warmly. We both signed the visitor register, then once again Ruth was off, down a long corridor, with me close behind. Pushing open one door she and ushered me inside. Ruth went over to Mother and kissed her forehead.

'Anna's here Carrie.'

Mother nodded.

'Come on Rachel, let's give Anna a couple of minutes.'

Rachel, who was sitting by the side of the bed holding mother's hand, glared at me. She leant and kissed her, then followed Ruth out of the room.

The silence felt oppressive. I glanced around. A low, mullioned window overlooked the grounds, and the wide sill was full of roses and freesias, releasing a heavy scent as the afternoon sun warmed their delicate blooms. I assumed the flowers were from Ruth and Rachel and again felt my apartness from the family. It was an attractive, welcoming room, comfortably furnished, like a hotel, though less formal. Not a bad place to die, I thought, turning my attention back to my mother. I didn't know why Ruth thought I needed time alone with her. I had nothing to say.

Mother's eyes were closed, but she didn't look peaceful.

Someone had brushed her pale brown hair into a fluffy halo around her head, giving the illusion of softening her pinched features, in a way that her usual coiffure could never achieve. Her skin looked pale, almost yellow, and under her eyes were dark rings.

She opened her eyes and looked intently into mine,

'I'm sorry,' she said.

I don't know what I was expecting her to say, but an apology wasn't high on the list.

I sat quietly and waited for her to say more.

'I did try; it was just…' her voice trailed off.

I felt sure that whatever was coming next, it would be my fault.

'I should have told you about your dad before.'

'Why didn't you?'

She looked at me, not with the usual reproving stare, but a sad, almost, or so I thought, gentle expression on her face. Then she shrugged,

'I just couldn't bring myself to,' she whispered under her breath.

'I was just a child,' I said, anger welling up inside me.

I could hear the murmur of conversation as people walked in the gardens below the window; perhaps it was Ruth and Rachel. I wished I was out there, anywhere other than this room.

'I'm so very sorry,' she said again, but this time I doubted the sincerity of her apology. Was it something about her tone, or was I being mean?

I looked at her ashen face. She was not an old woman, but today she could have passed for an eighty-year-old. I wondered if she really wanted to make her peace with me before she died, or did she just want to see the hurt in my eyes one more time. Perhaps I was too cynical. She looked at me, with an unreadable expression. Did she deserve an ounce of my forgiveness just because she was dying? All sorts of thoughts raced through my mind. If only I had known before, so many questions would have been answered. Her hand twitched on the bedcover, and I wondered if I should take hold of it. What was the point of bearing a grudge at this last stage in her life? I was about to reach out towards her when she moved her hand away.

'Well?' she said.

'Well, what?' I'd heard that tone before, as a child, when she wanted an explanation about some supposed misdemeanour.

'I said I'm sorry. Don't you have anything to say to me?'

'I don't know. I'm sorry you're ill. What do you want me to say?' Our eyes burned into each other, and I knew she was about to make another hurtful comment. 'I just can't understand why you didn't tell me about dad before. Why did you adopt me if you didn't want me?'

She paused for a while, looking straight into my eyes, then said,

'I knew your father would never forgive me if I didn't, and I couldn't lose him.' Her voice was again little more than a whisper. I tried to imagine what must have gone on and began to feel a twinge of sympathy. Once again, I thought about reaching for her hand, but she spoke, more loudly this time.

'You were a blight on my marriage, on my happiness. Every time I looked at you, I was reminded about... I wanted you to suffer, like you made me suffer.'

I couldn't quite believe what I'd heard. Had I heard right? Heat rose inside my body and my heart was thumping. Did she just say what I thought she'd said? Why had I come here, just to be further abused in her dying breath? No, her voice rang clear in my ears, and I refused to give her the pleasure of saying it again, by asking her to repeat it. She repeated it anyway,

'I wanted you to suffer. Just like your daily presence made me suffer.'

'I was a child. I wasn't responsible for how I came into the world.'

'A child, maybe, but you weren't my child.' She looked at me and her chest moved, jerking up and down, and it became obvious for some unfathomable reason she was laughing, her mouth a gaping hole. Not a happy laugh, but a sound that bore into the core of my being.

Fury consumed every part of my body. I leapt to my feet and, without even thinking, whipped my scarf from round my neck and stuffed it into her open, smirking mouth. She didn't resist. Then I whirled round, pressed the advance button, at least once, on her syringe driver before grabbing my scarf and striding out of the room without a backward glance.

Chapter 5

Some moments later, screwing my scarf into a tight ball and pushing it to the bottom of my bag, I walked out into the warmth of the afternoon; the sun dazzled my eyes and blurred my vision, matching my thought processes, which were shaken by the recent revelations and events. I walked across the manicured lawn and sat on a wooden seat, stared unseeing into space. I couldn't stop trembling and pushed my hands between my legs to stop them shaking. What had I just done? I couldn't let the images form in my mind. It was too awful, but they kept pushing their way to the front. 'You just killed your mother' a little voice whispered from the back of my mind. I put my head in my hands and sat waiting for something to happen, for what felt like a long time.

What happened next was not what I expected. Happy and somewhat inappropriate, or so I thought, loud shouts and shrieks of two young children running around on the grass infiltrated my thoughts. I looked at them, about to form a disapproving expression on my face, when I noticed a young woman in a wheelchair and a man, who I assumed to be her husband, beside her. I watched, fascinated, my own worries quashed for a moment. She must be the patient and therefore dying, otherwise she wouldn't be here. I could see a discreetly stowed catheter bag in a rack under her seat. She wore a blue spotted dress with a white cardigan around her shoulders; even from this distance, I could see she was painfully thin. She wore a white cotton sunhat, and I wondered if she had lost her hair. The children were throwing a soft ball to each other.

'Catch, Mummy!' one of them shouted, throwing the ball towards the wheelchair.

She laughed and held out her hands, but the ball fell to the floor and rolled along the grass. When she looked up, a smile of dignified serenity crossed her face.

Her husband retrieved the ball and threw it back to the children. As he turned, I could see his face was etched with worry and concern. The woman looked up at him and reached for his hand.

'You'll manage,' she whispered, so the children couldn't hear, but in the peaceful surroundings, I could hear her clearly. 'I know you will. You're strong. Don't let them forget me.' She looked towards the children and smiled.

He knelt on the floor and buried his head in her lap, and I imagined he was crying. She stroked his hair with such tenderness I did not dare breathe in case I shattered their moment of intimacy.

'Daddy, what are you doing? Come and play,' their small son broke the moment, and I breathed again.

I was sure they were unaware of my presence, and I didn't move. I didn't want to attract their attention. My heart went out to them, the man in particular. He was the one who would be left bereft and trying to cope with two little ones. I wasn't too familiar with children, but guessed these two were about four or five years old. Their happy innocence was heartbreaking and their dad, in contrast, must be fully aware that he, and they, were in for a tough time. They wandered away, treasuring their last moments as a family, and I watched them with an odd feeling of envy.

The image of the old man in the surgery waiting for news of his beloved dog came into my mind. There was so much love in the world, but at that moment, I felt as though every ounce had passed me by. The young family and the old man, they would all have treasured memories. I didn't let myself think about what I would have.

Left alone once again, I tried to think, but nothing made sense anymore. I would just wait. I felt sure any minute now the sound of sirens and police rushing across the lawn to arrest me would break the silence. I don't know how long I sat on the bench. No one else ventured into the garden; it was a haven of peace, and I felt I never wanted to leave, to re-enter reality. I stared at the trees swaying gently in the light breeze and the birds hopping on the lawn or perching on the edge of an old stone birdbath to drink.

The warmth of the day was seeping away when I noticed Ruth walking round the side of the building. I knew she was looking for me, but I didn't move. She scanned the garden and, spotting me, she quickened her pace and flopped onto the seat next to me.

'She's gone,' she said. 'It was very peaceful. I'm so pleased we made it back to her in time.' Ruth stared out across the gardens at the pattern of long shadows now dancing across the lawn. 'I thought about looking for you, but I didn't want to, well, you know, not be there. The nurse looked in the visitor's room.'

'That's OK,' I said, surprised Ruth wasn't saying more. I knew there was nothing I wanted less than to be in that room again. Self-pity again overwhelmed me. Mother and Ruth had that elusive bond of love, and Rachel, of course. I wanted to scream, but I didn't. Instead, I took a deep breath and reached for Ruth's hand.

'Was Rachel there?' I asked.

'Yes, she is very upset. She's gone home now. She'll ring tomorrow.'

I nodded again. Rachel, my newly acknowledged, not by her, of course, half-sister, rather than adopted sister, would not have relished my presence at her mother's bedside.

'I think she hung on until she could speak to you,' Ruth said.

At first, I thought Ruth was referring to Rachel and took a couple of seconds to realise it was mother she was talking about.

'Are you sure?'

'Yes, I'm sure. She was adamant she needed to see you. That's why I rang you at work. It was important. She seemed quieter after speaking to you. In fact, she never roused again. The doctor said it happened a lot. People wait for close relatives to arrive and just give in to death after they've said their last goodbye,' Ruth paused and smiled. 'Thank you for coming and listening to her, Anna.' She squeezed my hand.

I felt hot and uncomfortable, but I said nothing. My heart was pounding. Maybe Mother never roused, and the doctor suspected nothing. I felt sick, and started shivering all over and then, to my horror, I burst into tears.

'Oh, poor you, Anna.' Ruth pulled me into her arms and patted my back while I sobbed onto her shoulder. After a few minutes, she moved, wiped some tears from her own face and tried to smile. 'Come on, let's go, it's getting chilly. You will stay with me for a while, won't you? At least for tonight?'

I nodded. There were too many unanswered questions for me to leave now, and the last thing I wanted was to be on my own. My mind brimmed with confusion. Ruth tucked her arm through mine, and we walked back around the building to the car park in silence.

Chapter 6

In the end, I stayed with Ruth for several days, most of which went by in a haze of information about my actual mother and funeral arrangements for my adopted mother. No one commented about the circumstances of her death, and I decided, whether it was right or wrong, to bury my guilty secret.

Ruth and Rachel made all the decisions about the funeral. I just agreed to whatever they suggested. I didn't feel it was my place to interfere, or even voice an opinion, and they accepted that. The strangest decision to be made was what we wanted mother to be dressed in. I was surprised when the undertaker asked. After all, she was going to be cremated so I couldn't see it mattered, but Rachel agonised for ages over which dress would be best, even once asking for my opinion, as if I would have one. Every time the phone rang, I froze, expecting it to be someone saying that the funeral couldn't go ahead because of suspicion over her death. It never happened.

The funeral was arranged for early the following week, so I stayed with Ruth. The speed of the ceremony was to do with the undertaker's schedule, or some such thing, but from my point of view, the sooner the better.

The number of people who attended the funeral surprised me. Mother must have been more popular than I imagined. For the first time, I wondered who she was, beyond being a malevolent presence in my childhood. I had never thought of her as a person with interests and friends. One or two faces I recognised, but the majority were strangers to me, although not to Rachel.

Ruth spoke during the service, of the fun-loving sister who she would miss seeing on a regular basis. A well dressed, not unattractive man in his sixties also spoke. He was a close acquaintance, or even more, of Mother's and spoke of his devastation at losing such a close friend at a time when there was so much to look forward to. I looked enquiringly at Ruth, and she leant close to whisper that he and Carrie were just good friends, but he was hoping to become more. Rachel turned round and glared at us through red-rimmed eyes, for daring to talk. Ruth mouthed 'Sorry' towards her, but I ignored her. I assumed from Ruth's implication that mother's feelings were less certain about taking the relationship further.

Someone else read a passage from the Bible, and I began to feel restless, suffocated by the overpowering, grieving emotions I could not share. It felt as though I was at the funeral of a stranger. I didn't recognise the bright, caring person they were talking about. It was only when the vicar, in his address, mentioned mum's two loving daughters, Anna and Rachel, that I was connected to the funeral in any way. I squirmed at the irony and had an inward, wry smile to myself at being described as loving.

I wondered what all these people knew about me, or whether mother mentioned me at all. An overwhelming sadness swept over me, but I wasn't sure if I was just sorry for myself or sorry for not knowing, or even liking, the woman whose life we were commemorating.

The funeral wake passed by in a blur. More people, strangers, kept commiserating with me, as if they knew me. It was odd, but so far in my thirty-four years I had avoided going to any funerals, except dad's. This entire event felt contrived and otherworldly. The transition from the solemn service at the crematorium to what now felt like a party was disorientating.

Rachel appeared to be in her element, hugging everyone in sight, seeming to know all about them, and vice versa. The man who spoke was also, it appeared, a familiar visitor to Rachel's family and a friend of her husband, Jim. They all appeared to be sharing a joke and were laughing heartily. He shook my hand and said how pleased he was to meet me at last, and was sorry it was on such a sad occasion. I nodded but just wanted to get out, to be on my own.

As soon as was decent, I made my excuses. Ruth already knew I would go back to my house after the funeral and understood my haste.

'Take care, Anna. I'll try to find more answers about Debbie for you.'

'Thank you for everything, Ruth.' I hugged her and knew I would miss her.

'Keep in touch,' Ruth called as I drove away.

I drove round the corner, parked the car and burst into tears of loneliness, fear and self-pity.

Chapter 7

I drove home on autopilot. My mind was all over the place, focusing on aspects of the last few days. No matter how hard I tried to suppress the thoughts, they surfaced again. It took me a few moments to register that the blue, flashing lights behind me were following at my speed. My first instinct was to put my foot down and accelerate away, but sense prevailed, and I carried on. The police car, once the driver realised that I was aware of them, overtook and indicated for me to pull over onto the hard shoulder.

I stopped the car, my hands clinging onto the steering wheel. I felt numb, and my heart was pounding fit to burst. There could only be one reason the police were stopping me. I felt sick. A tapping on the passenger side window made me jump. A police officer was leaning down looking through at me. He indicated for me to open it. I pressed the button and as the window slid down, the wave of nausea swelled inside me.

'Afternoon, Miss. Would you mind turning the engine off and sliding across to get out of this side of the car.' It wasn't a question.

I fumbled with the keys and inelegantly scrambled across the seat and out of the car.

'Can you tell me your name, please?'

'Anna Fairbrother,' I said in a voice barely audible over the roar of the traffic.

'Have you got your driving licence?'

I nodded and scrabbled in my bag to find it. He took it and passed it to his colleague, who'd just joined him. He looked at it, nodded and handed it back.

'Do you know why we've stopped you?'

I looked at him, but my mouth was now so dry I couldn't answer, so, although I felt certain why they'd stopped me, I just shook my head.

'You'll be surprised to hear that we've stopped you for driving too slowly. Makes a change from speeding, but cars are expected to maintain the flow of traffic and you were driving between thirty-five and forty miles per hour. Which, on a motorway, can cause a hazard.'

I felt my mouth drop open, but words were beyond me. He pulled out a breathalyser and asked me to blow into it. I did so with trepidation, even though I'd only had one small glass of wine to drink at the wake.

'You were also driving with your indicators on for several miles. Again, this constitutes a hazard.' He looked towards the other officer.

'All OK,' he said, reading the breathalyser. Then looked towards my bag, which was hanging open, and back at me.

'Been to a funeral?' he asked, nodding at the order of service that was visible in my open bag.

I clutched the bag to me. 'My mother's,' I whispered.

The two officers looked at each other.

'Our condolences,' one of them said, and the other nodded. 'It's understandable that you're a bit distracted under the circumstances, but you must try to just concentrate on your driving. Have you got far to go?'

I shook my head, not knowing whether to laugh or cry. I wasn't being arrested for murder!

'I'm nearly home,' I said.

'OK, well, you take care. Put everything out of your mind, except what you're doing, until you get home.' He opened the car door for me, and I got in as fast as possible, took several deep breaths and started the engine.

'Follow us onto the carriageway,' he said, leaning through the still open window, before walking back to the police car.

Once out on the road, they waved, flashed their lights and sped off. Luckily my junction was close, and I made sure that my driving was impeccable for the rest of my journey.

Not long after the incident, I nosed my little car into the garage underneath my modern, terraced three-story town house, which sat just off the canal towpath. My sanctuary. I sat in the car without moving for a few moments. Being back home didn't make me feel any better. I could barely muster the strength to get out and open the front door. With a feeling of doom, I heaved my bag out of the boot and trudged up the stairs to my living room, where I dropped it on the floor. My bedroom was up another flight, but that felt too much. Perhaps I'm sickening for something, I thought as I dropped into the nearest chair and shut my eyes.

I must have slept, for the next time I opened my eyes I could see the reflections from the canal outside, on the ceiling, a sure sign that the sun was setting. I pulled myself up and went into the kitchen. I opened a few cupboards and looked in the fridge, but there was nothing to tempt me. Settling for a glass of sparkling water and chocolate biscuit, I made my way upstairs to my bedroom. I felt numb. Random thoughts floated in and out of my consciousness, but I was too tired to grasp them. I dropped my clothes on the floor and climbed into bed. I couldn't relax enough to sleep. The stories Ruth had told me all jumbled together and I couldn't make sense of them. Anger flooded my mind and engulfed me. I raged at everything and everyone, leaving me drained and exhausted until all I felt was self-pity.

For several days I moped around, not bothering to get dressed or showered, my hair scraped back into a ponytail. Nothing seemed worth the effort. I ate cereal in bed when I felt hungry and watched mindless daytime TV programmes about renovating houses or chaotic relationships. My phone ran out of charge, and I left it dead and useless on the bedroom floor. It suited my mood; I didn't want to talk to anyone. I didn't know who I was anymore.

I felt alone, detached from reality. I tried to tell myself that I was the same person I always was, only now I knew my history. That made a difference and no matter how much I wished it, I couldn't turn back the clock. I became maudlin and sorry for myself. Who was I? What were my achievements? I didn't even have a regular boyfriend. There had been some relationships in the past, some even felt like real love, with a hope for the future, but always they ended in tears. Not always mine! There was no one, apart from Ruth, who gave a damn about me.

Even the fact that, according to Ruth, who was mum's executor, I was now quite a wealthy woman did nothing to ease my despair. Mother hadn't used her spite to cut me out of her will, but I didn't want her money, although Ruth said it was in a trust from dad, which made it more palatable.

Chapter 8

I moped about for another evening, analysing and finding wanting every part of my life. Then a news item caught my attention on the television, a disaster that put my problems into perspective. Orphaned children with big, brown eyes stared from the screen; all they possessed were the clothes, no, you couldn't even call them clothes, the *rags* they stood up in. I looked at myself in the mirror, pasty, blotched face with a spot just beginning to appear on my cheek, tangled, greasy hair and sunken eyes. I felt quite shocked at how pathetic I looked and forced myself to have a shower.

Feeling better but still looking a wreck, I made myself a strong cup of coffee. The envelope, I had ignored several days earlier still sat unopened next to the phone. I knew who it was from, which was why I had pushed it out of my mind. I took a deep gulp of coffee and ripped open the envelope. All it contained was a photograph, with a sticky note on it stating: "This is your mother", in Mother's precise handwriting. By now, from Ruth, I knew much more about Deborah, my real mother. I even knew what she looked like from the one or two photographs in Ruth's albums.

I studied the photo, it showed four people; two girls with long straight hair parted in the middle, wearing long floaty cheesecloth skirts. A third had shorter curly hair and was wearing tight flared trousers and a loose smock top with what looked like embroidery all over it. The fourth was a boy, or young man, with shoulder length hair, wearing an embroidered T-shirt and flared trousers. All wore wide grins and the man's arms were draped around the shoulders of two of the girls. I turned the photo over; someone, presumably Mother, had written on the back:

"Glastonbury 1971
Me, Ruth, Pete, Deborah"

I remembered Ruth always used to have curly hair. I stared at it. There they all were, Deborah my real mum, Carrie my adoptive mum, Pete my supposed adopted, but in fact real dad, and Ruth my aunt. Ruth told me she and Deborah were friends, but seeing this photo shocked me. Did she tell me they were all friends? Ruth and Deborah were much younger than Mum and Dad. Why didn't anyone tell me the truth years ago?

Anger bubbled up again, this time directed towards Deborah. I was angry because she was a flirt and allowed herself to get pregnant. Angry that she went ahead and gave birth to me, and angry that she left me at the mercy of who knew what. I poured myself another coffee and curled up on the sofa. I needed to pull myself together and put the moping, self-pitying days behind me. A few sips from my mug and the caffeine quickly sharpened my mind. Now I needed to sit and piece by piece go over everything I could remember Ruth telling me that first night, and the following few days. I had absorbed the key details when she told me, but my overwhelming emotions then, since, and now, were confusion and anger. Anger that refused to be quashed.

I was angry with Mother for adopting me, and then not loving me. I was angry with dad for not being the hero I always thought he was. How could the wonderful man I adored be so callous? The full story was swirling around in a soup of emotions, and I now needed to pull it all together and reach some clarity. I leant back and closed my eyes, holding onto the now crumpled photo.

I grew up knowing my real mother had died when I was

very young, and that's why I was adopted; but now, replaying Ruth's story, I remembered her telling me Deborah had committed suicide. How could a fact like that have slipped my mind? Ruth told me she didn't know all the details, but it seems it was a combination of postnatal depression and something to do with the cause of her mum's death. Apparently, it was some sort of hereditary illness. Hereditary illness? I felt anxious. What could that be and what were the implications, if any, for me?

Ruth told me that dad and Deborah had a brief fling during a split from Carrie. So, Dad wasn't cheating on her, was he? I needed to maintain the image of Dad as an honest man. There was only one way to sort it all out. I needed to go back and see Ruth to ask her to go over some facts again; she would understand how I felt. I knew she would reassure me and look after me; perhaps I could stay with her again, just for a few days, until I felt calmer. I dressed as fast as I could, hurried to my car and sped off towards Ruth's apartment. Now I'd decided to go I couldn't get there quickly enough. I didn't ring to ask if it was all right, in case she said no, but I knew she would never say no. Just knowing I would soon see her made me feel better.

Ever since I was a small child, I had loved visiting Ruth. Her flat was one of half-a-dozen in what was a converted warehouse or an old mill. I made a mental note to ask her about the origins of the building sometime. Her apartment was on the top floor with a mezzanine level, which she used as her studio. The windows were sloping into the roofline and then dropped floor to ceiling on one side of the room. As a child, I dreamt that one day I would live in a place like this. The view from the window looked across the communal gardens and over sweeping lawns, to where a huge horse chestnut tree took centre stage. A stream bordered the far end of the lawn and meandered round towards the back of the building, where it magically disappeared underground and re-appeared some distance away on the other side.

I had spent many happy hours here as a child when Ruth

was babysitting, and later it served as my refuge. Back then I never wondered why it was only me who needed babysitting and not Rachel as well. I just loved being there. Ruth would often be painting and didn't ask awkward questions. Sometimes she would give me some brushes and a discarded canvas and ask me to paint something. I would put on a big old shirt and wield my brushes with dramatic flourish, but the result was usually a total mess. Ruth always looked for the positive aspects, but even at a young age, I knew art would not be my forte.

Ruth was out. I felt inordinately disappointed and angry that she wasn't at home. I kicked her door like a spoilt child. It was that or burst into tears, but I had done enough crying. I scoured the contents in my bag for my phone to ring her. It wasn't there. It was still lying uncharged on the bedroom floor. After hanging around on the doorstep for about fifteen minutes, I gave up. I scribbled a note on a piece of scrap paper and pushed it through the letter box before I drove back home.

Once home, I started to wallow. I was alone; there was no one who cared about me. I could feel myself about to plunge back into misery. After taking some deep breaths to keep myself strong, I began to clear up discarded clothes and dirty dishes. I switched on my computer and charged up my phone. It pinged into life delivering texts and voicemails. Several were from Ruth, concerned whether I was OK and asking me to ring her when I could. She sounded excited. I checked my emails and was surprised to find one from Ruth saying she was in Greece with someone called Alice, and I should join them.

I read the message several times and couldn't quite believe it. Ruth never mentioned she was going on holiday. I felt let down; how could she go away when I needed her. I wondered who Alice was; perhaps she was an artist friend, but why would I want to join them? Even as I was wondering, a bell was ringing somewhere in the depths of my mind. Alice?

wasn't she something to do with me? Of course, I remembered, Ruth mentioned an Alice, she was Deborah's sister, my aunt. That was why Ruth wanted me to join her; she must have tracked her down to Greece! From her email, she must have assumed I would remember that she told me who she was. The idea didn't seem quite so ridiculous now, and the thought of sunny skies and blue seas was very appealing. A holiday would do me good, although how much of a proper holiday it would be was debatable. I washed up my mug and rang the travel agent to ask about flights to Greece. I then rang work and negotiated some additional leave. More than anything, I wanted to be with Ruth.

Chapter 9

Ruth goes to Greece

Ruth felt exhilarated as she leant over the rail of the ferry; the warm wind ruffled her short hair. It was a spur-of-the-moment decision to board a plane and now be heading towards a lesser-known Greek island, on what could, probably would be a wild goose chase, but it appealed to her sense of adventure, and if nothing else would be fun. Looking around, she was certain, judging by the clear light and beautiful scenery, that it would re-energise her somewhat jaded artist's brain.

The stress of the last few months, coping with Carrie's illness and then supporting and explaining everything to Anna had left Ruth drained, with little time to paint or enjoy herself. Now she felt a delicious sense of freedom, tinged a little with guilt if she was honest, but she wanted to, no, *needed* to find answers for Anna. The guilt stemmed from her lack of pressure over the years, to persuade Carrie to tell Anna the truth. That Carrie left it until the last minute, which left Anna with no time to question her, felt almost unforgivable. Ruth pushed that thought away. She loved her sister and did not want her memory tinged with anger. Then there was this illness, or whatever it was, in Deborah's family. No one, as far as she knew, made any effort to discover what the condition was, and Ruth now felt it was her responsibility to find out. If she didn't, who could? She knew Anna would be worried. Ruth hoped to reassure her. She felt uplifted by the sight and sound of the blue sea and sky and smiled to herself. A short time later, the ferry bumped against the harbour wall of a small, pretty fishing port. Ruth decided not to let guilt and grief mar her newfound sense of optimism. At once, there were people everywhere, tugging on ropes, shouting to each other, and unloading boxes and crates from the boat.

The few passengers disembarked; most seemed to be tourists with the same holiday company. A young Greek woman, dressed in an incongruous smart red tailored suit and ankle boots, stood on the quay waiting to greet them and to tick them off on her clipboard before she dispatched them to their accommodation. A handful of local people, loaded with unwieldy parcels, hurried down the gangplank and made their way into the maze of little streets leading off from the harbour.

Ruth pulled her wheelie case along the quay. The heat bounced off the whitewashed buildings, causing her to stop and wipe the sweat from her brow. She would have to buy some sunglasses as soon as possible; she could still picture her own pair sitting on the table where she put them yesterday, to ensure she didn't forget them. Delicious smells drifted across from several small waterfront tavernas. She took a deep breath; grilled sardines, and she sniffed again, grilled meat of some sort. She was hungry. The bacon sandwich at the airport seemed a very long time ago. Resisting the temptation to sit at the nearest table and order an enormous meal, Ruth pulled her case further along to where she could see the tourist information sign. She needed to find somewhere to stay first. A couple of hours later, after a shower and quick nap in the tiny studio overlooking the bay, rented, to start with, for four nights, she ventured out to eat. Tomorrow she would look for Alice.

The next morning, feeling rested, Ruth sat on the harbour side at a small, painted wooden table enjoying breakfast. Some rich smooth honey perfectly complemented a dish of creamy, tangy yogurt; it tasted like nectar in her mouth. Followed by a cup of strong coffee and a glass of freshly squeezed orange juice, she felt back on form. She lingered, watching people go about their business. A young man was idly wiping the tables with one hand and smoking with the other; a couple of older, weather-beaten men were chatting as they hauled nets across to a boat whose faded blue and yellow peeling paint only added to its charm. To Ruth's inexperienced eyes it did not look very seaworthy, particularly not for men of their apparent age. Coiled ropes lay like snakes snoozing in the sun, coming to life with a sharp tug. Further along the harbour, a young couple were having a heated conversation. The girl was gesticulating with her hands; her shrill voice rising in frustration, while the boy smoked a cigarette and kept glancing out to sea, desperate to escape. It's strange, she thought, how romantic other people's everyday life was, when you couldn't understand the language.

The day was already beginning to heat up, and Ruth, absorbing the laid-back atmosphere of the island, decided to have a leisurely morning, perhaps a swim at the little beach she had spotted from her balcony. There was no rush to find Alice; later when it was cooler would be better. Every time she thought about Alice, a strange knot formed in her stomach. What if Alice didn't want to speak about her family, or worse still, wasn't there? No, whatever happened, Ruth would enjoy her few days in the sun. She could only do her best to find out the truth for Anna. The sea felt like silk over Ruth's skin, although the initial cold was a bit of a shock to the system. Ruth was a good swimmer and vowed to herself to swim at least once a day while she was here. She might even shed a few excess pounds.

Chapter 10

Much later, after a midafternoon nap, and with a mixture of excitement and anxiety, Ruth climbed out of a seen-better-days taxi. She breathed in the dusty, dry, late afternoon scents of pine, and sweetness from a small white flower that she could not identify. The taxi driver indicated that this was as far as he could go.

'Steps, too winding, not good for cars,' he said. 'Taxis wait here until late.'

There were already a few taxis parked up. Their drivers were sitting in the shade of a large tree, smoking, playing cards and chatting.

'Thank you.' Ruth handed him a few euros.

'No problem, see you later,' he said, going to join the other drivers.

The old town was a jumble of houses, some whitewashed but most were built of the old mellow local stone, with purple Bougainvillea clinging to walls and tumbling over small wooden and ironwork balconies. Ruth smiled to herself. As an artist, the unselfconscious beauty of the place captivated her. In her imagination she was already covering a canvas in a blue wash.

Ruth knew, or thought she knew, that this was where she would find Alice. She made her way up the steep cobbled path and into the town, serenaded by the chirruping of cicadas in the olive trees. There were just enough people around, without it being crowded, to give the place vibrancy. Most were tourists who seemed to be on a pilgrimage to the top of the hill to watch the sunset. The air felt light and dry, and a gentle breeze made wandering around the streets a pleasant experience. The charming, narrow streets appeared old, although she remembered reading in a guidebook, she had flicked through in a quayside gift shop, saying it was still being restored after an earthquake some years ago, and most of the buildings were new or rebuilt from ruins. Small buildings: some houses, some shops or tavernas, nestled into courtyards or jostled each other for positions along the steep cobbled streets, built, she presumed, from the original stone. Now and then, a gap in the buildings framed a spectacular view of the sea and islands in the distance.

Most of the small shops were catering to the visitors, selling a range of crafts, bags, and clothes. Ruth paid special attention to shops selling jewellery; her information was that Alice ran a jewellery shop or stall of some sort. No one in any of the shops looked at all like Alice, not that Ruth could be sure after all these years she would recognise her. Alice must be about fifty now and the last time Ruth saw her, she was a teenager. Thirst drew her to a shady taverna, where she sat for a while, once again watching the world go by. She could understand what drew people to this place; it felt like an oasis in the madness of the world. Even the tourists wandering around appeared peaceful and relaxed; most were couples, soaking up the atmosphere with nothing to worry about but where to eat that evening.

After her drink Ruth carried on wandering the streets, a little shop halfway along the main thoroughfare caught her eye; no one appeared to be inside, but she made her way down the uneven steps into the delightfully cool interior.

'Hi, can I help?' a beautiful young man with dark, wavy hair resting on his shoulders stepped into the shop from outside.

'Oh, I was just looking,' Ruth said, taken by surprise by his appearance behind her.

'Everything is handmade.' He indicated the cabinets and stands displaying a range of silver jewellery, strings of beads, necklaces, and earrings.

'It's lovely, beautiful. I love jewellery but I was looking for a person, not to buy anything,' Ruth said, smiling at the slim, handsome tanned man. Her fingers itched to paint his portrait, perhaps lounging in front of a seascape. She took a deep breath and blushed.

'Actually, I'm looking for someone called Alice Jenkins,' she said.

'You've come to the right place, then,' he said. 'This is Alice's shop.'

'Really? Does she make all this?'

'Yes, all of it, but she's not here.'

'Oh, no, that's a shame.' Disappointed, Ruth raised a questioning eyebrow.

'She's gone to Athens for supplies,' he said, studying Ruth with interest.

'Oh,' Ruth said again. 'Is she away for long?'

'Just a minute,' He went to the door of the shop and called across the street.

'Jorgy, when is Alice coming back?'

'Tomorrow or Wednesday, depending on flights or ferries. Why?' A voice with a Scandinavian accent came back across the street.

'There's a lady here looking for her.'

Another good-looking young man, except this one was fair-haired and a little shorter, appeared in the doorway of the shop opposite. He wiped clay from his hands as he came across.

'Are you a client or a friend?' he asked. 'We can sell things or take an order.'

'Not a client. I suppose I'm a friend.'

The man called Jorgy tilted his head with a quizzical look.

'You're not sure if you're her friend?' he asked.

'Well, no, I am a friend. It's just we haven't seen each other for a long time.'

'Would you like us to give her a message?'

'Yes, please, perhaps I could leave my mobile number so she can call when she gets back.'

'Good idea,' the dark-haired man started scrabbling around on the little counter looking for a piece of paper. At last, he found a scrap.

'Have you got a pen?' he asked Ruth.

Ruth searched her bag certain she had one but couldn't find it.

'Jorgy, have you got one?'

Jorgy raised his clay covered hands.

'Luke, look at me. How can I touch anything?'

'Isn't that one?' Ruth pointed to what looked like the end of a biro sticking out from under a pile of tissue paper.

'Aha!' Luke brandished the pen. 'Now then your name and number?' he asked, poised over the piece of paper.

Ruth gave him the details, thanked them both and made her way out of the shop and started to walk back down towards the taxis.

'We'll be sure to pass it on. See you again,' Jorgy called after her.

Ruth raised her hand in acknowledgement. There was nothing more she could do now but wait and hope.

Chapter 11

Ruth heard nothing from Alice the next day. She spent her time ambling around the small harbour, swimming in the sea, and reading her book in the shade; enjoying the opportunity to relax and take in the everyday life of the small harbour town. By lunchtime the following day, there was still no call from Alice. Ruth felt restless. What would she do if Alice didn't ring, or if she didn't want to see her? Ruth felt so near to answers for Anna. She didn't want to fail now. She sat in a taverna close to where the ferry docked, scanning from a discreet distance all the people disembarking to see if Alice was amongst them. There were a couple of likely candidates, but Ruth didn't feel sure enough to approach them. As late afternoon came around, with no contact, she decided to make her way back up to the old town. She could check with the two boys in the shop opposite to find out whether Alice was back.

Climbing up the cobbled street, feeling weary in the heat, Ruth doubted the wisdom of being there; she didn't want to look like she was chasing Alice. She should have waited for a call.

'Ruth! Ruth!' a breathless voice called from behind her.

She swung round and there was Alice, beaming, rushing towards her. Ruth recognised her at once. Alice was quite small with sun-bleached short, spikey hair. Her skin glowed golden in the late afternoon sunlight. She wore loose white trousers and a top that appeared to be made from two silk scarves.

'Ruth, how lovely to see you! You look just as I remember you.' Alice wrapped her arms around Ruth in a hug of genuine warmth, and all Ruth's concerns slipped away. 'I've been trying since I got back yesterday to ring you, but the boys must have written down the wrong number. Mind, it could be the phone signal; it's awful here,' she said, linking her arm through Ruth's and guiding her back towards her shop.

'Are you here on holiday?' She asked.

'Well, not really. I sort of came looking for you.' Ruth felt embarrassed and blushed.

'Really? How lovely, but why? Look, let me just close the shop, then we can go to my place to talk.'

They made their way into her small shop. Luke was there holding the fort and trying to manage a family of rather demanding American tourists.

'Ah, Alice! This is the lady that can help you,' he said to a large lady dressed in what appeared to be an old-fashioned swimming costume, with a brightly coloured sarong tied around her waist. He cast a relieved look in Alice's direction and took a step towards the door.

'Glad you found each other,' he said to Ruth. 'Catch you both later,' he called in Alice's direction, and hotfooted it back across the cobbles to where Jorgy, leaning languidly against the door, was waiting for him.

'Oh, it's so darn hot,' said the American lady. 'Honey, can't you just make up your mind, then we can go get a drink?'

'I'm trying, mom, but I like them both.' A young woman was holding one necklace, then another up against her neck whilst looking into a small mirror on the counter.

'Tell you what, baby, why not get them both? They both look great,' a man said.

'Oh, do you think I should?'

'Yes.' The mom and the man, possibly the younger woman's husband, chorused together. Alice shot a glance and wink in Ruth's direction.

While Alice dealt with the transaction, Ruth looked around the shop. Most of the jewellery was exquisite, intricate, without being fussy.

At last, the satisfied customers left, and Alice rushed to close the door and put the closed sign up.

'Are you sure?' Ruth said. 'I don't want you to lose business.'

Alice grinned. 'With the amount they just spent, I can afford an evening off!'

Chapter 12

Alice led the way through a small workshop at the back of the shop and up a whitewashed flight of external stairs to a beautiful terrace.

'Wow!' The view took Ruth's breath away. She leant on the low white wall, admiring the view that swept down to the sparkling coast below, and further along to the harbour where Ruth was staying. The terrace was large, with a table and chairs positioned under a canopy, covered in what appeared to be mature vines, which provided much-needed shade. An oven or barbecue was in the corner, seamlessly built into the wall, and painted in the same bright white. On the other side of the terrace, a large rambling bougainvillea tumbled over the wall and climbed up the side of the building, almost reaching the roof.

'It's beautiful, isn't it?' Alice stood beside Ruth. 'It's my piece of heaven. Here, sit and soak it up and I'll get us a drink.'

Ruth lounged in a comfortable chair; the sun was sinking and would soon be swallowed up by the sea. A gentle breeze fanned her face, and she couldn't remember when she last felt so relaxed.

'Do you like ouzo?' Alice called from the depths of the interior behind the terrace.

'I don't know,' Ruth called back.

'It tastes of aniseed. I'll bring you one.'

A couple of minutes later, Alice placed two glasses of

cloudy looking liquid and a bowl of fat, juicy olives on the table.

Ruth must have looked doubtful.

'Take a sip and see what you think. I've mixed it with lemonade, not the traditional way, but it's how I like it.' Alice raised her glass.

'Cheers, it's so lovely to see you.'

'Cheers.' Ruth took a tentative sip. 'Mm, not bad,' she said, popping an olive into her mouth. 'Goes well with the setting,' she raised her glass to the view.

'So, when did we last see each other?' Alice asked.

'Well, it must have been sometime after Deborah's funeral.' Alice nodded.

'I would have been about seventeen. Over thirty years ago,' she sat, silent for a few moments, considering times she may have preferred to forget.

'So, how is everyone at home? Carrie, Anna? I know about Pete, of course.'

'Carrie died recently,' Ruth said.

'Oh, I'm sorry, she can't have been very old.'

'Fifty-five, much too young. She died of ovarian cancer. It was all very quick.'

'I'm so sorry,' Alice said again.

She got up and lit some citronella lanterns, bustling around while the news sank in.

'Anyway, tell me about you. How have you moved from schoolgirl to being here?' Ruth asked.

'Well, it's a long story, but I'll try to cut it short,' Alice said, sipping her drink and reaching for an olive. 'After Debbie's death and Anna's adoption, my dad and I were distraught, heartbroken in fact, and we both retreated into our own worlds.' Nothing ever seemed quite the same again. In some ways, it was harder to cope with than losing my mum. I suppose after mum, Debbie was my support. Anyway, I absorbed myself in schoolwork and, to my surprise, and everyone else's, I excelled at maths. I got top grades in my A levels and ended up taking maths at university' Alice took another sip of her drink, and Ruth didn't interrupt. 'I loved university. It felt like a different world,' she continued. 'I wasn't one of the wild students, out drinking and partying, but I just loved the space and ability to concentrate on my work, and selfishly, I suppose, not having to worry about Dad. When I first left university, I worked for a high-flying firm of accountants in their Gloucester office, then in London. Dad, by then, was living with his sister. I bought a flat near Gloucester and commuted to London daily. It was good money, but stressful, and not what I wanted from life. Then, one weekend I went to a jewellery-making workshop for relaxation, found I loved it, and started doing more and more. I teamed up with another girl and we ran a stall together at the Saturday market. People seemed to like the jewellery I made, and then one day a lady started chatting about her holiday in Greece and how much art and crafts were developing on this island she'd visited. She showed me her photos, and, as I was looking for somewhere to go on holiday, I decided to visit. I fell in love with place and here I am,' Alice spread her arms wide.

'Did you just stay here?' Ruth asked.

'Well, no, I'm not quite that impulsive! I went back to England, worked out all the finances, weighed up the pros and cons. Dad had died by then. So, I thought, why not give it a go? I kept my flat on, as a sort of insurance policy.'

'I'm glad you did, that's how I managed to find you,' Ruth smiled.

'That's me. So, Ruth, what about you? Apart from when you used to call for Debbie, I didn't see much of you. I was just the kid sister not allowed to join in, and I'm intrigued to hear why you've come looking for me now.'

Ruth laughed,

'I went to Art College, and I suppose I was one of the lucky ones who went on to make a living from painting.'

'Really? So, you're a proper artist?' Alice asked.

'Well, it pays the bills. I was lucky, one of my paintings was used in an advert, so it got me noticed, but my bread-and-butter stuff is portraits. My real love is of landscapes and abstracts and here is just so inspiring.'

'It is a beautiful place. It bewitches you,' Alice said. 'Have you got children, Ruth?' she asked.

'No. I've never been in a meaningful relationship. I guess I'm happy on my own. How about you?'

'No children; I lived with a guy on and off for a couple of years, but it wasn't deep and never really felt right. I broke it off when he started pushing for us to make things more permanent.'

Ruth nodded and was about to ask Alice more when Alice started talking about the past again.

'You and Debbie fell out, didn't you? I never knew why, and Deb wouldn't talk about it.'

'Yes, sadly. I still feel bad about that, but I was mad at her for messing around with Pete. Officially, Pete and Carrie weren't going out at the time, but they soon got back together and shortly after, they got married. Anyway, I guess you know that? Then Debbie started going around with a different crowd, so we stopped seeing so much of each other. I think she thought I was overreacting.'

'Do you think Debbie thought she and Pete were serious about each other at the time?' Alice asked.

'No, at least I don't think it was that serious. I think it was a couple of mad moments for them both. Probably if Anna hadn't been born, they would all have moved on, and no one would have known anything about it.'

'And Carrie didn't know about them?'

'Not until the bombshell of Deborah's death. Followed by the bigger bombshell finding out about the existence of Anna.'

'I can't imagine how devastating that must have been,' said Alice.

'In fact, finding out about Anna was a surprise for Pete as

well. I gather he told Carrie that Deborah had told him she was going to have an abortion, not that hearing that appeased her at the time. Deborah obviously never told Pete about Anna being born.'

'Carrie's agreement to take Anna on amazed Dad and me. Wait a minute, let me get us some food and more drinks before we can carry on chatting,' Alice said.

The two women talked on for many hours in the soft warmth of the evening, getting to know each other properly for the first time.

Ruth spent the night in Alice's spare room, and the next morning they both went down to the harbour to collect her belongings. Alice wouldn't hear of Ruth staying anywhere else.

'Stay with me as long as you like,' Alice said, as she pulled Ruth's case up the steps to the terrace. 'Why don't you contact Anna and suggest she come over for a holiday, and then you won't have to rush back? I'd love to see her again and I can fill her in about the family.'

Ruth could think of nothing she would like to do more than to spend time in this beautiful place, getting to know Alice better. She would email Anna later.

'I'd love to stay. Perhaps I can do some painting and help you in the shop, and I know Anna has loads of questions she would want to ask you.'

'Yes, I'm sure she has. I'll do my best to give her answers. I can show you the rest of the island as well,' Alice said. 'I've made friends here, but it's special to have someone from home.'

'What's it like here in the winter?' Ruth asked, as she unpacked her small bag, realising that she didn't have many clothes for a long stay.

'It's very quiet, especially up here. Most places close at the end of October and open again around March. I go on holiday, make more jewellery, generally catch up.'

'Have you been back home?' Ruth asked.

'Once or twice, but there's nothing there for me now. This is home, for now. I don't think about the future or what happens when I get older,' Alice said. 'Come on, let me show you around the town.'

Later, Ruth sent an email to Anna, letting her know she was in Greece with Alice, and suggesting she come and join her.

Chapter 13

Anna arrives in Greece

I gasped as the heat took my breath away. The air was so hot it was almost palpable. Everywhere was dry and dusty and although it was an airport, there was a soporific feel to the atmosphere. It was early June, but already it felt like mid-August. I paused at the top of the aircraft stairs, squinting into the bright sunlight. My sunglasses were deep in my bag, and I didn't want to hold up the queue of people coming down behind me while I got them out.

Hitching my bag over my shoulder, I made my way down the steps onto the tarmac, quickly withdrawing my hand from the burning aluminium handrail. I walked across towards the terminal building, shrugging my way out of the cardigan that had felt so inadequate earlier this morning in Britain. Beads of sweat were beginning to gather along my hairline. I wasn't used to such heat but was looking forward to acclimatising. The automatic doors swished open, and as I walked through, a blast of icy cold air conditioning hit me, and I was soon pulling my cardigan back on.

The arrivals hall was small, and by the time I was through passport control, the bags were already trundling around on the rickety carousel. The air was full of the excited babble of holidaymakers, eager to get on their way to the beach and the bar.

Baggage reclaims have always made me feel nervous, after

one disastrous journey when I was the only person left watching an empty carousel long after all the other passengers, luggage in hand, had departed. It took three days to be reunited with my bag. Three days out of a one-week trip! But today my small blue case with the bright pink strap was already on its second rotation by the time I pushed my way through the throng.

Once all the passengers had claimed their luggage and dispersed, a small group of us waited outside the terminal for a transfer bus to take us the short distance to the port to catch the ferry. By the time I boarded the ferry, my clothes were sticking to me and my hair felt damp and heavy, hanging round my neck. I was gasping for a drink, so as soon as my case was stowed, I made my way to the small bar and bought the biggest bottle of water on sale. Resisting the temptation to tip some over my head, I took a big swig and found myself a seat near the rail under a canopy on the open deck. Not for the first time that day, I wondered what on earth I was doing. I wasn't prone to impulsive actions; but here I was, in Greece, less than forty-eight hours after receiving Ruth's email. The email contained scant information about finding Alice, my real aunt. Well, real in the sense that she was a blood relative. Ruth, to me, was my real aunt; I couldn't remember a time when she wasn't a part of my life. Who says blood is thicker than water? Although, hearing about Alice was the impetus for me to spring into action, after all, what did I have to lose? I presumed it was an impulse on Ruth's part as well, but then that was typical of Ruth.

There were still so many unanswered questions. Ruth had done her best, but I hoped Alice could tell me more. A slight shiver ran down my spine at the thought of what might be to come. I took another swig of water, regretting my decision to wear jeans and trainers with socks. I pulled off my shoes and socks and tipped some water over my hot feet, wriggling my toes with pleasure at the coolness. Feeling a little better I looked around and took in the beauty of the scene. The horizon melted into a hazy line of inky-blue ocean and azure sky. It was stunning. The ferry was skimming over the waves, sending tiny diamonds of spray up into the air which now and then reached the deck and my welcoming face.

'Look,' a child shouted, pointing over the rail. I looked to where he was pointing; three glistening, grey backs were visible. Dolphins rising above then dipping under the surface of the water as they swam, their skin like gleaming rubber. One leapt right into the air, landing with a splash, raising a collective 'ooh' from the transfixed passengers by the rail. I wasn't superstitious but couldn't help thinking their appearance must be a good omen. I needed one.

Already I felt calmer, just being out of the UK. Perhaps it was the sunshine or maybe it was just the distance. If nothing else I would try to enjoy it as a holiday, and a holiday was just what I needed. I leant back and tried to relax. The light sea breeze turned the oppressive heat of the day into a comfortable warmth, and for the first time in a couple of weeks, I felt at peace, or at least, less agitated.

Chapter 14

The journey took little more than an hour and was a delight. We passed close to one beautiful looking island with a tempting display of golden beaches and wooded hillsides, but didn't call in. Soon, we were slowing down as the ferry sailed close to the rocky shore, at the top of the island that was my destination. It then turned around the headland into the bay and a small port came into sight. As the harbour drew closer, my thoughts turned to seeing Ruth again and meeting Alice for the first time. It was unsettling to think that my life might be about to change based on the information of a woman I had never met. I couldn't imagine what she would tell me, and if I was honest, wasn't sure I wanted to know. No, I shook my head; I must know and know everything she could tell me, good or bad.

'Anna!'

Hearing someone call my name startled me, but in a second, I recognised Ruth's voice. Looking over the side, I spotted her on the quay waving madly, and waved back, surprised but delighted to see her. I wasn't expecting her to meet me. Not knowing what time, I would arrive myself, I couldn't tell her when I would reach the island and hadn't thought about logistics much beyond getting here. I was relieved she was there though; the island looked bigger than I'd imagined it would be. If I'd thought about arriving at all, I just assumed I would get off the ferry and find them without too much trouble. With shaking fingers, I gathered my bits and pieces and dropped and spilt my water bottle over my handbag. Pulling myself together, I ran down the ramp and into Ruth's arms, swallowing hard the lump rising in my throat.

'Alice guessed you'd be on this ferry,' she said, reaching for my bag. 'Come on, let's go and get a drink and some food. Alice thought it best if I met you alone, so we could catch up before we go to meet her.'

Our meal was a leisurely affair on the quayside and a cool glass of wine contributed to further my state of relaxation.

'How are you, Anna?' Ruth asked, in a way that meant she wanted to know. Not just asking as a reflex.

'I'm ok - now,' I said. 'It's been difficult. A lot to think about.'

She nodded and reached over to squeeze my hand. Her manicured nails and neatly applied deep red nail varnish were in stark contrast to my own, down-to-the-quick, nail bitten fingers, which I curled into my palm, out of sight.

'It's bound to take time, but this is a great place for freeing your mind,' she said. 'Have you seen Rachel since the funeral?' She asked, still holding my hand.

'No, no, I haven't. She left a message; I haven't been communicating with anyone much.'

'No, I noticed,' she said and squeezed my hand again. 'I tried to contact you. I was getting worried, but well, you're a grown woman and I knew you'd get in touch when you were ready.'

Ruth filled me in on what she'd been up to since mum's funeral, which already felt a lifetime away. She'd put her detective hat on, she said, and went back to the last place she knew where Deborah and Alice lived. The family was long gone, and the current occupants of the house were two or three on from them, and of course didn't have any idea where they might have gone. But Ruth remembered a family down the road, with a son the same age as Alice, so she knocked on their door and although that family had moved on, the lady living there now gave Ruth a phone number for them.

'I rang them,' Ruth said, taking a sip of wine before getting back into the swing of her story. 'They remembered the family, of course. Mr Jenkins died a few years ago, and they thought Alice was living in a small town in Gloucestershire. So, I looked up all the Alice Jenkins in that area on the electoral roll.' She took another sip of wine. 'It was quite easy to find her; I remembered her date of birth was New Year's Eve, and there was only one on the electoral roll, so I decided to contact her. At first, I thought I would send her a letter and then I thought, why not go to see her? So, I got the train to Stroud and took a taxi from the station straight to what I hoped was her house, well flat. I was knocking on her door when an arty looking chap appeared on the stairs. He knew Alice, but said she was now living most of the time in Greece, he knew which island but not much else.'

'Quite the sleuth, aren't you? So, did you just decide to come out on speck?' I asked, feeling impressed. I wasn't sure I would have set off with such scant information.

'Well, I tried to ring you a few times, as you know, to discuss what to do or to see if you fancied coming along.' She looked at me and smiled.

'Yes, sorry, you know how it was,' I said.

She nodded, 'Well, I've always been sort of impetuous, so I thought why not, why not have a bit of an adventure and see what comes of it. And here I am, here we are!' She smiled again, and I noticed for the first time how well she looked; being here obviously agreed with her.

'So how did you find Alice when you got here?' I asked.

'I knew she was selling jewellery, so I just looked around. She has a small shop in the old town. She's so talented and makes all the pieces herself. Her beautiful little, well, I suppose you'd call it a villa where she lives, is just behind her shop. She can't wait to meet you. You'll like her, I'm sure.'

I smiled. There was so much more I wanted to know but I didn't want to interrogate Ruth. There was plenty of time. Could the laid-back Greek atmosphere be working its magic already, or was it the wine? After about an hour, Ruth stood up, picked up my bag, and with a few butterflies in my stomach, we set off to meet Alice.

'Here we are. It's a bit of a walk from here.' Ruth parked Alice's little car in a space under the shade of a tree and climbed out. I was stunned by the view across the sea and up to the old town winding its way on up the hill.

'It's cobbles and steps from here, but it's not too far.'

Ruth pointed up to a whitewashed building as we rounded a corner; it was on the edge of a jumble of other buildings.

'That's Alice's place.'

I could see a pretty veranda shaded by a vine and bougainvillea.

'We'll go round this way, through the shop. I think I'll be losing weight all this up and down,' she said, pausing to catch her breath.

I followed Ruth, who, despite struggling, still insisted on carrying one of my bags. As soon as we turned into the narrow street, I could see a middle-aged, blonde-haired woman standing outside a doorway. She was small but quite slim and very attractive and bore no resemblance to her sister, Deborah, who I'd studied so intently when I was last in Ruth's flat. She waved as soon as she saw us and came rushing down. She had light blue eyes and a smile that chased my doubts away.

'Oh my God, it could be Debbie,' she said, standing a few feet away from me and clapping her hand to her mouth. 'Anna, it's so wonderful to see you.' She reached out for my hand. 'Last time I saw you; well, you could barely sit up. Oh, I can't get over how much like Debbie you are.'

I felt my stomach knot as I realised that this person, who I never even knew existed until recently, knew me, and must have been an important part of my life when I was born. She personified confidence and charisma, someone at peace with her choices in life. I warmed to her but felt a tinge of envy. I wanted that certainty back in my life.

'Go through with Ruth and make yourself at home. I won't be too long and then we can get to know one another again.'

Now we were here, I could think of nothing I wanted more than a shower and a lie down. I wasn't ready yet for more revelations and followed Ruth through the shop, taking in the attractive contents in the displays to the villa beyond. Ruth, understanding, left me to rest, but my mind insisted on trawling back over the events of the last few weeks. I must have slept, because I woke, feeling anxious after a vivid dream about chasing a woman down the street. Calling for her to stop and wait. She turned, an expression of total loathing on her face. The woman didn't look like Mother. She had long blonde hair, but I knew it was her. At last, she stopped, laughed a humourless laugh, turned and disappeared into thin air.

I sat, unmoving, for a moment, feeling shaken by the dream, and then went to find Ruth and Alice.

Chapter 15

Alice closed her shop early, and the three of us sat on her spacious terrace eating and drinking until late. She told tales of life on the island. Who she liked and who she avoided, and funny stories about tourists and the strange requests they made. She was eager to know about my life. What I did, did I have a partner, where I lived and how losing my dad at a young age affected me. Alice was fourteen when her mum died, only a couple of years older than I was when my dad died. We talked and talked but not, I felt, about the important things. I guessed that would come out as we got to know each other. There was no rush.

I slept fitfully that night, partly because of the large amount of wine I'd consumed and because of the feeling that I was in a different world. When I did sleep, I dreamt again. This time, bizarrely, about people in swimming costumes on my towpath at home, demanding jewellery in the shape of bottles and chairs. When I woke up the villa was quiet. I wasn't sure if Alice and Ruth were up, or still asleep. It was late, so I got up and made my way down to the terrace. I picked up a note that was resting on top of a plate covered with a cloth, on the table.

> *Anna*
> *Hope you slept well. Help yourself to a honey bun (delicious local delicacy) and anything else. Will be back about 11 to make lunch.*
> *Love Alice & Ruth xx*

I poured myself some orange juice and carried the plate of honey buns to the low terrace wall; the spectacular view captivated me. Staring out to sea, I tried to imagine how it must be to wake up to this every morning, and much as I loved looking out over the canal at home, waking up to this would be magical. I sat down on the smooth, white painted concrete bench built around the side of the wall. Brightly coloured cushions and rugs were heaped on the top and it was, to my surprise, nice and comfortable. Everything both inside and out was beautifully decorated. The white painted rooms were fresh and airy. The doors and edges of the steps were painted blue in the traditional Greek style. Large original paintings adorned the interior walls. I savoured a honeybun, which was delicious, and pottered about soaking up the peace and beauty, as well as the stunning view.

'Come and chat while I put some lunch together,' Alice said, when she returned a short time later with Ruth.

I followed her into the kitchen, where she started chopping and peeling vegetables.

'Here, slice this lengthways and we'll griddle it,' she said, handing me a glossy, dark purple aubergine. 'It's funny. I've often wondered about you over the years; what became of you; how you were.' She wiped her hands on a cloth and smiled at me before slicing an enormous tomato.

'You remind me so much of Debbie to look at. Have you seen a picture of her?'

I nodded. 'Yes, Ruth had some old photos. Tell me more about her.' I hoped she would paint a more endearing picture of her than Ruth.

'Well. She was almost four years older than me, and I looked up to her. I wanted to do everything she did. I must have been a real pain to her, especially when she had to look after me. When we were little, she sometimes used to let me play with her dolls, but only if I did things for her, like make her bed or pick her clothes up off the floor. Sometimes she treated me like a living doll, dressing me up and pushing me around in her doll's pram. I loved that.' She paused, mid chop, and smiled to herself. 'She was a bit of a daredevil, even a bit wild. I thought she was so clever. She and Ruth used to spend ages in the bedroom putting on make-up, trying on clothes and listening to Debbie's record player. Sometimes they let me in, but usually they pushed me out. They both looked up to Carrie. She was so grown up and sophisticated. I didn't know Carrie that well; she was eight years older than me and sometimes felt scary.

'Our mum was ill, but it wasn't until I was about ten, so Debbie would have been fourteen, that Mum became bad. I mean, her illness became severe. She couldn't look after the house, or us, properly. Dad did his best, and Debbie and I tried to help. Then Mum went into a home and Dad just seemed to give up. He would visit Mum and come home and cry. It was awful,' she said, not raising her eyes from her chopping board.

I listened without making a noise, not wanting to interrupt her train of thought; I imagined this wasn't something she spoke about often.

'Debbie supported me as best she could. She helped me do my homework, made sure my clothes were clean and cooked as best she could. We used to visit Mum. Sometimes with Dad and sometimes on our own. No one ever talked to me about what was wrong with her, but it got to the stage where I hated going. She wasn't our mum anymore; she didn't seem to know who we were; she couldn't speak and made all these strange movements. I've thought about it since, and I think it was around this time that Debbie went off the rails.

She was a teenager and wanted to be out having fun all the time, but she couldn't, because she had to look after me and Dad. So, the times when she did go out, she went mad. There were lots of boys and I suspect drugs, just dope and alcohol, nothing harder, I don't think. She didn't tell me much about what she did; she became quite withdrawn at home. Mum was in the nursing home for about a year before she died. It sounds awful to say, but it was a relief when she did. I was almost fourteen. Dad just went to pieces, and Debbie spent more time out. I was left to my own devices.

'Pass me those herbs, could you?' Alice asked, and it took me a couple of seconds to realise she was back in the present day. I handed her the herbs and looked at her willing her to continue.

'Sorry, I expect you're waiting for me to get to the point,' she said, and I nodded.

'But it's good to hear all the details,' I said.

'Well, it wasn't long after mum died that Debbie came home and announced she was pregnant. Dad was furious and at first Debbie wouldn't say whose baby it was.

Dad called her a whore and said he doubted she even knew whose it was. He told her to get rid of it. She spent ages crying in her room and I tried to comfort her. She considered an abortion, and I think she even went for an appointment somewhere, but in the end, she couldn't do it. I think she just wanted someone of her own to love.' Alice paused, gathering her thoughts, then continued.

'Somehow Dad found out that Pete was the father. I remember a lot of shouting and crying, but not a lot of detail. Anyway, later that year you were born.' Alice stopped chopping the herbs and looked at me. 'You were the most beautiful baby and so good. Debbie was so proud of you and loved you to bits, but things went wrong after a few months. Postnatal depression, the doctor said. Debbie started neglecting herself, and you, to some extent, so I did lots of things like feeding you, bathing you, taking you for walks. I moved your cot into my room so I could keep an eye on you at night and to let Debbie get some sleep. She became obsessed with the idea that she was ill like mum.'

'What was actually wrong with your mum?' I asked, not able to wait any longer.

'It was called Huntington's Chorea; they don't use the Chorea bit these days. It's hereditary, but quite rare, and in those days, I don't think even the doctor knew much about it. He said it was very unlikely that Debbie would get it and didn't really take her concerns seriously, even though we could see that she was getting more depressed and agitated by the day.

One day, I came home from school, and you were crying in your cot, Dad was drinking in front of the telly and Debbie seemed to be asleep on her bed. When I tried to wake her, she wouldn't wake up, she was cold; her lips were blue. I remember screaming. It must have been loud because Dad came running up.'

'She'd taken an overdose. There was no note, but it seemed obvious to me that her fears about her health, and her depression were the cause. The next few weeks felt like a blur. I couldn't believe Debbie would not be there anymore. Her funeral was the most tragic event I've ever been to, much worse than Mum's.' She paused and took a drink of water. I tried to imagine what it must have been like, and struggled to place myself, as the baby, in the scene.

'Are you OK?' I asked.

'Yes, fine, it just feels a little strange talking about it after all these years. Right, where was I? Yes, so after Debbie died, my aunt, dad's sister, came to stay for a while to look after us all. I don't know when, but not long after Debbie died, Dad must have contacted Pete, because I remember sitting on the stairs listening to a heated conversation between them, about you. I don't think Pete even realised you were alive. He thought Debbie had gone through with an abortion, and the poor bloke was in total shock. He kept saying, "Oh god what am I going to tell Carrie", and Dad was shouting, "She's your daughter. You need to take responsibility". He didn't want to see you, but Dad made him, and he called to me. I think he knew I was listening, and he told me to bring you in.'

'You looked at him, gurgled and smiled, and you could almost see his heart melting. Anyway, I don't know the details, but I would love to have been a fly on the wall when he got home. He contacted Dad some days, or maybe a week or so, later to say he and Carrie would take you on. I remember my aunt being shocked and saying, "What woman in her right mind takes on her husband's bastard". Sorry,' she said, looking at me.

I presumed she meant sorry for using the word bastard. I shrugged, unconcerned about that at least.

'So, the day came when we handed you over. I felt devastated. It was like another death. Apparently, Carrie didn't want any of your things. She insisted on having everything new, although I made sure your favourite pink monkey went with you. She didn't even want Dad or me to visit you, she just wanted to pretend you were hers, and we were nothing to do with you. I suppose looking back it would be the only way she could cope.'

'I don't remember a pink monkey,' I said. Not having that pink monkey felt symbolic of all the hurt in my childhood. I took a few moments to absorb all the information. I felt a deeper understanding and sympathy for Deborah. Alice was the only person who ever called her Debbie. I felt relieved that she wasn't quite the thoughtless flirt I'd imagined, but I was even less sure what to feel about mum. I wondered what my life would have been like if Deborah had lived.

Chapter 16

'OK, let's take this out onto the terrace,' Alice said, and picked up dishes of salad; whilst talking, she'd prepared a lovely-looking lunch.

'Ah, there you are,' she said to Ruth, who was sitting in the shade of the leafy canopy sketching.

'I thought you two needed to chat without me butting in, besides it got me out of helping prepare lunch.' Ruth winked, and relieved me of the dish I was carrying.

Once we'd all finished helping ourselves to food, Alice asked Ruth why she thought Carrie was prepared to adopt me.

'It's something I've puzzled about over for years. I know I could never have done it,' Alice said.

I felt odd listening to them discussing my past in this way.

'It was a shock to all of us,' Ruth said. 'I asked her why and tried to persuade her not to go through with it. It seemed a mad idea to me, but by the time I found out, it was all going through. Sorry Anna.' She gave me a half smile, realising I might feel awkward. 'The only conclusion I reached was that she was so desperate for a baby. It looked as though she couldn't have a baby of her own, and here was one handed to her on a plate as it were.'

'But how could she forgive Pete?' Asked Alice. 'I would have killed him.'

'I don't know how Pete persuaded her, but Carrie was besotted with him and didn't want to lose him. Perhaps a baby that was his seemed like a good idea, better than adopting one from a stranger. I don't know, who knows?'

'Do you think she regretted it?' Alice asked.

'I do,' I said, after listening quietly for a while. 'I don't think, looking back, that she ever came to terms with who I was.'

Ruth and Alice both looked at me.

'I wonder what would have happened to me if she had refused to take me on,' I said.

'I don't know. The only other option would have been adoption, through the social services, and that would have been awful. I was too young to look after you and Dad, well Dad couldn't manage.'

'You would still have become the lovely young woman you are now, but I wouldn't have been privileged to know you.' Ruth smiled at me, and I knew she was being sincere.

The simple lunch was delicious. The beautiful setting and warm sunshine added to the pleasure. We chatted about all sorts of other normal things as we continued eating. As we ended the meal, I steeled myself and asked Alice to tell me more about the condition that affected the family. It niggled in the pit of my stomach, and I needed to know more.

'Well, it is hereditary. I knew little about it when Mum was ill and couldn't find out much at that time. Then, I was watching TV one night, several years ago, and out of the blue a programme about it came on about Huntingdon's Disease. Apparently, although it is rare, it runs in families and all children with an affected parent are at risk. I went to see the doctor, but he just said it was a case of waiting to see whether I developed symptoms. He seemed to know less about it than me! I've read that there's a new blood test these days to test if you have the gene.'

'How does the condition develop? What does it do?' I asked.

'The symptoms?'

I nodded.

'Well, it seems to be different in different people, but with Mum she reached the stage where she couldn't walk or talk, and she kept jerking, which made her fall out of her chair. The nurses used to tip it back and put a strap round her waist, but she still slid out. It affected her mental faculties as well. It is like a type of dementia, I think. Sorry, Anna, I'm not very helpful, am I? I don't know the details properly,' Alice said. 'I've sort of stuck my head in the sand and tried to ignore it. I think there are special clinics in England now, where they look after people with it. Like most conditions, there's more understanding about it now, but I haven't kept up. In fact, I haven't given it a thought for years.'

I was hoping to feel reassured, but my anxiety levels were rising by the minute.

'I know a lot of research is going on now into treatments, and even an eventual cure,' she continued. 'After I saw the TV programme, I said to Dad that we needed to tell Pete and Carrie, just in case you got it. Dad wrote to them, trying to explain it. He showed me the letter, not very eloquent, but it got the point over that you could be at risk when you got older. He said he sent it, but I wasn't sure. Dad was so unreliable by that time, so I went round. Carrie was at home on her own and not very receptive, but I said what I needed to. I had the impression she knew about it, so she must have seen the letter.'

'Carrie never spoke about it,' Ruth said, imagining what a difficult meeting that must have been for both Alice and Carrie. Ruth felt surprised that Carrie never mentioned it to her. Surprised and disappointed. She always thought she was Carrie's confidant, even more after Pete's death. For some reason, she must have kept this information to herself. How could Carrie have been so selfish? Having taken on Anna, she was duty bound to look after her.

'Perhaps she never discussed it, even with Pete,' Alice said.

'I wonder. That's a big secret.' Ruth didn't know what to think.

I sat lost in thought for a few moments, not sure what to make of it all, except I was pretty sure I couldn't just bury my head in the sand like Alice.

'Are you worried?' I asked Alice.

'No, not now, not really. I went through a phase of wondering if I would get it, but what's the point of worrying about something you can't control? Anyway, I'm forty-five now and fine. Well, some people might say I'm mad, but I think that's just me,' she said. 'Try not to dwell on it. You could always talk to a doctor or someone to get the facts later, when you go back to the UK.'

'Hmm, I think I need to know,' I said. Knowing that for me, I couldn't live with the uncertainty; it felt like the sword of Damocles hanging over my head. I would make an appointment to see a doctor as soon as I got back home.

Alice and Ruth both nodded.

'But for now, I'm going to enjoy my time here,' I said. Indicating the old town and the sea. Sounding more upbeat than I felt at that moment. 'I think I'll go for a wander around, if that's OK?' I felt the need to be on my own. To have space to ponder all I'd heard.

'Good idea,' said Alice, understanding that there was a lot for me to think about.

'There are good views from the top of the street. We'll eat out later and we can show you round the rest of the town.'

Chapter 17

I walked up the hill to the top of the town and found a secluded spot beyond the church. Here I sank to the ground and leant against the old dry-stone wall, which radiated warmth absorbed by the hot sun of the day. The late afternoon was still warm, and the beautiful scene, spread before me like a painting, soothed my overactive mind. I gazed down the slope, covered with gnarled old grey-green olive trees. Their lengthening shadows danced across the dry earth in the light breeze. The trees became shorter and sparser and then stopped several metres before the shimmering blue sea took over from the land. The wide horizon rose into a clear blue sky, punctuated only by one or two lazily drifting clouds. These mirrored the progress of a yacht with bright white sails as it slid past the dark silhouette of an island far out in the bay. I watched a small lizard, oblivious to my presence, pause to catch the afternoon rays on one of the small rocks scattered amongst the sparse, scrubby shrubs.

Closing my eyes, I wondered what might be ahead of me. I was worried, but somehow, in this place, the worry felt unreal. So much had happened, so much had changed. I wondered what I would be doing now if I had never gone to see Mother that day, when summoned, if I'd just stayed at home. I would probably be getting in from work about now. My life wouldn't have changed, and I would be in blissful ignorance about Deborah and Huntington's Chorea. Ruth would be in her studio not searching out my birth relatives on a Greek island. I wondered, was that better? That was something I would never know, because here I was, and now I knew. I sat in the sun pondering the impossible and after a short time, instead of feeling anxious and wound up, I felt able to push those thoughts to the back of my mind. I locked them in a metaphorical cupboard marked 'issues for later consideration'.

That evening we went out to eat in a taverna that was perched on a small terrace, between the cobbled stepped street and the steep olive grove that dropped away towards the sea. The view was breathtaking, and we were lucky to get a table, because it was in a prime position to watch the sunset. An ancient tree that appeared to be growing out of the street shaded our table. The tension in my shoulders had eased, and I felt hungry, which was surprising after our lunch.

'Good evening.' A tall man in his thirties nodded towards us as he walked down the street.

I took a sip of wine and studied the man. He and Alice seemed to know each other well. He was tall and skinny, and attractive in a quirky sort of way. Scruffily dressed, he wore a dark blue bandana around his head. His reddish blonde hair was pulled back into a thin plait, which reached to his shoulder blades. A pair of expensive sunglasses hung from the neck of his once white T-shirt.

'Herman, join us for a glass of wine.' Alice pointed to an empty chair.

'I would love to, but I'm afraid I have got things to do,' he said, in an accent I couldn't quite place.

'Herman's from Germany,' Alice said, as if anticipating my curiosity.

'Oh, you don't look German,' I said, and could have kicked myself for being crass.

'Really?' He said, raising an eyebrow. 'And how do German's look?'

Before I could speak, he placed two fingers under his nose and lifted his arm into a Nazi salute.

I felt mortified and could feeling myself blushing to the roots of my hair.

'I'm so sorry, I don't …'

He threw his head back and gave a loud hoot of laughter, drowning out my apology.

'I have watched your Fawlty Towers,' he grinned. 'Don't mention the war!' He carried on laughing.

Alice and Ruth were also laughing, so I swallowed my embarrassment and laughed as well, mainly in relief.

'Herman, this is my good friend Ruth from the UK and Anna is our niece.'

I felt a swell of love for Alice for referring to me as 'our niece'. That simple phrase pulled us together as a family. I beamed at her, a warmth spreading through my body.

'How do you do, Ruth and Anna?' Herman leant across and shook both our hands. 'Are you staying long?'

Ruth, Alice and I exchanged glances. How long either of us was staying wasn't anything we'd discussed.

'I hope so,' Alice answered for us. 'As long as possible.'

'Ah good, we will meet again then.' Herman stepped back onto the cobbles.

'Enjoy your meal,' he said as he set off down the steep street.

'Herman's the island's vet,' said Alice, as we all watched him stride away.

'He doesn't look like a vet,' I said, and we all again collapsed into giggles.

'No, particularly not a German vet,' Alice said, laughing.

'Oh dear, I must learn to think before I open my mouth,' I said, wiping a tear from my cheek.

I composed myself, took a sip of wine, and surveyed the surroundings.

'I noticed when I was wandering around that most of the small shops are run by non-Greeks. Is that right?'

'Yes. Most are Brits and Germans,' Alice said. 'An earthquake destroyed the old town in 1965, and the residents moved down to the port and other parts of the island and set up homes and businesses there. The old town was left to the forces of nature. It is such a beautiful position that tourists soon discovered it and started buying up properties, renovating them and turning the town into the charming place it is today.'

'Aren't you worried about another earthquake?' I asked.

'There are often minor tremors that shake the earth for a couple of seconds. But, well, I'm a bit of a fatalist. Live for now and not worry about tomorrow.'

'I guess so, but don't the Greeks mind? I mean, don't they resent foreigners taking away their business?' I asked.

'You'd think they would,' Ruth agreed.

'Well, no, it's not like that,' said Alice, topping up our glasses. 'I think the locals were pleased that someone was prepared to restore the old houses; they didn't have the money themselves. Besides, the town as it is now, is attracting more tourists to the island, and so the whole economy benefits.'

A waiter brought our food, huge plates of moussaka and a bowl of Greek salad.

'Costa, this is my niece.' There was that warm glow again. 'She wants to know if you feel angry about foreigners like me setting up our businesses here?'

He threw his hands in the air,

'I love you all! This taverna wouldn't be here without you. It makes me happy. It makes my wife happy, and my children happy.'

He put our plates down and then returned with another carafe of wine. 'This is for my special English lady and her family, from me.'

'Oh Costa, thank you, that's so kind,' Alice said. He blew a kiss in her direction and went back to the kitchen.

'The Greek men can be such charmers.' Alice raised her glass. 'To Costa,' she said.

We all raised our glasses. I was feeling on the tipsy side.

'And to both of you,' I said, waving my glass towards Alice and Ruth.

Chapter 18

My worries about unknown health problems stayed locked away, most of the time, over the next few days; I became an expert at keeping them at bay, forcing them into the depths of my subconscious whenever they tried to take over. The island was so beautiful, and Alice and Ruth were such good company that I couldn't help but relax and enjoy myself. Sometimes, Alice asked the two guys who ran the shop opposite hers to mind her shop while she acted as our tour guide. We hired a small boat one day and motored to remote beaches and found tavernas serving fresh fish and surprisingly good wine. Alice seemed to be known and liked by a lot of the people we met, which added to our enjoyment and relaxation.

Sometimes, I lazed on the terrace reading, while Ruth painted, or we wandered the streets of the old town exploring the little shops or sat people-watching in a taverna, of which there were many. Tourists who ventured up to the old town were, in the main, couples; the different shapes and sizes fascinated me. American tourists, as a generalisation, were by far the loudest, huffing and puffing up the hill in the heat. British tourists spent a lot of time window shopping but bought little. The German and Japanese tourists were the ones with the money. One afternoon, fascinated, I watched a Japanese couple take photos of each other in front of every shop, and every gap between the buildings, where the sea shone far below, making sure they captured every scene for posterity. A weary English family with two small children, one in a buggy, struggled up the cobbled steps to find a vantage point ready for the sunset. The children looked and acted as though they would rather be anywhere else; the beach, I thought.

Most evenings, the three of us placed ourselves in a taverna or sitting on rocks under the old castle ruins for the stunning sunset across the sea. What is it about the sunset I wondered? It draws people like a magnet, romantic and mysterious. It amazed me how long it took for the sun's rim to touch the horizon, but once it did, the fiery ball sank into the sea in minutes, sending red and golden rays across the waves and then, within seconds, darkness. It never failed to move me.

The old town was charming. Some buildings had been restored using the original stone and others rebuilt, I imagined, with concrete and then whitewashed. The overall effect was timeless. Old olive trees grew up in small courtyards and spread welcome shade, but it was the twisting streets, some comprising only narrow steps and others cobbled, but all inaccessible to cars, which made the whole place feel authentic and tranquil. I felt happy and relaxed, but I knew it couldn't last forever. I would at some time have to go home to find answers to my questions.

After one of my wanders around, I retreated into the cool of Alice's shop. Not only did she have a skill in making the actual jewellery, but the displays in her little shop were also artistic and drew the customers inside. It always seemed to be busy and very few people left empty-handed. She created beautifully crafted pieces to suit all styles and budgets.

'Thank you, enjoy wearing them,' she said to a couple, leaving with a bow-topped bag and satisfied smiles, as I entered.

'Hi,' I said. 'Good morning?'

'Very good. People are in the mood for spending. But I'm in the mood for lunch,' she said, moving to close the door. 'I saw Herman this morning, you remember, the vet?'

'Yes, was he buying jewellery?' I asked, still feeling embarrassed at the memory of our meeting.

'No,' she chuckled at the thought. 'I bumped into him down the road. I happened to mention that you are a qualified veterinary nurse. He was very interested. He told me he goes to a rescue centre on another island; I'm not sure what he does there, but he wondered if you fancied going with him next time he goes?'

'That all sounds a bit vague, Alice. Are you match-making or trying to get me a job?'

She laughed. 'Oh dear, does it sound like that? No, neither, well more the job, I guess. He said he might come up later to ask you himself.'

'OK, I'll wait and see.' I played it cool, but my interest was sparked.

Everywhere on the island there were stray cats and dogs. Most of them looked in good condition but I wondered who looked after them if they became ill. One vet I worked with in England took a sabbatical when he was younger and worked in a rescue centre in Turkey. He told stories, hair-raising and heartbreaking in equal measure. It was where he said his skills were honed. I wondered if Greece would be similar and was eager to find out.

It wasn't until the next morning that Herman appeared. I was sitting on the step outside Alice's shop, chatting to Jorgy about his life. How he met Luke and came to be making pottery and silk-printing on a Greek island. The twists and turns in people's lives fascinated me more, now that my life was subtly heading in a different direction. It only takes one seemingly unimportant decision to change the course of your life. Certainly, for Luke and Jorgy, their relationship and current life seemed to hinge on Jorgy missing a bus one day in Stockholm. I was enjoying his story when Herman loped up the street.

'Hi,' I said, not getting up.

'Hi Anna, did Alice mention I might come to see you?'

'I better get back to work, see you later.' Jorgy stretched his legs, nodded towards Herman and disappeared into his shop.

Herman took the place on the step vacated by Jorgy and, without preamble, described the work he did at the rescue centre. Apparently, it was a tiny charity, run on a shoestring, and he offered his services every few months, free of charge. He was going over tomorrow, even though he wasn't due to go for a routine visit for another week. The person who ran the shelter had contacted him about an injured cat that needed his attention sooner rather than later. When I asked whether there was a vet on the other island, Herman shrugged his shoulders and raised his eyebrows, so I didn't pursue the topic. He just said he could do with another competent pair of hands and wondered if I would be interested in going with him. Not wanting to disrupt my holiday, he said he wouldn't be offended if I declined. Herman watched me with interest before I replied and seemed genuinely pleased when I said I would love to go.

Chapter 19

The next morning, I met Herman on the quay. I helped him carry several bags onto the small ferry we were taking to the neighbouring island. There was a large, wheeled, cool box, a big rucksack, and two large Gladstone-type bags.

'They have little equipment there, so I take what I think I might need,' he said.

I wondered how on earth he could manage all this on his own and, as if reading my mind, he grinned and said he wasn't asking me to accompany him just to act as a courier!

The ferry was quite a quick trip, and, on the way, Herman asked about my job in England. He seemed impressed with the range of work I carried out routinely and, for the first time since qualifying, I felt pleased that I had followed the degree course. He outlined the expected tasks for our visit. As well as dealing with the injured cat, if time allowed, we might spay a stray cat and dog while we were there.

'You never know what might be waiting. I must always be prepared for the unexpected as well,' he said.

The sun was sweltering, as usual, and the ferry docked in the small harbour under a cloudless sky. I smiled to myself; this was the best commute to work I could imagine. Herman handed me a bottle of water out of one bag and took another for himself.

'You must drink plenty, so you don't get dehydrated.' He took a long swig from his bottle. I did the same.

'Right, let's go. We'll take a taxi.' He waved to a driver lolling against his car in the shade. They knew each other apparently, as they shook hands and conversed in fluent Greek. His mastery of the language was another of Herman's skills, which impressed me.

We piled the bags in the car, and I squeezed into the back seat next to the big cool box. We took off at a speed that felt far too fast for the potholed state of the roads. Herman and the driver were chatting all the way, and, to my alarm, the driver kept waving his hands around while nonchalantly correcting the veer of the car with one hand. By the time we reached our destination, I felt as though I'd been through a spin dryer and was a nervous wreck. I drank the rest of my water, took some deep breaths and composed myself, leaving Herman to unload the car.

We were outside a traditional style villa, quite old and built out of mellow stone, which in the heat of the day seemed to melt into the surrounding garden. Before we picked up all the bags, a brown and white Saluki Lurcher cross type of dog came bounding down the path, barking excitedly and leaping around us. He was all legs and noise, which made it impossible for us to move on until we gave him lots of attention.

'Hello Frank.' Herman leant down and stroked the dog's long, silky ears.

'Frank. Komme!' A female voice boomed across the garden.

Frank stopped, listened, hesitated, and then bounded back up the path.

We made our way towards the villa, where a woman, with Frank, (who by then had flopped at her feet), stood by the door waiting for us. A large floppy hat and sunglasses hid her eyes; she was holding a scrawny cat in her arms. A broad smile lit up her face when we reached her, and she greeted Herman in German. The two chatted for a moment before Herman turned to me and introduced us.

'Anna, this is Ingrid, a good friend of mine and the owner of this sanctuary. Ingrid, this is Anna, a veterinary nurse from England.'

'Oh, how wonderful,' she said, removing her sunglasses and speaking English with barely an accent. 'I try to help but I'm a bit too… what's the word? I don't like the blood to be much help.'

'Squeamish?' I said, studying her. She must have been about sixty. Her skin was tanned and wrinkled from the sun, but her past beauty was still evident. Her body looked lithe and supple in her shorts and skimpy top.

'Squeamish, yes what a lovely word. Come on in. Would you both like a cold drink before you get going?'

I immediately said yes, and Herman said no, so Ingrid decided we should have a quick drink while we sorted everything out. Herman led the way round the back of the villa to an annex where, as soon as we drew near, we could hear a dog barking and a cat yowling.

'They don't like being inside,' Herman said, as he opened the door. There were four cat boxes on the floor, each with an annoyed cat inside. There was one dog in a penned off area, and in another pen, on the other side of the small room, was the cat who was yowling in distress. Its arched back and stilted movements showed it was in pain and frightened.

'A couple of tourists brought it in the night before last, but I haven't been able to get near it since,' said Ingrid, putting a tray with a jug and two glasses down on a small desk.

'OK, we'll have a look at it first.' Herman was already busy opening bags and taking out instruments and drugs.

'The treatment room is through here,' he said, indicating for me to follow. It was tiny, with old equipment and nothing like the state-of-the-art premises I worked in at home. There was a small fridge where we put the drugs and a couple of cupboards on the wall.

'I'll leave you to it.' Ingrid closed the door behind her. Herman flicked a switch, and a large fan started rotating on the ceiling, but it only stirred the warm air around. We observed the distressed cat as best we could. A large swelling on one side of its mouth indicated the problem.

'We'll have to sedate it before we can examine it,' Herman said, pulling a cylinder out of a bag and attaching a mask. He picked up a blanket. 'Can you try to get its attention?'

I started clicking my fingers and making high-pitched noises while Herman held the blanket out behind the box. The cat, just for a second, stopped yowling and looked at me. Herman gently threw the blanket over the cat and scooped it up, wrapping its legs inside so it couldn't scratch, while he tried to look in its mouth.

'OK, can you hold the mask over its nose?' The cat, still struggling in Herman's arms, soon became sleepy, and he could lie it down on the table and began examining it. It was a neutered male. The problem in his mouth became obvious: two broken teeth and a huge abscess. No wonder the poor thing was yowling in pain. I held the cat while Herman prepared both himself and everything he needed. Without fuss, Herman removed the teeth and drained the abscess. The stench of pus in the small, warm room was quite nauseating. After an antibiotic injection, the cat was soon back in the box to recover.

'Come on outside. We need some fresh air for a minute before we clean up and carry on.'

With relief, I followed him into the sunshine and took some gulps of fresh Mediterranean air. My shirt was sticking to my back, and I gulped down some more cold juice from the jug that Ingrid had thoughtfully topped up.

'Ready? Let's get on,' he said, putting his glass back on the tray. 'One day, maybe we'll afford some air conditioning, but for now, we sweat.' He grinned.

We cleaned the table, laid out instruments and scrubbed up. It felt primitive but, somehow, more real than the work at home. All the cats and the dog were male, so neutering was straightforward and quick. Herman was a very calm and efficient worker, and we soon returned all our patients back to their boxes and pens to recover, while we tidied everything away. Herman scrubbed the surfaces and asked me to check the drugs in the fridge, and to swap any that were near the end of their use by date with others from the cool box. It felt like we were a good team.

'Good work, thank you. Now let's find Ingrid.' Herman closed the door. 'We'll check on them again before we leave.'

Ingrid was sitting on the terrace reading and jumped up when we appeared. 'Come and sit down. I have some lunch ready.'

My stomach lurched and I realised I was starving when Ingrid brought out dishes of salad and traditional cheese and spinach pie. It was a very companionable lunch. Ingrid was quite a character with a great sense of humour; it turned out she used to be a dancer in a Burlesque club in Berlin.

'It's where I met my husband,' she said. 'He was a frequent visitor when he was in town. Said he liked the music!'

Herman laughed. 'I bet,' he said.

Ingrid's husband, she told me, was a pilot, and it was his idea to buy the villa in Greece in preparation for his retirement, which was coming up soon. 'We used to only come for holidays, but now I live here most of the time; with the animals it gets more difficult to leave. We have big plans to improve the animal area once Erich is here full time.'

Air conditioning would be near the top of the list, I was sure.

After lunch, which was nothing like the quick sandwich in the staff room I was used to, we went to check on the animals. Herman and Ingrid discussed their ongoing care and if possible, she would try to keep them in the centre for a day or two, but these were feral animals and used to being free. She told us that food kept them close by for a few days, and she hoped she would be able to entice the cat with the abscess to stay long enough to finish a course of antibiotics.

'I hope to see you again,' she said to me, as we loaded ourselves back into the taxi for the hair-raising drive back to the port to catch the ferry.

Chapter 20

Once back on our island, I helped Herman carry the bags back to his surgery, which was on the edge of the main town. It was well equipped and spotlessly clean, much more in line with the modern conditions at home.

'Anna?' Herman stopped as we were packing equipment away. 'Will you work with me? I mean, as a proper job. I know you're on holiday, but I sort of picked up that it was an open-ended stay, is that right?'

I laughed, surprised by the unexpected offer, but he appeared to be serious.

'It won't be full time, or much pay.'

'You're really selling it.' I laughed again.

'Well?'

'Well, it's incredibly tempting.'

'But?'

'Not a real but,' I said, my brain whirling. It would be a great opportunity, and I couldn't think of anywhere I would rather be now. 'But I need to go back to the UK soon, to sort some things out.' I knew that I must go back to be tested. Sooner rather than later. Herman's offer seemed to clarify my mind.

'When? Will you come back?' His directness forcing me to confront the issues myself.

'I just need to arrange my travel details; I'm not sure how long I'll be away, but I will be back,' I said with complete confidence.

'Good, so will you work with me when you come back? I have worked alone for a long time so I can wait.' He smiled, and at that moment I wanted to work in this amazing little surgery, more than anything.

'Shall I come in before I leave, to get a feel for it?'

'A feel for it, for what?'

'Sorry, figure of speech. To see what you do and what you would want me to do?'

'Yes, good, come on Wednesday morning.'

I walked back up to the old town feeling excited on the one hand, but anxious on the other. The cicadas surrounded me with sound as I climbed the path towards Alice's villa, and my head was aching. I wasn't sure if it was the heat or all the issues spinning around in my brain. How many more turns was my life going to take? I wondered. I needed to discuss everything with Alice and Ruth before I decided what to do. The three of us spent another evening on Alice's terrace, sipping ouzo and eating juicy olives.

The thought of me staying and working with Herman delighted them, but I told them I felt certain that I now needed to go back home to be tested. They were concerned but understood that I wouldn't be completely at ease until I knew. Ruth was content to stay longer on the island with Alice, she was beginning to be quite at home. I would be travelling back on my own.

The next day I bought a ferry and air ticket back to the UK for the following Saturday. Before then, Alice made sure I saw all the best places on the island. We ate wonderful food in tiny tavernas, beside the clear blue sea, drank wine, watching the perfect sunset and lazed and swam from golden beaches.

'I want to imprint on your mind how lovely it is, so you don't go back to England and forget us,' she said.

I was touched. I was certain I wouldn't forget.

As arranged, I spent a morning with Herman at the surgery, just as an observer. The morning wasn't very busy, routine vaccinations, and a dog that was vomiting after eating something disgusting on the harbourside. An English man, with a very overweight Labrador, came in for the dog to be treated for worms, to fulfil the conditions of his pet passport before returning to the UK.

'He is too fat,' Herman told the man, who ran an estate agency on the island, and was returning to England to attend his sister's third wedding. He seemed unimpressed and was reluctant to go, and said he used having the dog as his excuse for not going, but unfortunately for him, his sister knew the dog had a passport and insisted on him being there.

'It's too hot for him to exercise here,' he said in reply to Herman's comment.

'He needs less food then.'

The dog, a soppy golden Labrador, looked sadly up at Herman, as though he understood every word, then flopped onto the floor with a sigh.

Herman knelt on the floor and looked into the dog's eyes, 'Now you listen to me. You do lots of exercise in England and when I next see you, I want you to be a lot thinner. OK?' The dog thumped his tail on the floor, stood up, and gave Herman a sloppy kiss on the nose.

'Are you driving all the way home from here?' I asked.

He nodded. 'It's a bit of a nightmare journey, but at least, we don't have to do it often. My wife flew back yesterday. I expect to get home on Saturday or Sunday. It's all your fault,' he said, patting the dog on the head. 'I couldn't be without him, though. I often leave him here with my colleague, but he's very busy and we're going to be away for a couple of weeks. Anyway, I didn't want to be without him.'

The dog nuzzled his owner and wagged his tail even more.

'Good luck,' I said, as he left, clutching the correctly stamped passport.

Herman tidied up. 'Some days it's busier and sometimes I get called out to animals in difficulty, in remoter parts of the island. It'll be different working here than in England,' he said.

'I'm sure it will. I think it will do me good to see animals other than pampered pets.'

'This morning hasn't put you off?'

'Not in the slightest.'

'Good. So, you still don't know when you will be back?'

I shook my head and felt pleased that he asked when I was coming back, rather than when I was leaving.

'It depends how long I take to get everything sorted,' I said, but didn't elaborate and, to his credit, he didn't ask. I wasn't sure if in the same position I could have resisted probing a bit.

'Maybe I can check with Alice in a week or two? Goodbye and good luck.' He held out his hand, and we shook.

Chapter 21

I arrived back in England to grey drizzle and temperatures that felt more like October than mid-June. I'd been away for just over two weeks, but it felt like a lifetime. I doubted the wisdom of coming back the minute I stepped through my front door. All the old doubts and anxieties jostled for priority in my mind. I tried to push them away and instead wondered what Ruth and Alice would be doing now. I imagined them pouring a glass of ouzo and lemonade and relaxing on the terrace. I picked my mail up from the doormat and flicked through it before humping my bag upstairs. It was nearly all junk mail, which I left on the small table by the door, ready to go in the newly acquired recycling bin. The answerphone light was blinking, but I unpacked and made a cup of tea before listening.

The first message was from Rachel asking me to ring her. I deleted the message.

"Anna, it's Jen. Where are you? I need you. Sarah's rubbish. We've lost every game in the last fortnight. Call me, hope all's OK." I laughed. Jen and I played doubles tennis together, very badly, but it sounded like her sister Sarah was even worse. I made a note to ring her tomorrow; a game of tennis would do me good.

Another message was from the dentist reminding me of my appointment the following day, which was about a week ago, and the next message was from them again letting me know that because I missed my appointment, I would have to pay a fine or be struck of their books. I wondered if I could wriggle out of it by explaining that my mother recently died. Probably wrong, but worth a try, I thought.

I listened to the last message, and it reminded me of the real reason I had returned from Greece.

"This is Doctor Edward's surgery," a woman's voice said. "Doctor Edwards has referred you to the hospital. A copy of the referral letter will be in the post." I checked when that message had been left. It was four days old. I was impressed. After I decided to return, I had emailed the surgery from Greece, explaining my situation and stating that I wanted to be tested as soon as possible. I was dubious that I would get a reply or at best thought they would just tell me to make an appointment. I picked up the couple of letters that weren't junk mail from the kitchen worktop and found the doctor's referral. Attached to the letter was a handwritten note from the GP, inviting me to make an appointment if I felt the need to discuss the situation, either before or after my appointment at the hospital. My stomach contracted in fear. Doctors didn't make these offers unless there was something to be worried about. He hoped I wouldn't have to wait too long.

I read the copy of the referral letter, which included most of the content of my email, and requested an early appointment with a genetic counsellor. I felt anxious and echoed his hope of not waiting too long. Having decided to be tested, I wanted to know, now.

I needn't have worried. The next morning my phone rang; it was the hospital offering me an appointment for the following week. Once again, the speed of the response impressed me. I couldn't settle the next day and rather than contacting friends, I spent most of my time on the computer trying to find out about Huntington's. There wasn't much information, but what I discovered caused even more anxiety.

Knowing I couldn't put it off any longer, I rang Rachel. I knew she wanted me to help her sort out mother's house. I couldn't think of anything I wanted to do less, particularly with Rachel, but I knew I must. We arranged to meet at the house the following day at two in the afternoon. She sounded almost pleased to hear from me and was interested in where I'd been.

Chapter 22

I shuddered the next day, as I passed the end of the drive leading towards the hospice. I couldn't bring myself to glance up in the direction of the old house. I'd erased the memory of that last afternoon from my mind whilst I was away or at least pushed it into the dark recesses of my mind, but now it thudded back into my consciousness like a sledgehammer. My heart pounded in my chest, and I thought I was going to be sick. I vowed to myself that I would mention nothing to do with that day to Rachel.

Her car was already in the drive when I pulled in. Taking a deep breath to calm myself, I climbed out of the car and walked round the back to the kitchen. Rachel was sitting at the old pine table, surrounded by paper and old photos; she must have arrived long before two. I checked my watch. I wasn't late. She looked her normal pristine self; I don't think I'd ever seen her looking scruffy; she always looked like she was about to go to out for afternoon tea in some gentile establishment.

The old table brought back memories of heated exchanges over mealtimes. The meal I hated most was Sunday lunch, which, inevitably, ended with me stomping out of the room, feeling hard done by. Followed by barbed comments from Mother.

'Hi,' I said, trying to sound upbeat.

'Read this,' Rachel said without even looking up at me.

Not a good start. 'What is it?' I asked, looking at a sheet of writing paper on the table, covered in scrawled loopy writing.

'A letter about you.'

I couldn't quite work out whether her tone was accusatory or concerned.

'I found it in this box of papers in the sideboard.' She nodded towards an old shoebox on the table.

I felt an overwhelming instinct to turn round and walk straight out of the door. I assumed this was the letter Alice mentioned, but I wasn't sure I wanted to read it in front of Rachel. It was clear she had already read every word and was going to scrutinise me as I read it. I looked at Rachel and she edged a chair out with her foot. I sat down on the opposite side of the table. She pushed the letter towards me. The date on it was April 1977.

> *Dear Peter and Carrie*
> *I know you didn't want anything to do with us after you took the baby, but there is something you need to know. My wife died of a condition called Huntington's Chorea and there is a chance it might affect Anna when she is older. I don't know much about it, but you and your wife might like to speak to a doctor to find out the details.*
> *I hope Anna is well. I know it was the right thing for her to live with you.*
> *Yours,*
> *Bill Jenkins*

'What does it mean?' Rachel asked, childishly sucking her hair, a habit that always annoyed me.

'Bill Jenkins was my grandad. My mum killed herself and Dad, our dad, was my real dad, so he and Mum adopted me,' I said. 'I've only found out more details since Mum died.'

Rachel looked bemused. I felt quite impressed that I'd condensed the story into one sentence, but I knew that wouldn't be the end, and after what felt like an interminably long silence, she spoke.

'Blimey. Did you know?' she asked.

'Know?'

'Know Dad was your real dad?'

'Not until Mum told me that day when I came round. You remember? The day when you and Ruth were both here.'

I noticed she was blushing and looked uncomfortable. I wondered if she was remembering all those taunts of "he's not even your real dad," she used to throw at me when we were children.

'What's Huntington's Chorea?' she asked.

'I'm not certain; it's hereditary, so I might have it. I've got an appointment at the hospital next week; they can do a blood test to check.'

'You don't seem surprised,' she said, and picked up the letter to read it again.

'No, I'm not. Alice filled in the details for me,' I said. 'That's why I've come back from Greece.'

'Who's Alice? I had a card from Ruth saying you were both in Greece. She didn't mention anyone else.' She stared at me, but not, I thought, unkindly.

At that moment, I realised how quickly I'd accepted Alice as my aunt, and for a moment felt surprised that Rachel didn't know who she was. I wasn't sure I was ready to go into all the details with her, but for once, she seemed interested and even concerned.

'Well, Alice is my aunt, my real mum's sister. She lives in Greece and Ruth, and I have been to see her. In fact, Ruth is still there, and I plan to go back.'

'Blimey,' she said again.

I smiled to myself. Who says 'blimey' these days?

'That explains why Ruth wasn't in when I called round last week,' she said. 'So, let me get this straight. You resulted from a relationship Dad had and then when your real mum died our mum took you on? I'm struggling to comprehend. Why? When was that? Were you born after they were married?' A look of accusation flicked across her face.

I nodded and shrugged. 'I know it's hard to believe. I've only started to make sense of it all myself.'

'Who was your real mum, then?' she asked.

'She was called Deborah, and she was a friend of Ruth's.'

'Bloody hell, how did they keep all this secret?'

I laughed at her reaction but just shrugged again.

'But I don't understand how, or why, mum did it. God, if Jim announced he was father to a baby by another woman and expected me to look after it... I'd, well I'd go berserk. I'd kill him,' she said.

'I think that is most people's view. She must have been in an impossible position,' I said. 'I guess times have changed.'

Chapter 23

We sat in silence for what felt like an age, both contemplating the dilemma. Rachel started picking up more pieces of paper. I thought the questions had ended, so I followed her lead and reached for some papers.

'How are we sorting all this stuff?' I looked at a pile of documents that were old bills.

'I'm not sure. I suppose most of it will be rubbish. Just put anything that looks important in a pile, and we can burn the rest.' There was an accumulation of old letters from people unknown to us, and strangers in photos; some named, others anonymous. It seemed wrong, but there was no point in keeping them. They meant nothing to either of us, so they went on the rubbish pile.

'Look!' Rachel unfolded a newspaper article that was folded into the Order of Service from Dad's funeral. It was old, and the creases began to split as we opened it out.

I moved around the table and read it over her shoulder. As I read, I felt an overwhelming sensation of guilt that somehow his death was my fault. I was the catalyst for all this pain and unhappiness.

Man Dies After Pub Brawl

Forty-two-year-old father of two, Peter Fairbrother, died in an ambulance on the way to hospital after crashing his motorbike, following a brawl in the Golden Lion pub. Mr Fairbrother, who had been drinking heavily, caused a scene when the landlord, Ed Williams, refused to serve him. The situation escalated and punches were thrown.

A drinker in the pub said that Mr Fairbrother became abusive and lashed out at Mr Williams when he tried to throw him out. Other drinkers went to Mr Williams' aid.

Stella Arnold, a passerby, said she heard shouting and saw Mr Fairbrother get on his motorbike and skid out of the car park at great speed.

He swerved to avoid an oncoming car and rode straight into a lamppost along the road.

'He appeared very drunk, and agitated, and was swearing loudly. He didn't put his crash helmet on.' Ms Arnold said.

An ambulance was quickly on the scene, but Mr Fairbrother suffered severe head and neck injuries and was pronounced dead in the ambulance.

He leaves a wife and two young daughters behind.

There was a grainy photo of Dad inserted into the text. This was the first time, for me, I expect for both of us, that we knew more than that dad had died following a motorbike accident.
   'I remember that night, before he left,' I said, tapping the cutting.
   'Do you? Where was I?' she asked.
   'I don't know, at a friend's house, I expect.'
   'What happened?'

It was a sign of how distant we were that something as big as this in our lives had never been discussed. I cast my mind back eighteen years. I was almost twelve and Rachel was nine years old. Although I couldn't remember ever speaking to anyone about that night, each minute detail had seared itself into my brain, as though it were yesterday.

'I was upstairs in Mum and Dad's bedroom. I thought Mum was busy downstairs, so I sat at the dressing table and tried out her lipstick. It was deep pink. Even for me, I put it on quite expertly. I was pouting at myself in the mirror when Mum came up behind me. I hadn't heard her coming up the stairs.

"What the devil are you doing? How dare you!" she yelled at me. She grabbed hold of my hair and pulled me back off the stool.'

'I used to do that all the time. She thought it was funny, especially when I smudged it round my mouth,' Rachel interrupted me. 'Sorry, go on,' she said.

I took a deep breath and continued. 'She didn't find it funny,' I said, and hesitated. 'I don't know if she was about to hit me. It wouldn't have been the first time, or the last. I braced myself, but Dad arrived in the bedroom at that moment.' "Carrie. Stop. Leave her alone this minute," he shouted.'

'Mum let go of my hair and Dad told me to go to my room. They both went downstairs, and I could hear raised voices, but not what they were saying. The shouting seemed to go on and on, and then it went quiet. The next thing I heard was Dad revving his motorbike. I knelt on the bed and watched him screech off the drive, and ride down the road at top speed. That was the last time I saw him.'

'I must have come home. I remember Aunt Ruth coming here later, telling us daddy was in hospital,' Rachel said.

I nodded. I remembered Mum coming in through the front door later and throwing herself into Ruth's arms, sobbing that he'd gone, and she had never said sorry. I also have a vivid picture of Rachel sitting on Mum's knee being rocked backwards and forwards while Mum stroked her hair. No physical contact or words of comfort occurred between Mum and me. Aunt Ruth hugged me and explained about Dad's accident. She was around a lot after that.

'I'm so sorry,' Rachel said.

I nodded, although I wasn't sure what she was apologising for.

'Do you fancy a coffee?' Rachel asked after reading the article again.

'Yes please, shall we have it outside?'

'Good idea. I could do with some fresh air.'

We sat side by side on the garden bench overlooking the lawn. Looking at the once pristine, now tangled shrubbery and flower borders, drinking our coffee. It felt almost companionable.

'The garden's been a bit neglected since mum became ill. She loved this rose.' Rachel got up and snapped a rose off a nearby bush. She put it to her nose and inhaled. 'Lovely!' She passed the rose to me.

Its perfume smelt sweet and heady. It made me feel sad. There were so many things I didn't know. I felt like I had lived on the periphery of this family, always kept at arm's length. I twirled the pale pink rose between my fingers and sighed.

'We should have been friends,' Rachel said. 'Why weren't we?' She raised her eyes to mine.

'I don't know. It was complicated, I suppose.' I thought the reason was because Mum subtly, or maybe not so subtly, turned Rachel away from me. 'I think Mum wanted you all to herself,' I said.

'Poor you, I was a bit of a brat sometimes, wasn't I?' she said.

I didn't reply but agreed.

'Remember when you pushed me into the pond in my new dress?' she asked.

'I tried to make it look like an accident that I'd slipped, and you just happened to be in the way and lost balance.'

'I made a real fuss, didn't I? That dress was never the same.'

'Yes, and I got a sharp slap round the legs and sent to my room,' I recalled. 'Then when you pushed me in a few days later, Mum said it was my own fault, and you got away with it.'

'That was a bit unfair, wasn't it? I try so hard with my two to treat them the same.'

'Do you have a favourite?' I asked.

'No,' Rachel said, without considering my question. 'Of course not.' She sat thinking for a moment. 'Not a favourite, but I suppose I treat them differently. I worry more about Gemma. She's more highly strung, but Chloe's so laid back and funny I'm more relaxed with her, maybe because she was the second. I never expected having children to be so much hard work. Even when they were babies, it wasn't quite the beautiful experience I imagined. You know chubby cherubs wrapped in fluffy white towels, that sort of thing.'

'Did you go back to work?' I was surprised that I didn't know this basic piece of information about my own sister, well, half-sister.

'No, we thought it best for one of us to be at home and, of course, it was always going to be me. To be honest, I shouldn't say it, but bringing up kids is boring. I used to go to mothers' groups, but all they talked about was babies. I plan to do something, even if I can't recreate my career, when they both go to school full time. What about you? Do you want kids?'

'I need to find a man first.' I laughed, but having children didn't interest me much. I'd seen plenty of exhausted friends, and spoiled brats, to make it a less than tempting proposition.

'We had some good times when we were young though, didn't we?' She recollected family days out and holidays. She was right. I remembered some fun times, but only when Dad was involved.

'Do you remember when you got stuck up the tree?' Rachel nodded towards an old sycamore at the end of the garden.

I laughed out loud. 'You left me up there. I was so scared.'

'You thought I'd gone for dad to help you, but I just went to my room and watched you from the window.'

'That was so mean. I still don't like heights.' I didn't know why I was laughing, perhaps because it was such a typically normal sibling tale.

'Dad heard you shouting and got you down in the end!'

'He bought me an ice cream.'

'Did he? He didn't buy me one. That's not fair,' Rachel said with mock indignation.

I felt soothed by our conversation and think Rachel felt better for it as well. I smiled at her.

'Ready to carry on?' she enquired and stood up.

'I'll just be a minute.' I walked down the garden and looked at the pond. It was smaller than I remembered and muddier than it was when I'd given Rachel a push. I smiled to myself. At the time it was worth the slapped legs. I wandered across the lawn, now in need of a cut, and was sure I could still make out where the swing used to be with the brown, muddy patch beneath, where our feet scuffed and killed the grass. I remembered swinging so high that the pegs holding it to the ground loosened and the whole thing almost took off. I used to hang upside down off the sidebars and climb to the top and sit on the rail taunting Rachel, who was too afraid to climb up. I badgered Dad for a climbing frame, but he said the garden was too small. "There's a good enough park round the corner. I'm not having more clutter in my garden", I could hear mum's voice echoing in my ears even now.

I looked back towards the house. The light grey paint on the back wall now looked darker and grubby, mirroring my life inside. It didn't hold happy memories for me, and I wouldn't be sorry when it was sold. I could see Rachel busy through the window, and with a last look around, returned to help.

'What are we going to do with everything? I mean furniture, clothes and all that sort of thing?'

'We can divide personal items and valuables. I think Mum gave Ruth her jewellery before she died; it was all left to her in the will anyway, so there shouldn't be much of value left. Clothes to the charity shop and then a house clearance firm can take the rest before we put the house on the market, if you agree. Take anything you want first, of course.'

Rachel seemed to have it all worked out. I suspected that Jim, her solicitor husband, advised her on what to do. For my part, I just wanted to get it over with. All my personal possessions left with me long ago, and I couldn't imagine there was anything remaining in the house that I would ever want.

It all turned out to be less painful but more time consuming than expected, taking several days. We even shared the odd laugh over things we found.

'Isn't it sobering that all the things you treasure in life, in the end don't mean much to anyone else?' Rachel said, when we stood looking at the small number of boxes of mum's belongings worth keeping. We had deliberated over her collection of glass animals and decided that they should go to the charity shop, as neither of us wanted or even liked them.

'They were always a good fall back for presents, though,' Rachel said.

I nodded but couldn't remember when I'd last bought Mum a present.

'I'll take things to the charity shop and then that's it. Are you happy for me to arrange the clearance and get estate agents round?'

'Yes, of course.' I felt grateful and relieved that Rachel wasn't expecting me to be more involved. We loaded all the boxes, including the newspaper cutting, into her car. I would have liked the cutting, but every word was imprinted on my mind. She'd already given me Mr Jenkin's letter, which was tucked away in my bag.

'I'll keep you informed of progress.'

'Thanks.'

We exchanged a hug, the first for many years, and the first with genuine feeling.

'Bye then, you must come round and get to know your nieces better,' Rachel said, climbing into her car, and with a wave she was gone. I imagined her showing Jim the press cutting and relating all the events of the past few days over a nice dinner and a glass of wine. In the ensuing silence, I felt very alone.

Chapter 24

I walked up the stone steps into the old Victorian building. I was early for my appointment, but somehow, being there was better than hanging around at home. Next to the main entrance was a picture of a huge thermometer with sections coloured in showing how far towards, or rather, how far away from their fundraising target they were.

I felt sick and thought the next time I walk through these doors, on my way out, I would know whether I had the disease. The word 'disease' made it sound as though you could catch it and, therefore, be cured, but I knew it couldn't. It was ironic that the only thing that was making me feel ill was the thought of being ill. I was, in fact, very healthy and rarely succumbed to anything more than a cold.

Once again, I wished Mum had died before telling me about Dad. I wouldn't be here now. I wouldn't have known about being at risk, but then, neither would I have known Alice. I would have lived thinking that Mum disliked me because I was the unlovable child she told me I was. 'Evil', I remembered her calling me on more than one occasion. At least now I knew why she treated me like she did, and to a certain extent, when I thought about it unemotionally, I could almost understand her reaction. I wondered what I would have thought if I had seen Mr Jenkin's letter out of the blue when we were clearing out. I struggled to imagine the shock and the effect of total panic and confusion.

I picked up an out-of-date magazine and flicked through

the glossy pages, looking at ridiculously expensive clothes on stick-thin models, to take my mind off everything.

'Anna Fairbrother?' A young woman in a pale blue, flowery summer dress and shoulder-length brown hair smiled in my direction.

'Yes,' I said, putting down my magazine and getting to my feet. Her appearance surprised me. I was expecting a nurse, but this person wasn't wearing a uniform.

'I'm Hayley Jones, the Genetic Counsellor,' she said, holding out her hand.

'Would you like a cup of tea?'

'Oh, yes, please.' I didn't really want one, but the question surprised me and 'yes' was my reflex answer.

'OK, I'll be two ticks,' she said, and disappeared through a nearby door.

I had just sat down again when she reappeared, balancing a tray with two steaming, white mugs and a plate with a few biscuits on it. She had a folder that I hadn't noticed before, tucked under her arm.

'Here we are. It's just through here.'

I followed her down the sterile-looking corridor, and opened the door she indicated, standing back to let her go in first. She put the tray down on the small, round coffee table and sat in one of the three armchairs. I sat in the one on her right. I glanced around the room. It surprised me, as I was expecting a treatment room where my blood would be taken. Perhaps it wasn't a blood test or perhaps I would go there next. The room was painted a not unpleasant shade of pale turquoise, and along with the coffee table and three chairs, there was another small table with a discreetly placed box of tissues and a jug of water with two glasses. An inoffensive picture of an English landscape was on the wall. There were striped curtains at the window and a vertical blind positioned so that no one could see in, or out, for that matter. It was a carefully arranged room for delivering bad news, I thought.

Hayley smiled at me. 'So, Anna, I understand you would like the genetic test for Huntington's Disease.'

'Yes, I would please.' I nodded and hoped this wasn't going to take ages.

'I couldn't find any record of your family history, so can you tell me about your family and the links to HD?'

'HD?' I queried.

'It's the abbreviation we use for Huntington's Disease,' she said.

'Of course.' I felt rather stupid for not guessing or remembering from previous on-line trawling.

She smiled at me. A well-practised, reassuring look on her face,

'I understand your mother was positive, so are you aware of any other relatives?' she asked.

'Relatives?'

'Yes, aunts, uncles, cousins, grandparents,' she said, responding to my blank look.

'I'm not sure. I mean, I don't know, I'm adopted. I've only just found out about my real mother and met my aunt for the first time a few weeks ago. She didn't mention other relatives. No one ever established whether my mother was affected. She died young. It was her mother, my grandmother, who was ill.' It hadn't occurred to me to ask Alice about other family members, or if they were affected. In some ways, I didn't want to know. I was happy knowing Alice, and wasn't sure I wanted there to be lots more relatives, not yet anyway.

'OK, that's fine, why don't you just tell me what you do know?'

'I'm not sure where to start,' I said, more to myself than to her.

'Start anywhere. I'll be scribbling down a few notes while you talk.'

'Well.' I took a deep breath and launched into my story.

When I stopped, I felt as though I'd been talking for hours. I felt drained, but strangely, I felt better to have offloaded all my concerns. It was quite cathartic, pouring out everything to an attentive stranger.

'Thank you, well done.' She put her pen down. 'That's quite a story. You must still be reeling from the shock. It is a lot to take in, in such a short time.'

I nodded, and to my horror, burst into tears, real sobbing tears.

'It's OK.' She reached for the strategically placed box of tissues, pulled out a couple and passed them to me, leaving the box on the coffee table in front of me. 'Would you like a glass of water?'

I nodded, nearly choking with the irony of it all. After a few sips and noisy blows into a tissue, I composed myself again.

'Why do you want the test?' She asked.

I looked at her as if she was mad. After everything I'd just told her, she wanted to know why I wanted the test.

'I need to know if I've got it.' I wanted to add, isn't that obvious, but held my tongue. 'Doesn't everyone get tested?' I asked.

'Well, no, in fact I would say more people don't.'

'Really, why not?' I felt myself getting hot, and my heart started pounding. This was the only reason I'd returned to England so soon.

'It's quite complex, not the test itself,' she said, anticipating my next question. 'But the result, and how people come to terms with knowing, particularly if they are positive.'

'I'm not sure I understand,' I said.

'HD is a degenerative disease.' She looked at me to make sure I understood what she meant.

I nodded.

'At the moment there is no cure, although progress is being made on treatments to manage the symptoms, and into research, which should in the future be able to switch off the gene which causes the symptoms.'

'What causes it?'

She nodded, 'Good question.'

I looked at her and wondered how often she went through all these details with people. She looked quite young, younger than me, I thought, but she was very composed, not too clinical, just confident in her role, and assured as to the depth of her knowledge. She carried on explaining about a mutation in a gene, proteins, and something to do with the protein repeating itself.

'Don't worry if you can't take it all in,' she said, taking in the stunned look on my face. 'I have a leaflet I can give you, which explains everything.'

'It's OK, I'm following so far.' I tried to smile, but my mouth felt numb. I didn't want her to think I couldn't understand.

She carried on talking about how people with this mutant gene were positive for HD. They might not develop symptoms for a long time, years maybe. She paused for me to ask more questions. If the test is negative, the person hasn't got Huntington's, will never develop symptoms, and can't pass it on.

I just nodded. I wanted to know exactly what would happen, but my voice wouldn't form the words.

She smiled when only a sort of croak came out of my mouth.

'Don't worry.' She carried on explaining that the symptoms could appear at any age. I thought of Alice's assumption that because she didn't have any symptoms at forty-five, she must be all right.

'Your grandmother, it seems, had early onset, but some people don't develop symptoms until middle age or even until they are quite elderly, and some don't show symptoms at all in their lifetime,' she said, and carried on outlining the range of symptoms and what the effects could be.

I took a sip of water and struggled to overcome the urge to get up and run out of the room. What would I tell Alice if she asked, and I was sure she would?

Hayley looked at me. 'Are you OK to carry on or do you need a break?' She must be a mind reader.

I took a deep breath. 'I'm OK, just some water, please.' I was determined to carry on.

She poured me a glass and with a shaking hand I took a gulp.

'HD is what's known as a dominant gene. That means if only one parent has the gene, any of their children have a fifty-fifty chance of having it as well.'

'So, I've got a fifty per cent chance of having it,' I said, almost to myself. Which means, so has Alice, I thought.

'Well, only if Deborah was positive herself and from what you've told me, it wasn't certain that she was. She was obviously frightened when she found out what her mother's condition was, and in those days, I doubt there was much information or support to help her. We are learning more all the time.'

'She must have felt sure she had it,' I said.

'Yes, she must, but you also said she had postnatal depression. She might not have been thinking logically. It is possible she was developing symptoms, but not likely.'

'Might they have tested her blood after she died? There might be a record somewhere?' I thought if Deborah had been tested at postmortem and found to be negative, then I would know I was OK. It felt like a lifeline but was soon dashed.

'No, not back in the seventies. You said she died in 1977?'

I nodded.

'The gene hadn't been isolated then. So, although the condition was recognised, she wouldn't have been tested, particularly not after death.' She glanced at her notes.

'You mentioned Deborah had a sister. She might have noticed if she was showing any symptoms?' Hayley suggested.

'Alice, her younger sister, but she hasn't said there was anything wrong with Deborah. She didn't even know what was wrong with their mum until much later.'

Hayley nodded. 'Has Alice been tested?'

'No, she doesn't want to know,' I replied.

She nodded again. 'And how do you feel about being tested now?'

'I need to know.' I couldn't believe that after all this time, she was still doubting my need to be tested. I just wanted my blood to be taken and go, but she was talking again.

'What difference would it make to you if your test was positive?'

I thought for a while. 'I suppose it would make me get on with things, make sure I do all the things I want to do and not wait until I couldn't. Make the most of life, I guess,' I said.

'What's stopping you from living that way now?' she asked.

'I don't know.' I felt jolted by her question; what was stopping me? Echoes of Alice's comment that night in the taverna came back to me.

'It's quite a good philosophy to live life by for anyone. After all, none of us know what's round the corner. You said your mum died from cancer at the age of fifty-eight.'

'You're about to use the old cliché I could be run over by a bus tomorrow,' I said suddenly feeling confused.

She smiled. 'No not that, but anything could happen to anyone at any time.'

I sat without speaking for a while, just trying to think everything through. To her credit, Hayley didn't rush me, although I felt sure I must be well over the time allocated for my appointment.

'Do you have a boyfriend?' she asked out of the blue, and to my mind, rather irrelevantly. I thought perhaps she was winding the consultation up with a bit of small talk.

'No, not at the moment.'

'I'm not being nosey,' she said, picking up on my body language. 'It's just that if you were planning on having a baby, then testing would be more relevant.'

'What difference would that make? If I haven't got it, neither will the baby and if I have it would have a fifty per cent chance as well?'

'If you had a positive test result, and in the future, you wanted a baby, you would have the option of IVF. There are procedures these days that can screen the embryos, so that only negative ones are placed in your uterus. That means if you became pregnant and the embryo is negative, the baby won't have the disease and won't be able to pass it on.' She looked at me and a sympathetic smile hung on her lips.

I shook my head. It was all getting too much. I was feeling stifled in this contrived room and wanted to get out in the fresh air. The last thing I wanted to think about was having a baby. All I had wanted, or so I thought, was a quick blood test and an answer one way or the other. Not all this complicated information.

I think she sensed I was beginning to suffer information overload. 'I suggest you go away and think about everything. I'll give you some booklets to read and you can ring me anytime if you have questions.'

'So, you won't do the test now?' I asked, already knowing the answer.

'No, we never test anyone at the first appointment. You need time to absorb everything, and remember, if you were to have a positive result, you can't go back. You can't unknow the result. Try to think about whether it would negatively impact on your life; whether you would think every clumsy move or dropped spoon was the start of symptoms.'

'Won't I think that anyway?' I didn't expect an answer and didn't get one. I took the booklets from her and got up. 'Thank you,' I said.

'I expect you're feeling a bit overwhelmed and drained?'
I nodded.
'Is there anyone you can talk to?'
I shrugged. There was, but they were in Greece.
'Well, don't forget you can ring me anytime, and if you

decide you want the test we can meet again, and then if you're sure, I can arrange it for you.'

I nodded again. 'I don't feel quite so sure about anything now,' I said.

'Think about it, read about it, and if you can, talk to someone you are close to. Remember, there is no rush to do anything. Nothing will change, apart from your perception of yourself.'

We shook hands, and she walked me to the door of the clinic.

'Take care Anna, see you again.' She half waved her hand in goodbye.

Chapter 25

I walked out of the clinic into a long, bustling corridor. Once Hayley shut the door, I leant against the green painted wall and breathed in the unique hospital smell, a mixture of antiseptic and anxiety. I felt dizzy and could happily have slid down the wall onto the floor and just sat there, but already people were giving me strange glances, so I walked on and then out through the main doors, without the answer I thought I would have when I walked in a while ago. A light drizzle was falling and there was an unseasonal chill in the air. Everywhere seemed drained of colour. Even the people in the street, who when I entered the hospital were rushing around in bright summer clothes, now appeared dull and grey.

    I hesitated at the top of the steps, unsure of what to do. Hayley's words were whirring around in my head, and everything felt unreal. I pulled my cardigan tight around me and ran across the street. I needed a drink but wasn't sure whether I wanted alcohol or a coffee. In the end the rich aroma of coffee won, and I slipped into a coffee shop and sat down with a strong double espresso and a comforting slice of chocolate cake. The leaflets Hayley had given me were in my bag, but I couldn't face looking at them. Instead, I eavesdropped on a couple of women about my age, sitting at the next table, and envied them the trivia of their conversation. I sat for over half an hour making one cup of coffee last; listening to and watching people come and go in the cafe. I almost felt too numb to move.

At last, I got up and went back home; at least the weather was better now. Once home, I made another coffee and took it out into my postage stamp of a garden to soak up the last rays of warmth from the sun; I was missing the Greek climate. I looked through the post, more junk mail, as usual, except for a cream envelope that felt thick and expensive. I tore it open. It was a wedding invitation. Of course, Leila and Tom were getting married, not until December, but I knew Leila was well into planning mode. Inside the embossed invitation was a scribbled note saying to call her when I got back from my holiday. Leila and I went to secondary school together, and she was my oldest friend. She was at Mum's funeral service and her quiet support that day touched me more than I expected.

Reading the note again, I wasn't sure how she knew I'd been away, but now I wanted to see her. Hayley had suggested speaking to someone close. At the time I dismissed it, not being able to imagine talking to anyone other than Ruth or Alice, but now I wanted to talk to Leila. I picked up my phone to call her. Her warmth and excitement when I told her I was back home was touching, and she insisted I went over straight away. She said she was only planning an evening slouching in front of the telly as Tom was going out.

'Are you OK?' she asked, picking up a hint of anxiety in my voice that I wasn't even aware was there.

'I'll fill you in when I get there,' I said, putting the phone down and rushing to get ready. I walked the mile or so to her house, in anticipation of drinking the bottle of wine in my bag. My spirits rising with each step. I should have spoken to Leila when all this came to light, but, well, I suppose I just wasn't thinking straight.

'Anna, I've missed you. Fancy vanishing off to Greece without telling me.' Leila hugged me, and once again I bit my lip to stop the tears from coming.

'I'm sorry, it was all a bit of a rush. How did you know I was in Greece?'

'I bumped into "The Perfect Miss Rachel" in town,' she said.

We both laughed at the nickname we secretly used to call Rachel, when as children she could do no wrong and I could do no right. I would spend hours at Leila's house after school and at weekends. Her mum was understanding and was always so kind. I treated their house like my second home, along with Ruth's of course. Mum never objected to me going for tea or sleepovers. In fact, I think she was happier when I was out of her sight, and now I knew why. Leila and I shared all our teenage secrets, and our friendship stood the challenges of us going to different universities and following different careers. She was now a family solicitor with a big firm in town, which was where she met Tom, her fiancé, also a solicitor.

Leila led the way into her elegant, minimalist sitting room. A bottle of wine and two glasses were already on the glass coffee table.

'Right', she said 'tell me all about this mystery trip to Greece. I hope it involves a handsome Greek playboy! I was worried about you. I had to rush off, so I didn't get a chance to talk to you at your mum's funeral. Are you OK?'

She curled her long legs under her on the soft cream leather sofa. She did look as though an evening in really was her plan. The jogging bottoms and what looked like an old shirt of Tom's weren't her going out attire. She had scraped her long dark hair back off her face in a ponytail and her pretty face was devoid of make-up. I followed her lead and curled up in the big armchair.

'No Greek Adonis, sadly.'

'Did you go on your own? Why was it so sudden?' she asked, then took a breath. 'Sorry, I'm bombarding you. OK, start at the beginning. I want to know everything that's happened since your mum's funeral.' She settled back and took a sip of wine, looking at me expectantly.

'I want to hear about the wedding plans as well,' I said.

Now I was here, I was in no rush to start my tale. Although just being there with Laila, who I knew would understand everything, made me feel at ease.

'Yes, I'll tell you later, but you go first. Then I'll bore you with table decorations, flowers, and the nightmare it was trying to decide on the guest list, and who sits next to whom,' she said.

I took a deep breath and told her about Deborah. Then I told her about the letter and newspaper cutting Rachel and I found in amongst mum's belongings. I didn't tell her about that last afternoon at the hospice. That was never to be spoken about - to anyone. I went into detail about how Ruth tracked Alice down to Greece, resulting in us both going out to meet her. Then I told her about Deborah's death and her fears about Huntington's disease, and the implications for me. I told her everything I could remember Hayley telling me that afternoon. Was it only this afternoon it felt much longer ago? Leila was an excellent listener; she said very little, just asking the odd question for clarification, and nodding in encouragement, when I faltered over a small detail.

'So that's about it,' I said, after a long time. I couldn't remember the last time I had spoken so much about myself, or at least about things that affected me.

'Oh Anna, poor you.' Leila was about to get up, to comfort me.

'Don't be nice to me or I'll burst into tears,' I said. It was such a relief to be with her and tell her everything. Well, almost everything.

She knew nothing about Huntington's, which wasn't surprising as it isn't that common, but she quickly grasped my dilemma over whether, or not, to be tested. She didn't offer advice, or even an opinion on what I should do, but I felt whatever I decided, she would support me.

'What's your gut feeling about it?' she asked.

'Well, when I first found out, I was certain that I wanted to know, but now I feel confused. It's not like screening where if it's positive you can have treatment, and everything is sorted. With this, there's nothing much they can do. You just know, and then you wait for something to happen.'

'It must be difficult being in limbo, but I suppose there's no rush to find out. Is there?'

'I suppose not. What would you do?' I asked Leila, knowing it was unfair to put her on the spot.

'I don't know, I really don't. Talk to Tom, talk to you. Make sure I enjoyed every minute of life,' she said.

'You're doing a pretty good job on that front.' I laughed. Although nothing had changed, I felt more relaxed about needing to be tested and, I could always change my mind later.

'Right, now I want all your news.'

I stayed until late in the evening, listening to and discussing the wedding plans, and having a sneak preview of the dress on a video taken at a fitting. Leila was going to look stunning.

'Mum was in pieces when she saw me in that one. So, I knew it was right. I tried on hundreds, and she would say "that's beautiful dear" or "you have to feel happy in it", which I took as she didn't like it. So, when she burst into tears seeing me in this one, that was it. I couldn't believe there were so many dresses. I thought it would be easy.'

Leila was relishing every detail of the preparations for her big day. I couldn't help thinking, if ever it was my turn, I would opt for something different. Less lavish and much less expensive. It did me good to be chatting about normal things. We sent out for pizzas and sat eating them on our knees. It felt like we were sixteen again, and although I'd only been away a short time, there was a lot to catch up on.

Leila offered me a bed for the night, but I preferred to go back home. Persuaded by Leila, I called for a taxi after she convinced me it was too late to walk home alone. While I waited for it to arrive, she used all her skills to persuade me to go out with them the following evening. I really didn't feel up to it and protested.

'It'll do you good. I'm not listening to any excuses. We'll pick you up at seven thirty.'

They were going to a new comedy club in town. Leila assured me it wasn't a romantic night out, so she immediately rejected my excuse of not wanting to play gooseberry. When I arrived home, I pushed all the HD leaflets in a drawer. I couldn't face looking at them yet. My sleep was disturbed, bothered yet again by erratic dreams, and I woke early, feeling less than refreshed and with a headache. The temptation to ring Leila and cry off was strong, but I knew it would be to no avail. So, by seven thirty that evening, after a day of jobs and mundane tasks, I was ready and waiting to go out.

Chapter 26

'This is Dan.' Leila introduced me to a dark-haired, attractive looking man, as I slid into the back seat of their car next to him.

'Dan's an old friend of Tom's, and he's going to be the best man at the wedding. We're meeting a few other people at the club as well. It'll be quite a party.'

'Hi, nice to meet you,' I said, trying hard to not show my disappointment. Leila had failed to mention the previous night that it wouldn't just be the three of us. I wasn't sure I was up to being in a big group.

'Good to meet you too.' I could feel him looking at me as I struggled with my seat belt and felt annoyed with myself for blushing.

'You and Leila go back a long way, I understand.'

'Since school. How long have you known Tom?' I asked, trying to move the focus away from me.

'We met at university, not quite as long as you two, but long enough.'

'Don't get them started on university stories.' Leila looked over at us in the back and gave a mock yawn.

'You know you love hearing about our fascinating student escapades,' he said. 'Anyway, you wait for my best man's speech.'

Leila and Tom both groaned and laughed in unison at that.

The comedy club was tiny, and our party made up about a quarter of the audience. I'd met a couple of the group, colleagues of Leila and Tom's, before. It turned out to be a convivial evening. Some acts being funnier than others, but by the end of the evening my face was aching from laughter. For a couple of hours, I had forgotten my problems.

'See, I knew it would do you good,' Leila said, and draped an arm around my shoulder as we walked to the car. Dan cadged a lift with another of Tom's friends, who was going in his direction.

'Hope to see you again, Anna,' he called as I climbed into the friend's car.

'Bye, see you.' I didn't expect to see him again and surprised myself by thinking that I wouldn't mind if I did. It must have been the endorphins from laughing so much.

That night I went to bed and slept peacefully for the first time in weeks; could it be down to the power of laughter? The next day, Leila sent me a text. Dan was asking for my number, and she wanted to make sure I didn't mind her giving it to him. Her message ended with a row of exclamation marks. I laughed. Why not? He seemed a nice guy and I could do with a bit of distraction. I texted back, yes. It could only have been an hour later that my phone rang, and it was Dan asking if I would like to go out for a drink that evening. His speed surprised me, but as I wasn't doing anything that night, I agreed. We walked along to a pub beside the canal and sat outside in the none too warm British summer evening. Conversation was easy and relaxed. He didn't enquire too much about my circumstances, and I didn't ask about his.

We walked back along the towpath to my house. I asked him in for coffee, but he declined on account of work the next day. He suggested meeting up again at the weekend and I felt a buzz of anticipation. He just gave me a friendly peck on the cheek before he climbed into his car. I felt pleased that he wasn't the pushy type. Too many of my previous relationships had started with an explosion of romance, and then after a few weeks, or occasionally months, imploded into resentment and pain.

Dan and I saw each other often, and I grew to like him more each time. He was head of IT in a National Health Service Trust, but was looking for another job, finding the bureaucracy of the NHS too stifling. He was good company and almost old-fashioned in his manner, but it was clear he liked me as much as I liked him.

We didn't discuss previous relationships or anything to do with the future. There would be plenty of time for that later. For now, we just enjoyed the present, although I was curious whether someone had hurt him in the past, hence his cautious approach. Perhaps I could ask Leila.

Our dates were light-hearted and fun, and I jumped at his suggestion of the cinema one evening. We sat near the back of the theatre, in large comfy seats. I'd been looking forward to seeing the film, but was looking forward even more to seeing Dan. We hadn't seen each other for a few days. Part way through the film, which wasn't as good as I'd hoped, Dan slipped his arm around my shoulders. I leant closer and his fingers slid under the neck of my T-shirt and under my bra strap. I snuggled even closer. The film at once seemed irrelevant.

'Shall we go?' he whispered.

'Yes, let's.'

As quietly as we could, we made our way out of our seats, and pushed passed a couple of people who tutted as we momentarily blocked their view, then skipped giggling, like naughty school children, out of the cinema. I had a problem getting my key into the lock when we reached my house; I was almost shivering with anticipation and desire. We ran up both flights of stairs until we reached the bedroom, where we flung ourselves hungrily on each other.

Later, sitting together on the balcony, sipping cold white wine in the, for once, balmy evening, I felt the happiest I could remember being for a long time. We spoke little, but the silences felt companionable and held us together; set apart from the rest of the world. We swayed back and forth in my swing seat and before resting my head on his shoulder, I stole a glance; he was one of those men who was good looking in an everyday sort of way, but whose self-confidence made him even more attractive. It was confidence, not arrogance, I thought, remembering one ex-boyfriend whose arrogance detracted from his physical good looks once I got to know him.

Dan spent that night and the following morning at my house. I felt as though my heart would burst with happiness and desire. Making breakfast together in my small kitchen, we felt like a proper couple, and I dared to hope. I still hadn't told him about my family or that I might have HD. Plenty of time for that, although I felt the time was getting nearer. I just wanted to enjoy getting to know him first and thought he must feel the same way, as he didn't talk much about his family either. It was just the two of us in a bubble of romance; all the everyday pressures and complications could come later.

Dan went off to work, and I floated through a range of chores that normally would bore me, singing to myself as I worked. Today, even the washing and ironing seemed pleasurable.

Chapter 27

The more time Dan and I spent together, the less rush I was in to return to Greece. I would go back, but not for as long as I'd planned. I hadn't mentioned anything to Dan, but I wondered whether he would like to come out with me. It would be fun to show him around and introduce him to Ruth and Alice, but I kept quiet for now. It was early days, and I didn't want to break the magic spell. I didn't dwell on it, but thought I would not be working with Herman when I returned. A shame but... I didn't want to think too far ahead.

"*Meet me at Tortorino's about 7pm xx*" Dan's text read later in the day.

Tortorino's was a little wine and tapas bar in town, newly opened, and very trendy. I went early to do a bit of shopping. Buying clothes felt different now, wondering if Dan would like them. I didn't know his taste yet, as he seemed to like whatever I wore. With an effort I tried to pull myself together and not be so dippy and girly and just to buy what I liked, but everything I tried on, I couldn't help twirling around the changing room wondering if Dan would like it. For once I felt good about myself and thought I looked attractive, partly down to the lasting glow of my Greek tan and my newly acquired inner glow.

I reached the wine bar just after seven. Dan wasn't there, so I ordered myself a glass of Sauvignon Blanc and found a seat where I could see the door. I was halfway through my drink when my phone bleeped.

"*Sorry darling, held up at work, don't think I'll make it. Will contact you later xx*"

I felt disappointed, but it wasn't the first time his demanding job caused him to be late. I hoped he would find a new one soon. He was even discussing setting up his own business, which I guessed would demand even more of his time, so I needed to get used to it.

"*Poor you, speak later xx*", I texted back.

Reluctant to leave, I lingered over my wine and convinced myself that everything was fine, and of course he couldn't just drop everything to meet me. I contemplated having a second glass and people watch for a while but made my way back home just in case Dan might call round later.

I pottered around once I got back. I tried on my new clothes again and put them away, then made myself a sandwich and sat down to watch a bit of TV before going to bed early. I woke late and was surprised when I looked at my phone that there wasn't a text or message from Dan. I got up, made some toast and switched on my computer to catch up with emails. I deleted the few standard junk mail and spam emails and was about to click delete on another when I realised it was from Dan, sent late last night. It was the first time he'd emailed me, and I didn't recognise his email address.

> "*Anna, darling, please forgive me. I haven't been entirely open with you. I've been separated from my wife for over a year now and I promise you I thought our marriage was over. We have a young son, who today has been taken into hospital with suspected leukaemia. I can't leave Karen to cope with this on her own, and we have decided to try again for our son's sake. I hope you understand. I'm sure you will, as I know what a lovely, caring person you are. I didn't mention my situation before because I didn't want to put you off. Much as I would love to, I don't think we should see each other again. I am so sorry. Please don't think too badly of me. Dan x*"

I read his email several times with rising fury. I know I should have felt sympathy for his son, but I didn't. How dare he keep something so important from me? How dare he! Rage consumed me. I slammed my fist on the table and swept my arms across the surface, sending my coffee and toast crashing to the floor. Jumping up, my chair spun backwards against the door, cracking the glass. I didn't care. I felt like wrecking everything around me. What a coward, emailing, not even having the guts to tell me himself. I gave no consideration to how he might be feeling with a seriously ill child, or to the obvious fact that he wouldn't want to leave him to come and have a potential scene with me. I sat back at the table and banged out a vitriolic email in reply. With the final full stop, I broke down and sobbed, a split second before pressing send.

What felt like an age later, my eyes red and puffy, nose running, and head banging, I calmed down, deleted the email and cleared up the carnage from my fury. I decided I would not dignify him with a reply but clicked the read receipt. I didn't want him to be in any doubt that I knew about his wife and child.

It was drizzling outside, but not caring, I pulled on my coat and set off for a walk along the canal path. I needed some fresh air and exercise to help me think. I strode along the path, blind to everyone, even a neighbour who was walking his dog and was ready to stop for a chat. A group of friends were trying to moor a hired narrow boat and seemed to find it hilarious every time the boat banged into the bank. They were blocking the path. I glared and tutted at them as I stepped off the path into the long grass to get past, getting my feet wet in the process.

'Oh, don't mind us enjoying ourselves.' One girl said as I went past. The urge to turn round and push her into the canal was almost overwhelming, but I resisted and walked on. My brain felt as though there was a blockage in it, stopping me from thinking clearly. Fury and self-pity were fighting each other to claim my conscious thought. The drizzle stopped at last, and the sun shone on the canal through a break in the light cloud, turning it into a silver ribbon. Under normal circumstances, I would have been reaching for my camera to capture the beauty, but these were not normal circumstances, and I failed miserably to recognise beauty in anything.

After about half an hour, I reached The Lock Keeper, a pub popular with walkers and boaters, and not the one Dan and I had first visited together. I felt in my pocket just enough change for a half of cider. After the brisk walk, I felt the need to sit down and have a drink. I sat in the garden, on a damp bench, nearest to the water, and took two big gulps of cider before putting my glass down on the table.

The garden was almost empty, apart from one or two smokers under the canopy by the door. It suited my mood to be alone. As the fog cleared in my brain, I wondered why Leila hadn't told me that Dan was married. I toyed with the thought of ringing her to demand an explanation, but I recognised I was being irrational before I did anything hasty. She wouldn't welcome being disturbed by a ranting friend while she was at work.

I presumed Leila thought the marriage was over, and she might have expected Dan would tell me himself. I could hear her saying it wasn't up to her to tell me. Just as I didn't want her to tell Dan about me. I felt empty and alone. The numbing cider was taking effect on my empty stomach, and I felt marginally calmer. I checked the money in my pocket, not enough for another glass.

Chapter 28

I started to walk back, more slowly this time, contemplating why I was so unlucky with men. By the time I was in sight of my house, my walk had become a trudge, and self-pity was in the ascendancy. It just wasn't fair. Didn't I have enough to worry about? My phone bleeped with another text, but I resisted taking it out of my pocket in case it was Dan with another apology and excuse. I looked at the open bottle of wine on my kitchen worktop, knew I shouldn't, but what the hell, I poured a large glass and slumped in front of the TV, flicking through the daytime channels. I plumped for a quiz show and stared at it without really watching.

When at last I plucked up the courage to check my phone, the text message was from Ruth, "*Just touching base hope everything's OK,*" she said. I felt guilty. Ruth and Alice would be wondering about my clinic visit and in my misguided romantic haze, I hadn't even contacted them to let them know. Without giving it too much thought, I texted back to say I was returning in a few days once I could sort out flights. Her reply was almost instant, and her delight at the thought of seeing me soon warmed my heart. She said she would email me a list of art supplies she needed, if I wouldn't mind taking them over for her. She was running out and was planning to stay on with Alice for the rest of the summer. I pushed away the image of Dan and me strolling through the old town and sharing a drink, watching the sunset in a romantic glow, with all the other loving couples.

It would be good to see Ruth and Alice. Everything came flooding back, and I realised I needed to discuss my clinic visit with them before I decided what to do. I couldn't arrange a flight until the following week, which annoyed me because now, having made the decision, I just wanted to go. As I didn't know how long I was going to be away, I sorted the house out and asked a neighbour to keep an eye on things for me, and to contact me if there were any problems. I called round to see Leila. She knew about Dan, of course, and was upset to have been party to my distress.

'I really thought it was over between him and Karen,' she said. 'Karen left him. Apparently, there wasn't anyone else. At least, that is what she said. She was very demanding, and I don't think she thought Dan came up to the mark. He felt devastated at the time. Tom and I were so pleased when he started seeing you. We thought you would be perfect together.'

I wasn't sure Leila's explanation was helping. I didn't want to think of him going back to this Karen, who sounded quite calculating.

'Why didn't he tell me he had a child? I could understand not wanting to tell me about his wife. She hopefully would be off the scene, but a child. You never let go of a child. Did he think I would stop seeing him because he had a child?' I was getting into rant mode, but Leila just let me continue. 'If she left him, he must have hoped they'd get back together. The child being ill sounds like an excuse to me. What happens to them when he gets better? Or what if he doesn't get better and they're left on their own?' I stopped, realising the implications of what I'd just said. 'Is he that ill? Could he die? Oh my God, do you think he could?' I asked Leila. A mixture of shame and remorse rose up inside me.

'I'm not sure,' she replied. 'Tom spoke to Dan yesterday. He was extremely anxious. They were waiting for test results.'

'Oh dear, I'm being a selfish cow, aren't I?'

'I think it's natural to feel angry and cheated,' she said quietly.

'But try not to think too badly of him. He is genuinely a nice guy.'

'Too bad I've lost him then,' I said, struggling to feel benevolent towards him even though my bitterness was subsiding.

'What now? Are you going to go back to work?' she asked.

'I'm going back to Greece,' I said. 'I was on compassionate leave, but now I have negotiated unpaid leave, and they said yes, up to a year.'

'Lucky you, make the most of it, but make sure you come back for the wedding.'

'Of course,' I said, but didn't relish the thought of seeing Dan as best man, even less with his wife in tow.

Leila gave me a tight hug as I left and made me promise to keep in touch.

I nodded but wanted more than anything to get away and not return.

Out of duty, I met Rachel for lunch in town when I was shopping for Ruth's art supplies. Despite parting on better terms after sorting out Mum's house, I still felt less than enthusiastic about seeing her, but knew I couldn't go away without making contact. As it was, we enjoyed a relaxed lunch. Rachel was very chatty and seemed pleased to see me. I told her about Alice, but not about Huntington's, nor about Dan. She told me that the house clearance went ahead without a hitch, and it wasn't as traumatic as she imagined it would be, and the house was now ready to go on the market. The estate agent's valuation was a surprise, and I felt even more surprised when she told me Mum's will split everything equally between us. Rachel showed no sign of resentment, and I wondered if my image of her as a selfish brat who hated me was just in my imagination.

'I miss Mum so much,' she said. 'So often, I do something, or see something, and think, I must tell Mum or show Mum that, and then I remember she's gone.'

I felt sad that I couldn't share that feeling. In fact, Mum not being around anymore made little personal impact on me. The shallowness of our relationship meant there was very little left to miss.

'What will you do with your inheritance?' she asked.

'I have no idea. I haven't given it any thought,' I said, which was true. With everything else going on, it was the last thing I even imagined happening. 'How about you?'

'Well, we might move to a bigger house or use it to put the girls through school,' she said. 'Jim's keen that they go to High Cliff Park. He went to private school of course.' She nodded as if to justify the decision.

'Or you could go mad and blow it having a good time,' I said, only a little provocatively. Rachel and her family were my idea of middle-class dullness. Nice house, nice car, nice children, nice husband with a nice respectable job, but I wondered was there a hint of envy in my scorn? Would I swap my life for hers if I was given the chance? No, the answer came to me almost before the question. I didn't want to be on my own forever, but I didn't want to become Mrs Conventional.

'Well, you never know,' she laughed. 'Watch this space.'

We kissed goodbye, which was a first.

'Give Ruth my love,' she said. 'Keep in touch. Please. I mean it.'

I nodded, waved, and we went our separate ways. I would keep in touch, I decided; after all, she was my half-sister.

Chapter 29

Once again, the shimmering Mediterranean heat hit me like a wall as I reached the door of the plane. This time, I was expecting it and welcomed the heat on my face. In the throng of passengers grabbing bags and rushing off to start their holidays, I seemed to be the only single person. In normal times it wouldn't bother me, or even be noticed, but since Dan left me, I felt my aloneness all the time.

There was an hour to wait for the boat, and those of us making the onward ferry journey were deposited at the small port. People settled into cafes to drink and snack, and while away the time until the ferry arrived. I bought a bottle of water and a cheap sun hat and wandered along, watching the boats bobbing in the tiny harbour. There were a couple of expensive looking yachts, but most were small, local, pleasure boats, and a few decaying fishing boats. The heat was intense, which made me feel sweaty, tired, and grubby. I returned to the quayside and sat under the sparse shade of a dusty old tree, watching a column of ants as they marched around the base picking up twigs and leaves twice their size, before disappearing into a hole under a stone.

A family I recognised from the bus walked past. Grandparents, daughter and grandson, I assumed. The young woman looked about my age and was trying to stop the small child from running off. The more tightly she held onto his hand, the more he pulled and protested. He was on the verge of a full-blown tantrum when his grandfather scooped him up, swung him onto his shoulders and strode off down the quay. The child's tantrum instantly changed to delighted giggles.

'Let's get a cold drink, dear,' the older woman said to the younger, steering her into a small cafe behind where I was sitting. The young woman looked pale, and she seemed distracted, barely acknowledging the older woman who was speaking to her. She fascinated me, and I whiled away the time creating an imaginary tragic life for her, which, at least, stopped me from dwelling on my own problems.

At last, the ferry gave a blast on its horn. People, both tourists and locals, sprang into life and converged from all directions to board the boat. At first, I sat under a canopy on the lower deck, but the diesel fumes and smell of hot bodies overpowered the fresh smell of the sea. A wave of nausea swept over me. I moved up onto the open top deck, where the breeze soon restored my equilibrium. I felt the exhilaration of returning to the island. With no actual plans for when I would go home, I felt free. There was nothing at home for me anymore. Already, the sun and sea were working their magic and everything about the last few weeks seemed to fade, as though I was drawing a net curtain over my past.

My ticket was one way. The compassionate leave from work and now the period of unpaid leave made me feel almost as though I'd left altogether, but a job of some sort was there for me if I wanted to go back. I couldn't imagine going back. The thought of returning to my old job felt like slipping back into a parallel universe, but who knew where the future was headed? Certainly not me.

I dozed, rocked by the gentle swell of the boat and the warmth of the sun, and only woke when I sensed the movement around me of fellow passengers starting to shuffle and gather their belongings together. We were just rounding the headland and entering the small harbour. It looked even more beautiful than I remembered, and my spirits rose.

Scanning the crowd on the quayside, I soon spotted the

figure of Ruth, standing in full sun waiting for the ferry to dock. She was wearing a loose Kaftan; her face shaded under a wide-brimmed hat. She looked every inch the English artist abroad. Spotting me leaning on the rail, she waved and rushed forward. I felt a rush of love for her. Her joy at my return made me feel quite humble and made me certain returning was the right decision. I felt closer to Ruth than to any other person. She was my real family. I dashed away a stray tear, took a gulp of water from my bottle and waved vigorously back.

Most of the passengers were gathered along the deck watching the approach, and causing a definite tilt to the boat, but no one seemed concerned. First-time visitors looked excited and were eager to get off, so they could discover the beauty of the island. Returnees pointed out key landmarks, houses, and people waiting to collect them, to each other. At last, the ferry docked, and the crew lowered the ramp. Passengers jostled for position to be the first off. I saw Ruth position herself near the bottom of the ramp, ready to greet me. I didn't push and soon I was off, clasped in her bear hug of a welcome. Slipping her arm through mine, we set off along the quay towards the town.

'It's so lovely to see you again. How are you? I can't wait to hear all your news. Now, shall we have a drink here before we go up? Alice didn't come down; the shop's quite busy today.' She gabbled away, not leaving me a chance to answer, but I was content just to listen. I felt like I was home.

I agreed to a drink, and as we were heading towards the nearest taverna, the family with the sad-looking young woman and toddler caught my attention. They were amongst the last to disembark.

'Ah there's Spiros. Spiros, here we are!' The older woman busied herself directing a wiry, middle aged Greek man to load their luggage into a car. They fascinated me and I stopped to watch them for a few moments. It was clear they had too much luggage to fit in the car. The young woman, carrying the now sleeping child, showed no interest in the goings on, or her surroundings, but just stood to one side while the other woman, probably her mother, fussed and remonstrated. The man looked exasperated, but he also stood aside, letting her get herself hot and bothered, before offering a logical solution. He could have offered this sooner if the woman had not insisted on trying to squeeze everything in. His solution was the luggage in one car and them following in a taxi. 'Second homeowners, I bet,' Ruth said, following my gaze towards the family.

I smiled at her slight hypocrisy but nodded and turned my attention back to her. Soon, sat in a taverna, I relished the tall, cold, glass of fresh orange juice that the waiter placed in front of me.

'Tell me what you've been doing since I left,' I asked, more as a delaying tactic to prevent Ruth from asking me about my time in England. I needed to be more settled before I started on that tale.

'I've been painting, hence needing more supplies.'

'That's good. I've got everything on your list,' I patted my bag.

'Bless you. I've started painting more landscapes. It's impossible not to with this amazing light and beautiful scenery. I've even sold a few from Alice's shop.'

'That's great. I can't wait to see them.'

'And Herman's been up a couple of times, asking when you were coming back. I think he's keen for you to start work; it seems he's getting busier. Are you still interested?'

'Yes, I think it'll be good. I'll call in at his surgery tomorrow,' I said.

'That's good.'

We sat sipping our drinks watching the harbour, now quiet after all the ferry passengers had dispersed.

'Right, shall we get going? I won't give you the third degree until later. Alice is itching to hear your news as well.'

Chapter 29

It was late by the time the three of us sat around Alice's table on her terrace. The sunset, as beautiful as ever, had faded long before, and the terrace twinkled with a string of lights around the canopy. Several citronella candles on the wall and the table flickered to keep the bugs at bay. In the warm, calm air, chatter and laughter from the tavernas and other terraces carried through the air, mingling with the cicadas, whose chirruping seemed even louder than I remembered. It felt good to be back. Already, leaving home felt a very long time ago.

'So,' Alice said, as she placed the last dish on the table, and our glasses were full of wine. 'How did you get on? Did you have the test?'

Her direct question took me by surprise, but in some ways, it was a relief. I told them everything. Rambling between my dilemmas about the testing, to my short-lived relationship with Dan. Going from confused, to angry, to maudlin as the wine took effect.

Ruth and Alice listened to, and commented on, everything I said. Voicing their opinions about Dan, and what a fool he was to let me go. They felt his marriage was doomed, and would inevitably fall apart again, once the crisis with his son passed.

'Serves him right when he turns round and finds you gone,' said Alice at one point.

Alice was interested in everything I could remember Hayley saying about Huntington's, and insisted I left nothing out. She nodded in agreement when I mentioned living for today.

'It's what I try to do,' she said. 'How do you feel now?' she asked me and just nodded again when I voiced my confusion.

'There's no rush and here you'll have plenty of time to think without all the distractions of home.'

I told her about the leaflets that I had brought with me. She twirled her glass and appeared to study the swirling red wine. After a moment she looked up and smiled. She agreed to read them carefully and suggested we could talk about it again, at any time. I wondered if my dilemma over whether to be tested would unsettle her, but she appeared quite comfortable and calm with her decision not to want to know. I envied her self-assurance and wished I could switch off the niggling doubts that came unsolicited to me at all times of the day and night.

Ruth asked after Rachel and seemed pleased when I told her about our lunch and that she sent her love. It dawned on me that although my relationship with Rachel was less than warm, she must have been as close to Ruth in her own way as I was.

'I'm glad you two are getting on a bit better,' was all she said, reaching to squeeze my hand.

That night, although I was exhausted and felt calmer than before, I struggled to sleep. About three thirty I got up, quietly, not to wake the others, and went out onto the terrace. The night air felt almost as warm as the day. I felt sure the heat contributed to my restlessness. Everywhere was still and quiet, even the cicadas were quieter. I leant against the wall and looked out across the sea, glistening almost black under the moonless sky. Further out, a few specks of light twinkled, fishing boats, I assumed. Another cluster of lights in the distance marked a settlement on one of the other nearby islands.

There were a very few lights on in the old town, rising behind the villa and to my right, but everywhere else was in darkness. The lack of ambient light meant that the stars shone brightly and provided a magical picture above my head. The Milky Way swept across the sky and individual stars winked and blinked. I remembered when I was a child, dad spent many a frosty evening pointing out the different stars to Rachel and me.

I stared upwards and thought I could recognise the Plough, the Great Bear, and Orion's belt. I was never certain which was which, even when Dad was patiently describing them, but I just loved the excitement of being out in the garden in the dark with him, sharing his enthusiasm. I wondered if Rachel remembered and treasured the same memory. I thought she would, as she was always as enthusiastic as me when Dad suggested we went star gazing; in fact, I think she was a better and more dedicated astronomer than me. The beauty of the sky mesmerised me and, even though my neck was aching, I didn't want to look away. I was rewarded by a shooting star and an involuntary 'ooh' escaped into the night.

Even though it was night, the air was full of scent from the flowers on the terrace, the olive trees hugging the slopes down towards the sea, and especially the dry pine aroma I associated more than anything with Greece. A cat yowled somewhere out in the olive grove, calling for a mate, and I wondered how long it would be before it became a patient of Herman's spaying programme. I yawned and a wave of tiredness swept over me, so I made my way back to bed hoping to catch the sleepiness before it wore off.

The next day, I visited Herman's surgery. He was enthusiastic about my return, and very grateful that I was still willing to work with him. I agreed to work three mornings a week and maybe go in to help if there was an emergency. The arrangement suited me perfectly. It gave me a feeling of purpose and belonging, rather than just being a tourist, but allowed me plenty of free time to explore and relax. As the days went on it became easier to forget about my anxieties, and I looked forward rather than backward. Maybe I could make my future here, just like Alice.

Chapter 30

'Today I'm going to drive further up the island to do some painting. There's a place Alice and I visited while you were away. There's a beach nearby if you fancy coming?' Ruth was already gathering her paints and other equipment together and arranging them in a big canvas bag.

'Sounds great! I'll just get my things. Is there a taverna there or do I need water?' I called from my room. I didn't have any plans for the day and, despite a restless night, was ready to explore an unknown part of the island.

'Best bring everything you might need,' she called back.

It was a companionable, if bumpy, ride in Alice's old car, as we wound our way to a more remote part of the island, that I hadn't seen before. The coast was rockier, with cliffs tumbling down into the sea. They looked inaccessible, but now and then, down a steep path, I caught sight of tiny, empty, golden beaches. My mouth watered at the prospect of being on one of them. The journey took longer than I expected, and we passed many places that I would have liked to stop, but this was Ruth's expedition, and she knew where she wanted to be.

We passed a few scattered villas but no real settlement that I could see, and I expected we would reach the far tip of the island, but Ruth eventually pulled off the road and stopped. The view over the sea was breathtaking, but apart from a scattering of olive trees, there was nothing there. I couldn't see the promised beach or a path anywhere.

'My vantage point is just down here, and the beach is that

way. It's not too far,' Ruth said, pointing along to the right. I'll see you back here in a couple of hours?'

'OK, do you need any help to carry your equipment?'

'No, I'm fine, thanks. See you later.'

I watched Ruth expertly hitch her large bag over one shoulder and her portable easel over the other and, with purpose, make her way in one direction, while I set out in the other, to find the little hidden beach she had talked about. I checked my bag, water, bag of crisps, sun cream, book, and towel.

'Don't get sunburnt.' Ruth called over her shoulder. She was almost at the edge of the cliff and was striding out as though the scorching sun and her load were nothing. She was eager to start painting, and I looked forward to seeing the finished picture.

I waved, pulled my sun hat down hard, to stop the breeze sending it flying down into the sea, and made my way along the path. Well, path was a bit of an overstatement. I pushed my way through the scratchy scrub and clambered over boulders. Dripping with sweat, I wondered if I was mad, but Ruth had implied it was worth the effort, although she didn't say she'd been to this beach herself, so I kept going.

A lizard, sunning itself on the path, scuttled off under a stone disturbed by my footsteps. I doubted there was a way down at all, until at last I reached a position where I could see a tiny cove, with sparkling, clear sea lapping onto golden sand. Ruth was right. It was beautiful. Worth the scratched legs. I scrambled down the rocks, the steepest part of the walk yet, and dropped my bag onto the sand. I kicked off my flip-flops and pulled my dress over my head before leaping into the sea. It was cold, but not breathtakingly cold, and after a few strokes, it was sheer delight. I ducked under the shimmering surface, came up and rolled onto my back, luxuriating in the sun's warmth on my body through the water. The air was clear, and the scent of herbs, maybe thyme or oregano, drifted across on a gentle breeze. This was my idea of heaven.

Feeling refreshed, I waded out and scanned the small beach for a good place to sit and read. It was then that I noticed another person, a young woman, she was sitting at the back of the beach in the only patch of natural shade, cast by some large rocks. She must have been there when I arrived but, in my haste to get in the water, I hadn't noticed her. She was watching me and raised her hand in acknowledgement when she realised that I had seen her.

'Hi! Sorry, I didn't think anyone else was here,' I said, as I walked towards her. What else could I do? I really needed to sit in the shade and there wasn't anywhere else.

'Don't worry. You looked in need of a swim,' she moved over, indicating that she wasn't averse to me joining her.

'I hope I'm not disturbing your peace?' I noticed she didn't have anything with her, no towel or book, but was just sitting on the sand in her shorts and T-shirt and I thought, or hoped, that she wouldn't be staying too long.

'No, it's fine. I come here to get away from …'

She left who, or what, she was getting away from hanging in the air. It was then I recognised her.

'Away from your toddler?' I asked.

She raised a suspicious eyebrow, and her gaze turned cold.

'I was on the same flight and ferry as you, and saw you had a lively little one.'

'Oh, you're not a journalist, are you?' She looked as though she was about to get straight up and leave the beach.

I wished I hadn't said anything, and reprimanded myself for being insensitive, but now I couldn't help being curious why she was so jumpy.

'A journalist? Goodness no. I'm a veterinary nurse. What made you think I might be a journalist?'

'Sorry, they've plagued me lately. My parents brought me out here to get away for a while. Anyway, I'd better go,' she said, but didn't move, just looked down and curled her feet into the sand.

I kept quiet and looked at her more closely. I assumed she

must be someone famous. She looked a little familiar, but my knowledge of celebrities was ropey. She was attractive with long dark hair tied back in a ribbon. There wasn't a scrap of makeup on her face, not even lip balm, and her lips looked chapped and dry from the sun. Glancing up, she noticed me scrutinising her, even though I thought I was being very discreet. She self-consciously rubbed her nose with her hand, and I noticed her fingernails were bitten, and her hands looked rough and uncared for. There were no rings on her fingers.

'Don't worry, I'm no one famous,' she said, as if reading my mind.

'You look familiar,' I said, cringing with embarrassment. 'Why have journalists been hounding you? Sorry, I don't mean to be nosey.' By now, I was intrigued and wanted to know her story. I wondered if it would resemble any of the stories, I'd made up about her while we were waiting for the ferry the day we arrived.

Chapter 31

'It's OK! I'm just a bit wary around people these days.' She paused and now scrutinised me. 'Actually, it would be good to talk about it. My parents tiptoe around me as though I'm an invalid and I'm going a bit stir crazy. They don't like me going out of the villa. Well, out of their sight if I'm honest. I know they mean well, but…' she stopped, looking at me as though trying to weigh up whether she could trust me. 'Do the names Edwin Smythe and Garfield Rochford-Davies sound familiar?' she asked at last.

I thought for a moment. 'Yes, I think they do, but I'm not sure why. Oh, wait, was it something to do with a murder? I remember because the names are, well, quite unusual.' I was going to say posh but thought that might be rude.

She smiled. 'They sound like characters out of a Dickens novel, don't they? Well, Edwin was my husband,' she paused again, probably to gauge my reaction was. I nodded.

I remembered now; it had been all over the papers and on the television for days. It must be a year or so ago, I wasn't too sure, but I remembered the story. Edwin Smythe was having an affair with Garfield Rochford-Davies' wife, and if I remembered correctly Garfield stabbed his wife, and then shot Edwin, and then shot and killed himself.

'I read about it all in the papers. How dreadful for you. So, you're Lucy Smythe?

'Lucy Davidson now, I've reverted to my maiden name.'

'I'm Anna, by the way,' I said.

Lucy nodded in acknowledgement and carried on talking.

'Edwin had been having an affair with *Her* since before Tommy, my little boy, was born. I found out just after Christmas. I found a Christmas card tucked into a book on his bedside table. Full of gushing twaddle and sexual innuendo. So, I confronted him with it.'

'That must have been a shock,' I said. She looked up, surprised, almost as though she'd forgotten I was there. She scrunched her toes in the sand again, and I imagined in her mind she relived that moment.

'We said some terrible things to each other. He told me I was boring and a prude and that *She* was fun and knew what he liked. I felt crushed, and it was as though my love for him evaporated at that precise moment. I hated him and wanted to hurt him, to get back at him, more than anything. He stormed out of the house, and I phoned the Rochford-Davies' house. We knew them a bit, not friends or anything, but enough to have their phone number. Garfield answered, and I told him everything I knew. He was stunned. He thanked me, but in such a quiet, chilling voice, I almost immediately regretted calling him. I still feel responsible for all the carnage; if I'd kept quiet, they would all still be alive, I'm sure.'

'You can't blame yourself; anyone would have done the same,' I said. 'I'm sure I would.'

'Would you? That's what most people said, but there's no getting away from the fact that my phone call was the trigger. I feel as though I killed them.'

I felt a pang of sympathy, or was it empathy with her, but for once I said nothing, just waited for her to continue.

'Apparently Garfield went berserk; neighbours said they could hear shouting and screaming. Somehow during all that turmoil, she must have phoned Ed because he turned up at their house quite quickly. Either that, or it was where he was going when he walked out on me. Anyway, she must have been dead by the time Ed got there and Garfield, who apparently legitimately owned a gun, was waiting for him. He shot

Ed at point blank range before turning the gun on himself. The police said it was so quick Ed probably knew nothing about it. But I didn't care. I wanted him to suffer. Now I feel bad about thinking that. His parents were devastated, of course, and continually tried to contact me, but I refused to see them. My parents took control at the time and still are in control to a certain extent, hence escaping here.'

I watched her as she spoke and could see the waves of pain and self-recrimination form and then fade from her face. She did not look at me, and I could tell in her mind she was back in that time. I didn't know what to say. Words seemed inadequate. We sat in silence for a few moments. I let the warm sand run through my fingers as I tried to imagine the scene she described.

'It makes me sound awful, doesn't it?'

I shook my head. 'No, I don't think it does. It all sounds horrific, but your reaction was what most women would have felt and done.' I wasn't certain it was, but it felt probable, and the right thing to say.

'The worst thing is…' she started to speak again, more quietly this time, and her voice cracked, making me think she was about to cry. 'I don't feel the same towards Tommy anymore. I know he's not much more than a baby, and I am trying, but every time I look at him, I see Ed. I can't get it out of my mind that he was with *Her* when I was carrying Tommy. Even when I felt so low after he was born and really needed his support, he was with *Her*. How could anyone do that?'

It was a rhetorical question, so I didn't reply.

'Tommy looks so much like Ed. I try not to compare them, but it's hard. Do you think that's awful of me? I haven't told anyone that before.'

Her words took me straight back to mum, and when she told me how every time she looked at me, she saw Deborah. 'I think it's perfectly natural,' I said.

'Do you? Do you really?'

I told her about my mum and dad, and before I knew it, I was pouring out everything. Well, almost everything, about how I came to be here, about Huntington's and even about Dan, but not about that afternoon in the hospice.

She reached over and touched my arm. 'I'm so glad I've met you; I feel like a weight's been lifted off my shoulders just sharing everything and hearing about your family as well.'

I looked at Lucy and thought she looked different, more confident maybe, from when I first saw her sitting huddled on the sand, but perhaps I was just imagining it.

After our mutual confidences we continued talking about many other things. She was easy company. Lucy told me she was an archaeologist. Her career before having Tommy was fascinating. She described the thrill of finding ancient relics on a dig, and all the places she had travelled to over the years. She said she was itching to get back to her work once things had settled down, but for now she resigned herself to hiding here for a while.

'Anna?' I looked up. Ruth was standing above the cove waving. 'I'm thinking of going back,' she called.

'Ruth, sorry! I forgot the time.' I called up to her and jumped to my feet. 'That's my aunt. She's an artist and has been painting further along the cliff. I'd love to meet up again, Lucy,' I said.

'Me too,' Lucy said, and she also stood up. 'I feel better than I have in months. I'll remember what you said about the way your mum felt about you and make sure I remember Tommy is his own person, not a replica of Ed.'

We swapped phone numbers. Lucy didn't have any paper, so I scribbled my number on a corner of my book and tore it out, writing hers on the back cover.

'Promise you'll keep in touch?'

'Of course,' I said. 'If you're in the old town, my aunt's shop is on the main, cobbled street, but I will ring.'

'My parents' villa is just off the road up there.' She pointed to a small track leading up from the back of the beach. 'I'd better get back. I've been gone quite a while. They'll be getting anxious.' She moved towards the track.

'See you soon,' I said, and made my way back up the rocky path to where Ruth was sitting waiting and watching curiously.

'Sorry Ruth, I lost track of time. How has the painting been?' I asked as we followed the scrubby path back to her car.

'Excellent, I'll show you.'

When we reached the car Ruth unwrapped one complete and one half finished painting that she had placed on the back seat. They were beautiful, capturing the mood of the day to perfection.

'How did you get on?' she asked once we were settled.

I told Ruth about Lucy as we bumped over the potholed roads. She, like me, recalled the story of the murder from the news, because of the men's unusual names, but neither of us could remember the other girl's name. Lucy only ever referred to her as Her.

'Lucy's story sort of puts things into perspective a bit.'

Ruth looked across at me and after a short pause asked. 'So how are you feeling about things in general?'

'I'm still not sure what to do. I mean, I guess I'd like to know about Huntington's, but only if the result is negative. I'm not sure how I'd feel if it were positive. But being here I feel there's no rush. What about Alice? Has she mentioned anything since I gave her the leaflets?'

'I think she feels about the same as before. Although, she always thought if she was going to get it, she would know by now. I think because of her mum being quite young when she developed symptoms, she thought she would be the same. The information in the leaflets has made her think about it more.'

I nodded. It was the reason I knew I needed to give her the leaflets, even though it felt mean putting doubt in her mind where none had been there before.

'I think that surprised her, but I know Alice's philosophy is to live every day as it comes, and not to worry about things before they happen. She's a strong woman.'

I sat lost in thought for the rest of the journey. There seemed so much to think about. When we arrived back in the old town, and as soon as we were out of the car, Ruth pulled me into her arms and gave me a hug.

'Try not to worry; it's early days, all this information is still new. And remember you're not on your own, I'm here,' she said.

'Yes, you're right, thank you, and being here is a great help.' We unloaded the car; I carried the bags, and Ruth carried her canvases up the cobbles to Alice's villa.

Chapter 32

One sultry afternoon, I made my way to the spot behind the old church that I had found on my first visit. Being away from the main track meant other people rarely found it, and I now thought of it as my place. The ground was soft to sit on, and I leant against the old stone wall. It was still warm from the heat of the day. I closed my eyes and listened to the sounds of the island, voices from the village, the ever-present background noise of cicadas, and the distant lap of the sea against the rocks. It was blissfully peaceful, but my mind was churning. An unfamiliar noise made me open my eyes, and I was surprised to see Alice heading for my spot against the wall.

She looked up and was equally surprised to see me.

'Anna, hello! I see you've discovered my thinking space!'

'Hi Alice, sorry. I stumbled on it the first time I was here. I was about to go back, so we can swap places.' I made to get up, but she raised her hand to stop me and sank onto the ground next to me.

'I daresay we're both here mulling over the same thing,' she smiled, and touched my arm.

'I'm sorry if the leaflets I brought back have unsettled you. I wasn't sure whether to give them to you.'

'I'm glad you did. I don't think knowing the facts changes anything, except that now I know I'm not free from it, just because I'm older than mum was when she had it.'

I said nothing, and Alice sat staring at the view for a few moments, then she asked me what I was thinking of doing now. I told her I wasn't sure, but that for the time being, I was content to just be here and do nothing about finding out.

She nodded. 'Good idea,' she said.

'Are there any other relatives with it?' I remembered Hayley asking about the wider family and at the time, I realised I knew nothing about them.

Alice sat thinking for a minute, then looked at me. 'You know, I'm not sure. I don't remember anyone, or anyone saying anything about Huntingdon's before Mum, but it must have come from somewhere. My mum had a brother, older than her. He was in the army, but he died quite young. I never knew him. He fell off a roof somewhere. My grandparents, your great-grandparents.' she turned and smiled at me at this point. 'They were OK, as far as I remember. Gran died of a stroke and Grandad died in his eighties. He was doddery, but I've never connected that to anything other than being old. But one of them must have had it, mustn't they? There isn't anyone else on Mum's side.'

'Are there other relatives on your dad's side of the family?' I felt the urge to know everything about my heritage.

'Well, Dad had a sister, Connie. We saw little of her, but she was nice, always brought us sweets. I never met Dad's parents; his dad came from New Zealand. I think he came over after the war. He died before I was born. It's possible we've some Kiwi relatives. I remember my other granny, just. She always seemed ancient and aloof. They lived in Sunderland, so we didn't see them often.'

'Have you ever thought about going to New Zealand to find out if there's anyone left out there?' I already imagined a trip to uncover long lost cousins.

Alice laughed. 'No, to be honest, I haven't given them much thought. You're so like Deborah in so many ways. She was the one with the enquiring mind, always wanting to know about everything.'

I felt delighted. I liked to think I was like my actual mother.

'You've got her sense of humour as well. Ruth and she

were always laughing about something. Well, when they were younger, that is.'

I remembered Ruth telling me, when I stayed with her after mum's death, that she and Deborah had gone their separate ways, that Deborah became a bit wild after her mum died and began going around with people Ruth didn't like.

'Did you like Deborah?' I asked, then wondered if that was an unfair question when Alice didn't answer straight away.

'Yes, I adored her, as only a younger sister can. I think she found me a bit of a pain. I always wanted to be involved in whatever she was doing, but she rarely let me. She would have been a lovely mum, if…'

We left the "if" to hang in the air and both sat lost in our own thoughts for a while. Not for the first time, and I knew not for the last. I tried to imagine what my life would have been like as the daughter of single mum Deborah, but no pictures formed in my mind.

Chapter 33

Life soon settled into a very pleasant routine. We would do our own thing in the daytime, then meet on Alice's terrace for food and drink in the evening and swap our stories of the day.

Working with Herman was very enjoyable. It was demanding in a different way from my job at home. He involved me in all aspects of the work, and I felt that he trusted me. During my second week at the surgery he asked if I would take the ferry to the rescue centre on my own. Paperwork required by the Greek authorities bogged him down and he didn't want to miss the deadline for filing them. He said he would come if I felt it would be too much for me, but I felt a surge of excitement and agreed to go. The work was well within my capabilities, and I felt pleased that Herman trusted me enough to ask me to go alone. There would not be any surgical work, of course, just checking up on the animals there. I knew my knowledge and experience impressed Herman, and I was delighted that he treated me as an equal, often asking my opinion regarding cases, and eager to know about new techniques and treatments used in England. My self-esteem was repairing, and I was thinking I wasn't such a bad person after all.

The other bonus would be seeing Ingrid again. So, the following morning, armed with the cool box, Gladstone bag, a rucksack, and Herman's instructions for each animal in my pocket, I caught the ferry. Soon I found myself being driven up to Ingrid's villa, unfortunately by the same crazy driver as before. He asked after Herman and wanted to chat when I would have preferred that he concentrated on the road, but we arrived in one piece and Ingrid was waiting at the gate for me.

'Anna, how lovely to see you again, Herman rang to say you would be coming on your own. Can I do anything to help?' Ingrid picked up the bag and led the way round to the animals.

'See my new resident?' she said, pointing to an extremely thin, moth-eaten looking donkey grazing in a penned off area of the garden. I walked over to the fence to get a better look.

'What's his story?' I asked, wondering whether I should have a closer look at him.

'His owner, an old man, died, and no one thought about the donkey, or more like didn't want to be responsible for him. He was tethered to an old shed in an olive grove, and someone out walking heard him braying and went to investigate. At least they had the sense to contact me when they found him, otherwise, I dread to think what would have become of the poor thing.'

I shook my head. 'Poor old boy, how is he now?'

'Getting better. Herman looked at him when he was last here. He just needs food and love.'

I smiled, knowing he would get plenty of both with Ingrid.

'I'm worried he's lonely, so I'm keeping my ears open for a friend for him.'

'He's a lucky boy,' I said, as we made our way round to the kennel and clinic area. I unpacked the cool box and bag and consulted Herman's note. Amongst other things, there were five cats all needing stitches removed after having been spayed, and a check over before release. There was a dog with an injured paw to be assessed and re-dressed if necessary. He had also written to check on any other animals that might have come in.

'It all looks straightforward,' I said to Ingrid. 'What will happen to the dog? Will you just let it out to roam again?'

Ingrid gave me a sharp look.

'No, sorry, I wasn't criticising.'

'Oh no, I'll keep him here to see if I can re-home him, but it is difficult keeping them all. Now, there are five dogs here. A couple are just old and need a bit of care and a good bath. Then, fingers crossed, someone will adopt one of them,' she said.

'Do you manage to re-home many?' I asked.

'It's getting easier. The problem is often that if the new owners fall on hard times, the first thing to go is the dog and they get pushed back out to roam. There is one dog in here that a Dutch couple are interested in adopting. Herman saw him last time he was here, but could you check him over and give him his vaccinations?'

'Yes, of course. I think Herman mentioned him.' I checked his notes again and found the dog listed as needing a vaccination if in good health. 'What else do they need to do to adopt him and take him home?' I asked, wondering whether he would need a pet passport.

'Nothing else, they just need to work out how to get him back home from here. He can stay until then. They've made a big donation,' she smiled. 'It helps.'

'Well, I hope he travels well. It will be a long journey, and he'll need lots of stops. Do many foreigners want to adopt animals?'

'Some do. Sometimes tourists fall in love, usually with a dog, on their holidays and want to take them back home, but it's not always easy, especially for British people and it's not cheap for them. Only the committed ones do it.'

She was right. It wasn't an easy option, and I wondered if it was the romance of being abroad that was part of their motivation. After all, there were rescue centres overflowing with unwanted dogs back at home.

Ingrid stayed to help while I worked and was an expert assistant, despite her protestations the first time I visited. In no time the cats were all ready to be released. They all had small nicks in their ear, carried out by Herman while they were under anaesthetic to show that they had been spayed, so that if they were picked up again, it would be obvious that they didn't need to be operated on.

'It feels strange just letting them go,' I said, thinking of the detailed instructions we gave to worried owners collecting their pets from the surgery at home.

Ingrid agreed. 'They often stay around the garden for a day or two, especially if I put food out.' Ingrid laughed. 'I know I shouldn't, but poor things.'

I checked the dog with the injured paw and left the dressing off as it was healing well, then examined the dog due to be adopted. Looking at him, I could see why the Dutch couple had fallen for him; he was a small, sandy coloured boy, with one ear standing up and one flopping over, giving him a comical look. He was very friendly, rolling on his back to have his tummy rubbed. I checked with Ingrid that she was sure he wasn't someone's lost pet, but she was aware of him hanging around the tavernas and being chased away by the waiters. He was used to being stroked and fed by tourists and was becoming a nuisance with his begging. I wrote a report on Herman's headed paper for the couple to take away, giving details of the dog's weight, suggesting a sensible amount of food and tips for the long journey home, as well as the details of the vaccination for them to give to their vet in Holland.

Chapter 34

After I finished, I recorded everything, checked the fridge, and sorted and put away the equipment ready to take back. Then I took the dog with the injured paw for a short walk so I could assess his mobility. Ingrid pointed out a path leading up a slope from the back of the property, where she said the view was wonderful.

'Come round to the terrace for a bite to eat and a drink, after you put him back,' she said. 'There's plenty of time before you need to catch the ferry.'

The dog hesitated at first; it wasn't used to being on a lead and refused to move, but with a bit of encouragement and a handful of treats, he was soon trotting along beside me. We reached the top of the slope, where someone had balanced a piece of wood across two large stones, making a perfect seat. I sat down for a couple of minutes drinking in the island's view and sparkling sea, which, as Ingrid promised, was worth the walk. The dog sat beside me, and then with a sigh, lay down with his head on his paws. Such a beautiful place to live, but I wasn't sure I would like to live here on my own, like Ingrid appeared to. After a while, I walked the dog back to his kennel, happy that he wasn't limping or in any pain.

'Good boy,' I patted his head and gave him another few biscuits, then went in search of Ingrid. She was sitting on the terrace, swinging back and forth on a blue and white striped swing seat. She had changed into a long cotton sundress and tied her hair back with a bright pink chiffon scarf. When she saw me come round the side of the building, she hopped off the swing and ushered me to the table, where an assortment of snacks and a big jug of water with slices of lemon and ice were waiting.

'So, are you back here for a holiday, or did you go back to England for a holiday?' Ingrid asked once we had settled.

'Good question,' I replied. 'There were things I needed to sort out in England, but I'm back here for the rest of the summer, at least.'

'That sounds good,' she said, passing me a plate of delicious Greek nibbles.

As we ate, she told me that Erich, her husband, was joining her the following week for a holiday. Then, after that, he only needed to work one more rota before he retired and would spend most of his time here with her. They were planning to rebuild the kennels to make them more weatherproof and easier to keep clean.

'Do you ever get lonely or nervous here on your own?' I asked.

'Not really, I love my own company and my animals, but I am looking forward to Erich being here most of the time. I don't get nervous. I have lots of friends and we aren't as isolated as it seems. There is a little village just down the hill with a taverna and shop.'

She chatted about her life here and seemed very self-sufficient and happy. She told me that Berne, their son, was coming to visit with Erich.

'I'm hoping Herman can come and see him while he's here. I know he's my son and I love him very much, but he is such a bore.'

I laughed at Ingrid's openness. 'Why?'

'If he hadn't been born at home, I would believe someone in the hospital swapped him at birth; a changeling, he has nothing of me, no artistry, no …' She waved her hands as if to catch the right words in English.

'Flamboyance?' I suggested.

'Yes, flamboyance,' she agreed.

'What does he do?'

'Oh, something to do with advising the government on economics. It sounds deadly dull and very serious, so it suits him well. I'm hoping being here will help him relax.' She paused for a moment. 'He considers the animal shelter to be madness; he'll tut and mutter about it and tell me it's not economical. I say to him not everything needs to make a profit, and he should do things for the joy of it, for love. He just raises his eyes at me.'

'Is he married or anything?' I asked.

Ingrid threw her hands up. 'Divorced, but I can't be sorry. She was just as dull, dreadful woman. She would never just sit and talk with me like this, and no sense of humour. I think sometimes Berne might have a sense of humour, but it is buried deep. He needs to find someone to bring it out.' She gave me a knowing look. 'You could come and meet him when Herman comes.'

'Oh no, I'm definitely not in the market for men at the moment.'

Ingrid looked sadly at me, and then we both laughed.

'Do you have any other children?' I asked.

'Oh no, once was enough. I wasn't one of those women who bloom during pregnancy and childbirth. I hated it, feeling sick and fat, very overrated I would say.'

I chuckled. I was warming to Ingrid more and more.

'And being at home with a small child,' she continued. 'It was so boring and hard work. No one warns you. I'm surprised so many women go on to have another.'

'Did you go back to dancing after he was born?'

'No, my figure was ruined,' she said, running her hands over her slim body. There wasn't an ounce of fat on her, and she looked amazing for her age.

'I'd never know,' I said.

'In those days, if you weren't like a stick, you were fat, and the choreographers wouldn't tolerate fat. I tried giving dance classes, but I'm not a born teacher. I used to get so impatient. It's not a good idea to send your pupils home in tears,' she laughed. 'Then I worked with Erich's sister for a while; she made wedding dresses, and I helped her with the books and orders, it wasn't fulfilling but it fitted with Berne's school hours and Hella was fun to be with, so it wasn't too bad.'

'How long have you been living here?' I asked.

'Let me think. We came first on holiday in 1996 and then bought this place in about 2000, so just about six years, and then the rescue centre just sort of evolved. It started with one stray and grew from there.'

'Was Frank a stray?' I asked, looking at Frank sprawled on the terrace, wagging his tail at the mention of his name.

'Frank came from a rescue centre in Germany. He's almost eight now and has calmed down a bit from when we first got him,' she tossed a bit of food in his direction, which he caught without moving, stretched, yawned and rolled in the sun as if knowing he was now living the dream.

'So, tell me a bit about you.' She leant forward on the table with an expression that invited disclosures. I told her that my parents were both dead and that I didn't get on too well with my sister, but didn't mention Deborah or Huntington's. Although I didn't know Ingrid well, I felt very comfortable chatting to her, but I didn't feel ready to discuss the more complicated areas of my life. I told her about my relationship with Dan and how angry and upset I was when it ended. She listened, nodding from time to time but didn't interrupt.

'He must have liked you a great deal,' she said, after I told her about Dan's wife and child.

'What makes you say that?' Her response surprised me.

'Well, to think of you at such a traumatic time, I know it seems cowardly and impersonal to just send an email, but at least he contacted you and didn't just leave you guessing.'

I wasn't sure I agreed, but I suppose she was right. For him to think of me at all with his son very ill must indicate something.

'Hmm, I'm not sure. Anyway, I'm over him now,' I said.

'There's always Berne,' she said, with a twinkle in her eye.

I laughed but didn't answer. Berne certainly did not sound like my type.

'Well, I could stay here all afternoon, but I had better get everything together and head back for the ferry.' I said at last.

'I'll drive you down,' Ingrid said. She needed to pick up some provisions, so it would not be inconvenient. We gathered all my bags, and along with Frank, piled into her little car. Frank on the back seat rested his head on my shoulder, occasionally licking my ear with his slobbery tongue and sucking my hair. Much as I liked him, I could have done without this much affection, but I didn't want to offend Ingrid by pushing him away. As soon as I was on the ferry, I headed for the tiny toilet and swilled my face in the sink.

Chapter 35

Herman found Ingrid's matchmaking with Berne very funny when I related the events of the day to him back in the surgery.

'Berne's OK. I have met him once. He has lots of money,' he said, as if that would sway me.

'I don't think so,' I said. 'Money or not.'

I was still smiling to myself as I made way back up the hill and climbed up to Alice's terrace. Ruth and Alice were out. A note under a pot on the table told me they were on the beach. Before deciding whether to join them, I switched on my laptop for the first time since returning to Greece. There were several emails, including one from Leila, hoping I was OK, and filling me in with news of various friends and her wedding plans. She also said that to everyone's relief, Dan's little boy was responding to treatment. She apologised, as she wasn't sure I would want to know, but on balance decided it was best I did. I replied, telling her my news and about working for Herman. I felt I didn't want to know anything about Dan or his family, but remembered Ingrid's comments, and felt a tiny bit more benevolent towards Dan. Adding to my email, I asked Leila to pass on my best wishes to him and to tell him I was pleased the treatment was working. Try as hard as I could, I found it difficult to conjure up a clear image of his face. Instead, Herman's face kept blocking my mind.

Another email from Rachel informed me that Mum's house was under offer, and because it was in the price range we had agreed, she had accepted it. The sale should go through in a few weeks, and the solicitor would transfer the money to my account once everything was complete.

She told me about a nightmare, family camping weekend they went on with the children, where it rained all the time, so much that the tent leaked. She and Jim were ready to pack up and go home, but the children loved it and wanted to stay and were now asking when they could go again. I must admit the idea of Rachel camping, in any sort of weather, was a hard image to grasp and made me laugh. She hoped I was enjoying myself and asked me to pass on her love to Ruth. I sent an unusually chatty, for me, reply to her telling her about the surgery, my trip to Ingrid and about meeting Lucy on the beach.

I closed my computer and relaxed on the terrace for a while, then felt the need for company. Ruth's note was not specific which beach, but I guessed it must be the small one down a track from the edge of the town, which few tourists ever found.

I hurried to my room and put on my bikini under my dress, slung a towel over my shoulder, and set off. This was my favourite time of day. The late afternoon temperature suited me more than the scorching heat of the middle of the day, and there were still several hours of daylight left. I walked up the cobbled street and followed a narrow path behind the tiny, whitewashed church, close to my thinking place. It meandered downwards, winding round gnarled old olive trees and aromatic pine trees. Between the trees, the blue sea glittered, and I increased my speed, as much as the uneven, steep ground would allow.

The last part of the path turned into more of a climb over several large boulders. At the very end someone had tied a thick rope around a tree and, by hanging on to the big knot in the rope, I swung myself onto the soft golden sand. The beach was tiny and there were several large boulders around the edge and two even bigger ones several yards out in the crystal-clear water. I could see Alice sitting on top of one boulder, looking out to sea. As I watched, she stood up and jumped off the rock into the water, joining Ruth, whose head I could just see bobbing above the gentle swell. They had spread their towels on the shady side of the beach; I threw mine down near theirs and pulled my dress off before running into the sea. There was not another soul on the beach. It was our paradise.

I chose the easy route into the water, straight from the beach, rather than jumping off the rocks, but being a strong swimmer, I soon reached them. It was wonderful. The cool water felt delightful over my warm skin. Ruth and Alice swam towards me, pleased that I had joined them. After I greeted them, I floated on my back in the clear water, rocked by the gentle swell. I could not have been happier. I tried to imagine what I would be doing at this time on a Tuesday afternoon at home, but the images that drifted through my mind were hazy. It felt like another world; one I wasn't in too much of a hurry to return to.

I turned over and swam back to the beach. I could see Alice swimming ahead of me and Ruth was already standing in the shallows, waiting. Ruth was looking slim and healthy, I noticed. This lifestyle and being with Alice were obviously agreeing with her as well. We pulled our towels into the sun to dry off and Alice produced some water and juicy peaches from her bag. The sweet sticky juice ran down our chins and fingers and we ran back to the sea to swill it off. I recounted my visit to Ingrid describing in detail the animals in the rescue centre, Ingrid's house and her stories about her family. Like Herman, they found Ingrid's matchmaking very amusing.

'You should meet him. He might be a real Prince Charming,' Alice said.

I shook my head. 'Not according to Ingrid. He isn't.'

'Well, you never know unless you go.'

'Stop it.' I laughed. 'I want to be man free for a while.'

'Hmm, I must say I've always found them overrated,' chuckled Ruth.

'Well, I suppose I had better wander back to open the shop,' Alice gathered her things together. 'I think it'll be a busy evening, lots of people coming up for the sunset.'

'Come back with me, Anna, and see the paintings I've been finishing,' Ruth said as she pulled a kaftan over her head.

'They are amazing,' said Alice. 'Her best so far.'

Ruth smiled with pleasure, and I was sure I detected a little blush.

'Are you going to sell them?' I asked.

'Not the one of the castle,' Alice said. 'I want that on my wall. The colours are just gorgeous.'

'OK, you can have that one.' Ruth looked like she was going to burst with pride. 'But I need to make some money, so the others will have to be sold.'

We strolled up the path after heaving ourselves over the rock using the rope.

'Luke put the rope here, so we don't get stranded,' said Alice, puffing in the heat as we picked our way through the rocks.

The early evening air was heady with the smell of pine and olive trees and the sweet scent of wild honeysuckle; the sound of the cicadas beginning their nightly serenade filled the air.

'Look,' Alice stopped on the path and pointed to the ground a little way ahead. Ruth and I peered over her shoulder and watched a long adder slither across the path and disappear into the scrubby undergrowth.

'They're all right as long as you don't stand on one,' Alice said. 'They're usually more eager to get out of our way than to bite us.'

I wasn't afraid of snakes but stepped warily past the place where it was last seen.

The honey-coloured stone, white walls and terracotta roofs of the old town glowed in the evening sunlight, looking more like a film set than a real working village. As we approached, delicious smells of cooking from the tavernas drifted down and made my mouth water.

'Shall we eat at Dimitri's after I shut the shop?' Alice asked, as the aroma of the food worked on her taste buds as well.

'Sounds good. I'll pop down and give you a hand after I've changed, and seen Ruth's paintings,' I said.

'That'll be lovely, thanks.'

Ruth and I both went into the shop later, and, as Alice had predicted, it was heaving. Tourists were making their way back down through the town after watching the sunset, and the array of attractive shops enticed them in. The shops sold more than the usual tourist souvenirs. I loved helping Alice. Her jewellery needed no hard sell, and people who were relaxed and in holiday mode seemed eager to spend. I helped a young couple choose a necklace and matched it with a pair of earrings that once seen they could not resist. I put them in a little box tied with a ribbon, and they went on their way, delighted.

'Well, that was a good evening's work. Thank you, Anna.' Alice closed the door behind the last customer and turned the sign to closed. 'Looks like dinner is on me as a thank you for your excellent sales skills.'

Chapter 36

Herman and I were packing up equipment and finishing paperwork after a quiet, but steady morning of routine patients and tasks. I had spent most of the time sorting out Herman's cupboards and shelves, labelling boxes of equipment and arranging everything so that it was easier to find, as well as listing everything that was in his stock cupboard.

'There, that should make it easier to keep track of everything and know when we're running low.' I felt very satisfied with my morning's work.

Herman wasn't disorganised, but his practice lacked the organisation I was used to. He knew where everything was, which was fine working on his own, but we both agreed there could be a better system; I was used to working in a very organised practice, so took up the challenge of sorting everything out with relish.

'That is so much better, thank you.' Herman opened a cupboard and admired the tidy shelves where I had labelled and dated everything. 'I would never have got round to sorting it all out myself. I sort of held in my head the dates, but this is perfect.'

Just as I went to collect my bag before leaving, the door burst open and a man with a dog in his arms rushed into the reception area. A crying child came running in after him. The man was shouting something in Greek and although I couldn't understand a word of what he was saying, it didn't take too much detective work to realise the dog, a young female, was in labour and having problems. She was panting and looked totally exhausted. Herman was there in seconds, speaking to the man in calm, fluent Greek, and asking lots of questions.

'We'll need to do a caesarean. Can you prep the dog?' he said to me over his shoulder, while lifting the dog from the man's arms and handing her to me, as he carried on talking in Greek. The man and child were much calmer now the dog was in a safe place, and after a few more questions and answers they left, looking relieved.

Herman locked the door behind them and rushed into the part of the surgery used as an operating room, where I was already shaving the distressed dog's stomach while trying to keep her calm.

'I'll scrub up. Can you make sure she's safe and then prepare the instruments?' Herman was already washing at the sink, and although the dog was too weak to move, I placed her carefully in a crate on the floor. I washed my hands before I opened the sterile packets of instruments and placed them on a trolley, making sure I didn't touch anything in case I contaminated them. I placed a pile of towels nearby ready to wrap the puppies in as soon as they were born and lined a box with more towels.

As soon as everything was ready, I lifted the dog back onto the table, cleansed her skin and covered her with a surgical sheet. Herman pulled on his surgical gloves and anaesthetised her. Once satisfied that she was stable, he set about delivering the puppies.

The first puppy was stillborn, but four others were born alive. Herman handed each one to me and I wrapped it in a towel, vigorously rubbing until it gave a reassuring newborn cry, and then placed it under the lamp to keep warm while I dealt with the next one. Herman worked with speed and efficiency, and soon the mum, who he also spayed, was recovering in a warm whelping box. We put the puppies to her nipples as soon as possible to stimulate her milk production, and encouraged her to drink as soon as she was able. We cleared up and then sat on the floor with a cup of coffee, watching our patients.

'Cheers, good work. Sorry you had to stay late, but I'm glad you were here.' Herman raised his coffee mug, and I felt a warmth of pride and camaraderie. 'I was worried we might be too late and be delivering them all stillborn; she must have been in labour for a long time.' Herman leant over the box and gently touched the mother's head. She lifted her tail in a weak wag. His eyes glowed and a contented smile played on his lips.

'Good girl,' he said to the dog.

I watched him and understood his passion for running this isolated surgery. I felt privileged to be working with him. Staying over my time seemed irrelevant.

'I think she'll be fine,' he said, looking up.

'What did the man who brought her in say? Is she his dog?' I asked.

'No, his child found her in some rough ground behind their house. Luckily, she went back home and told him there was a sick dog. He went to investigate, more worried that it might be a risk to his little girl I think, than worried about the dog. He was going to leave it, but the child became very upset, which forced him to do something. The dog's a stray, so there won't be any money paid. We'll keep them here and try to find homes for the puppies.'

'Keep them here, but...' I was about to say there wasn't anyone here at night to watch over them, when Herman interrupted me to say he would sleep in the surgery for the time being.

'I've done it before; there's a pull-out bed in the back. I lived here when I first started,' he said. 'I don't think there will be any complications, so it won't be for long. You can relieve me in the mornings, so I can get showered and ready for the day, if you like? I will ask one of my friends if his daughter can help as well, when the puppies get bigger.'

'Of course, no problem, I can take more turns at baby-sitting if you like, until they are on their feet.' My admiration for his dedication grew even more.

The vets at home where I worked, were just as dedicated to their patients, but somehow here with Herman it felt more real, less like a business. I couldn't imagine any of them giving up their beds to look after stray puppies who would not be paid for, but then there was a fully staffed veterinary hospital at their disposal.

'It is good, us working together, don't you think?' he asked.

'I was just thinking the same thing,' I said.

'You aren't missing the drama of a big, busy surgery?'

'I think this is enough drama to keep me happy.' I nodded towards the box.

'Good.' He smiled. 'Right, let's clean up and then work out a plan. I won't ask you to do too much, but having your help will be good. Thank you. I appreciate it.'

Chapter 37

'Anna!' Herman burst into the surgery in a state of high agitation. He had been called out earlier to a donkey that had got trapped between rocks on the side of a ravine. I would have gone to help but needed to stay with the puppies.

'How was the donkey?' I asked.

'No. Not good, it didn't survive.' He paced around the room.

'Here, sit down! I'll make some coffee.' I knew Herman cared about all animals but seeing him in such a state surprised me.

'No, I don't want coffee,' he said, but sat down anyway, and I was already boiling the kettle.

'Anna, I've found my cousin.'

'Really? That's good,' I said, at a loss to know what else to say. It was the first time I'd heard him mention a cousin, missing or otherwise.

'No, you don't understand. My cousin, Andreas, was, um, what's the word, you know... entführt, kid...'

'Kidnapped, lost, stolen, abducted?' I guessed.

'Yes, all of those,' he said.

I smiled into my coffee and hoped that my face looked more composed and serious when I glanced back up.

'Someone abducted Andreas,' he said, selecting the word he thought fitted best. 'He is a baby, and now he is in the taverna.'

'Are you sure? One baby looks very like another,' I said, trying not to sound as confused as I felt.

'No. No, he's not a baby now.' He threw a withering glance

at me. 'Andreas is about my age now. He was a baby when they took him.'

'But what makes you think he's in the taverna?' I looked across at Herman and bit my lip in an effort not to laugh. He looked serious and seemed quite agitated, so I composed myself and made myself listen to his explanation.

'All my life, my family has been looking for Andreas. Everywhere we go we look for him.' He took his wallet out of his pocket and pulled out a crumpled, laminated, black-and-white photo and slid it across the table to me. I stared at the grainy photo of a baby, who looked about a year old, but the striking thing about him was his hand. The baby held a cup, and his partly formed hand was clearly visible.

'See his hand?' he stabbed at the photo with his finger.

I nodded.

'The waiter in the taverna has this hand. He has Andreas' hand. All the family carry this photo to remind us of his hand, and he, the waiter, has this hand.'

I studied the little boy's hand. His middle and ring fingers on his left hand were fused together, and the little finger was just a limp appendage, making it appear as though there were only two fingers and a thumb.

'I never knew him, of course, or at least I don't remember him; he was born a month after me.'

'I don't know much about hand deformities, but is it that uncommon? Couldn't it just be a coincidence?' I asked.

He picked up the photo and looked at it again. 'It might be, but he has fair hair. The waiter has fair hair, just like Andreas, not many Greek people have fair hair.' He jumped to his feet, walked to the desk, and picked up the phone, then put it down and walked back to the table. He stopped, looked into space with a furrowed brow.

'I must go. I must contact my friend about this,' he said, and walked towards the door then stopped. 'Anna, will you come with me to the taverna? We can go tomorrow, and you can see for yourself.'

'Yes, of course I'll come.' I was intrigued and excited about being involved in his drama. And it would be a chance to see more of the island, which was always welcome.

'Oh, by the way, was everything OK here?' he asked as an afterthought, and I realised that this issue about his cousin must be serious, as the surgery was always his priority ahead of anything else. I assured him all was well.

'Meet me here tomorrow at ten, OK?' he said, as we closed and locked the door.

'That's fine. I won't be late.'

'Thank you,' he said and rushed off down the street.

I watched him go, wondering who this friend was that he needed to talk to about his discovery.

The next morning, I was sitting on the step of the surgery by quarter to ten, enjoying the sunshine and watching the world go by, with a feeling of anticipation about what the day might bring. I'd already been inside and made sure the mother and puppies were going to be all right until we got back.

With a roar, Herman arrived on an old motorbike. 'Are you OK on the bike?' he said, offering me a crash helmet, assuming I would say yes. 'It's better than the car and quicker,' he said.

I must have looked a bit dubious. In fact, I was dubious. Motorbikes made me wary as I associated them with Dad's death. As a teenager I went out with a boy who rode a motorbike, and I went on the back partly because Mum said I couldn't. The relationship was short-lived, and if I'm honest, I hated the bike and felt terrified most of the time.

'I'll get the car if you prefer,' he said. 'I won't drive fast.'

'It's OK, but not too fast. I'm a bit scared of bikes,' I said, as I put the helmet on. 'Am I OK like this?' I asked, pointing at my shorts and T-shirt but noticing at the same time Herman was also wearing shorts.

He nodded. 'I'll be very careful.'

He was careful, and anyway, the condition of the roads did

not allow any great speed. We wound our way along minor roads that were pitted with potholes and went high above the coast. Herman stopped so I could appreciate the view down to a tiny bay, with a small traditional windmill perched on the rocks. I found this touching knowing he was in a hurry to get to the taverna. We carried on, following part of the same route Ruth and I took the day I met Lucy on the beach. Then we took a different road, and dropped down to yet another idyllic beach setting, with two tavernas almost next door to each other, both competing for the tourist custom, of which there was plenty.

Chapter 38

Herman stopped outside the furthest taverna, and we climbed off the bike. I stretched, and the heat hit me; the bike having generated its own breeze. Tourists occupied almost every table, but after a few minutes, we found one in the corner with a wonderful view of the beach and on out to sea. A cat lay on its back on the small wall beside it, lazily licking its paws. It paused mid lick as we sat down, raised its head and then returned to the task in hand. A young woman came to ask what we would like, and we ordered Greek salads, a bowl of chips and two cold drinks. Herman was scrutinising everyone to see if he could see the waiter, who he'd convinced himself was his cousin.

'I can't see him,' he said, shuffling in his chair.

The young woman brought out our food, followed by a fair-haired man carrying our drinks. Herman kicked me under the table, but I already guessed that this must be him. He handed me my drink and I could see the fused fingers of his left hand; it looked very similar to the photo of the baby Herman carried, except for the strange little finger, but I expect it had been removed, as it would have been more of a nuisance.

'Thank you,' I said, as he put my glass down, trying not to stare.

'You're welcome. Are you on holiday?' he asked.

'Work and pleasure,' I said. 'This is a wonderful place to live.' I indicated with my hand towards the beach. 'Are you

Greek?' I asked and was aware of a sharp intake of breath from Herman.

'Ah, so many people ask me that. It's because of my hair.' He raised his hand and patted his head of light brown hair. 'My mother says I was found under a gooseberry bush. He laughed accidentally knocking the table and slopping our drinks. 'So sorry,' he said, wiping the glasses with a cloth. Herman looked as though he was about to have apoplexy.

'What?' I asked once we were on our own.

'The glasses! He touched them, but he wiped them.' He was whispering but almost spluttering with frustration. 'My friend, the one I rang last night. We were at university together. He studied forensic science.'

'Ah, forensic science,' I said, more to myself as it confirmed why he rushed off to speak to a friend yesterday.

'He said on the phone I must get DNA. Something he has touched, or something with his saliva on it or his hair. The glass would have been good.'

'Oh, I see, well, we might get something else, but we can't just walk off with a glass.'

We ate our lunch in almost total silence. Both with our eyes searching the inside of the taverna and the kitchen area, but the waiter, who we ascertained was called Christos, didn't come back to our table.

'There he is,' I said, inclining my head towards where Christos was sitting on the wall, smoking a cigarette and chatting to someone. We watched him, and as soon as he finished smoking, he threw the butt on the floor. Before I could stop him, Herman jumped up out of his chair and ran round to where the still smouldering butt was lying on the floor. He bent down to pick it up.

'No, no please, I'm sorry. He is so dirty.' The young woman who originally took our order rushed forward and took the butt out of Herman's hand, and carried it off to throw it away.

He stood, open mouthed, staring after her, and then sheepishly sat back at the table.

'It's not funny,' he said, seeing my attempts not to burst out laughing.

'It is,' I said. 'She must have thought you were mad.'

'But it was his cigarette. It would have been perfect.'

'I think you'll have to be a bit more patient,' I said. He nodded, looking crestfallen.

'Anna, quick look.' He whispered. I followed his gaze. Christos was drinking a glass of water and put the empty glass back down on a table.

'Quick, go and get it,' Herman hissed.

'I can't just go and take his glass,' I said.

'Yes, you can. Look, he's not looking.'

I got up as casually as I could, walked calmly towards the table and picked up the glass.

'Please, that one is dirty! Here, let me get you a clean one.' The young woman took the glass from my hand, giving me a strange look, and handed me a clean one.

I thanked her and returned to the table and sat down. Herman looked in disbelief that I had failed such a simple task. It was too much. I could feel laughter welling up inside me and could not suppress it.

'OK, we need to think of something else,' he said, drumming his fingers on the table.

We sat for a while longer, but there was a limit how long we could sit there not eating or drinking anything. We were just contemplating ordering another drink, when a young man in a battered old car pulled up beside the taverna, wound down the window and called to Christos, who, after a brief conversation with the woman, hopped over the wall, jumped into the car and was gone. We rode back across the island. Herman was disconsolate, but I was feeling exhilarated, not only because of the motorbike ride, which, once I relaxed was very enjoyable, but having a day concentrating on someone else's problems rather than my own was quite uplifting.

'Well,' Herman said, dropping me at the bottom of the old town. 'Perhaps we can try again.'

I looked a bit sceptical. 'I think they'll start to get suspicious if we keep appearing in their taverna doing weird things.' I laughed, but I could tell he didn't see the funny side.

'Tell you what, I'm going to meet my friend Lucy soon. I could suggest lunch in that taverna.'

'Yes, good, that would be good. Thank you. When will you see her?' he said.

'I'll ring her to arrange something. OK, then. See you in the surgery tomorrow morning.' I handed back the crash helmet and wound my way back up the steep street to Alice's shop. Part of me couldn't help thinking that all this would come to nothing, but Herman was so determined, and I was happy to help. Although, I would never say to him, I was finding the whole escapade great fun.

Chapter 39

'I feel like a spy,' Lucy giggled. 'Which one is he?'

'Christos? He's the fair-haired one, over there by the counter. See his hand?'

'Oh yes. He's very good looking, isn't he? Does he look like Herman?'

'No, not at all!' I whispered.

'Do you think he really is Herman's long-lost cousin?' she asked.

I shrugged, looking at Christos it was hard to imagine. 'Who knows? I suppose stranger things have happened.'

'Well, it's a bit of intrigue, anyway. I have to say my parents' molly coddling is getting a bit wearing.'

We both watched Christos chatting to customers, taking orders and slowly moving towards us.

'So, what do we need to do again?' Lucy asked in a too loud voice. I put my finger to my mouth. 'Sorry,' she whispered.

'Just try to pick up something he's touched, something that might have his DNA on it, but we need to be careful not to contaminate it.' We watched, and just as Christos was about to reach our table to take our order, someone called from inside the taverna, and he disappeared. The young, pretty, dark-haired girl, who was waiting when Herman and I visited, came over to ask what we wanted. We later discovered she was called Maria and was Christos' wife,

'Um, oh I think I'll have a coffee. Lucy?'

'Yes, coffee, please.'

'Now what?' asked Lucy, as we sipped our coffee.

'We'll have to wait and see if he comes out again. I'll go to the loo in a minute and see if he's in there.'

We chatted about other things, drinking in the scenery and warmth, while we both kept watch to see if he reappeared. I went towards the toilet but there was no sign of Christos inside the taverna. I could hear voices from the kitchen and presumed he must be in there. I was just about to peep through the chain fly curtain over the door.

'Can I help?' The gloom inside the taverna, which contrasted with the bright sunlight outside, hid the elderly man sitting at a table next to the back wall, from my view. I jumped in surprise when he spoke to me. He was sitting on an old wooden chair, passing a string of worry beads rhythmically between his fingers.

'I, um, I'm looking for the toilet,' I said unconvincingly, considering I was standing right outside the door. The man looked at me with an expression of indifference. He pointed to the door without changing his expression. He gave the impression that he considered tourists, and their antics, to be beyond him. I suspected he longed for the days when his taverna was only here to serve the fishermen and locals.

'Thank you,' I said and opened the door. Once inside, I leant against the wall, feeling a fool. I hoped Herman appreciated the lengths we were going to, to help him with what could be a wild goose chase. After a minute or two, I flushed the loo and readied myself to face the old man again. If this was going to work, it was imperative we didn't arouse suspicion, and I feared we were failing. I was already worried that Maria remembered me from my visit with Herman. I thought she gave me a strange look when she first saw me. When I sat back down at the table, Lucy was ordering more coffee and a baklava each.

'I thought we better have something else if we're going to stay awhile.'

The baklava, when it came, was delicious, stickily oozing honey all over our fingers.

The breeze was getting up, like it did most afternoons, and we sat watching a couple of overweight men attempting to windsurf. Their attempts were hilarious. Every time one of them, the older one, stood on the board and heaved the sail up out of the water, the wind caught it, and spun the sail round flinging him back into the sea. To his credit, he didn't give up and time and again he clambered back onto the board. Two women watching from the beach shouted words of encouragement between guffaws of laughter. The younger man was managing to sail, but he started shouting that he didn't know how to turn round; he was clinging onto the boom for dear life as he was being propelled away from the beach. Eventually he let go and fell into the water and swam the board round before trying again.

'I didn't expect a cabaret performance,' Lucy said, catching the napkins that were about to blow off the table. 'Have you ever tried?' she asked.

'No never, I can't decide if it looks fun or a bit of a nightmare. Have you?'

'Yes, it's great fun, but hard work when you're learning, the sail's heavy when full of water, so you soon get tired trying to pull it up. I remember once when we were on a lake in France, we ...' Her voice trailed off and I guessed she was remembering a time when she was with her husband. She shook her head as if to dislodge the memory and stared back out to sea. 'Never mind, but it is good fun.'

I leant across and touched her hand. 'It's OK, it's still one of your happy memories,' I said, hoping it was the right thing to say.

She nodded. 'You're right, we were happy then, but I feel every part of my life that he touched is contaminated, even times before... Well, you know.' She put her finger to her mouth and started nibbling at her non-existent nail.

I resisted the urge to pull it away and glanced at my own nails. They were now looking quite respectable.

'I feel so angry,' she said. 'How dare he do this to me, I couldn't even challenge him because he is dead, and then I couldn't mourn him properly because I hated him so much and now, he's destroyed the way I feel about everything, about my memories.'

I thought she was going to cry; her eyes were blazing, but it was with suppressed fury, not tears.

'Sorry.' She looked at me with a wry smile. 'I didn't mean to have an outburst, it's just that my parents won't talk about him or what happened, and I feel like I'm living in a bubble, and it's got to burst sometime.'

'I expect they don't want to upset you.'

'I know, but I feel like I need to be upset, to be angry, so I can get to the next stage. Do you know what I mean?'

'I think so,' I said, trying to put myself in her shoes, but all the time thinking about Mum's story.

'Why don't you try writing him a letter?' I suggested.

'A letter?' she looked at me as though I was mad, but I could tell she felt intrigued, so I carried on.

'I know it sounds weird, but I read a book once, which was a letter from a wife to a husband who had died, and it was just pouring out all her feelings. It was very moving, and I remember thinking, what a good way to get things off your chest. You could write to Ed, explaining how everything that has happened has affected you. You wouldn't need to show it to anyone or even read it again yourself, but it just might help you sort out your own feelings, get it all out of your head.'

Lucy sat looking thoughtful for a while, but didn't reply.

'Do you think you would still be together if he were alive?' I asked, more out of curiosity that anything else.

'No, definitely not. Well, probably not. I'm not sure. I felt so betrayed. He was a bit of a flirt, but to do it while I was pregnant, and after Tommy was born. I don't think I could ever forgive him. Sometimes, I've wondered if he would have told me or left me for her, if I hadn't found the Christmas card, or whether it would have just fizzled out and I would have been none the wiser. Until the next one.'

She looked sad and tortured as she spoke. Her pain felt so real.

Chapter 40

'Look,' Lucy nodded towards where the taverna opened onto the beach. 'The reason we're here.' She smiled.

I turned to see Christos walking through the gap, where he paused and watched the windsurfers, laughing and shaking his head at their antics.

'Mad men. Look at them,' he said to no one in particular.

He caught a plastic chair as it blew over in the strengthening breeze, and as he pushed it under a nearby table, a strong gust sent a parasol flying, catching Christos on the head and sending him sprawling to the floor. Before anyone could react, Lucy was on her feet.

'I'm a first aider,' she shouted and reached Christos' side before anyone else moved. She helped him onto a chair; a thin trickle of blood was visible and ran down his cheek.

'Anna, hand me my bag,' she called across the tables. I was at her side in a flash, handing her bag to her. She whipped out a pair of nail scissors and cut a lock of blood-stained hair from his head.

'Let me get a better look,' she said, handing the scissors and hair to me. This all happened in the blink of an eye, and the lock of hair, wrapped in a napkin, was safely in my pocket before anyone else really knew what was going on. Christos was sitting up and being tended to by Lucy by the time his wife and mother appeared on the scene with a first aid kit.

'It's only a minor cut, but there might be a bit of a bump,

and I expect he'll have a headache.' Lucy sounded authoritative and in control, with everyone deferring to her.

'Thank you, thank you.' Christos' mother supported her son as he stood up, guided him back into the taverna, and, talking non-stop in Greek, gestured to Maria, expecting her to do something. Maria shrugged and followed. Christos, like most men, appeared to be enjoying the fuss. A couple of other tourists picked up the fallen parasol, and between us we lowered the others, which were over the tables nearest the beach, and most likely to catch the wind.

'Well done, that was amazing,' I said, once Lucy and I were sitting back at our table.

'Did you get it?' She asked.

'Yes,' I patted my pocket. 'Quick thinking on your part. Good job you're a first aider,' I said.

'Well, I got my badge in the Brownies when I was about eight,' she said, and we both collapsed into giggles.

'Goodness, what was that all about? We saw the rumpus from the beach?'

A man I recognised as Lucy's father loomed over the table. I didn't remember him being so tall. Behind him, her mother with Tommy in her arms, was twittering around asking if everyone was all right.

'A parasol blew over and hit the waiter, cutting his head,' Lucy said.

'Not a cause for such hilarity, I wouldn't have thought.' He looked at both of us and we giggled helplessly again.

I couldn't remember having a fit of the giggles like that, since Leila and I were sent out of a maths lesson for pinning a girl's long plait to the back of her chair with a stapler.

'He's OK.' Lucy got out between gasps.

'Well, I suppose it's good to see you laughing.' Her father pulled out a chair and indicated for his wife to do the same. He seemed stern, but I could see a twinkle in his eye and the corners of his lips twitching.

'You must be Anna?' he held out his hand. 'I'm Edward

Davidson, Lucy's father. This is Patricia, her mother.'

We all shook hands rather formally, then settled back at the table.

'Thank you so much. You were so quick, so efficient. Thank you,' Maria, Christos' wife, was standing beside the table, her mother-in-law behind her, smiling and nodding her thanks as well.

'Please let me get you all a special ice cream to say thank you,' she said.

'There's really no need, but that would be lovely. We all love your ice cream. How is he?' Lucy was gracious in her acceptance of their gushing thanks.

'He'll be all right. His mother will fuss him a bit, and he'll make the most of it,' Maria said, first pulling a face then smiling before following her mother-in-law inside to prepare our special ice creams; and special they were.

After a while, Tommy became restless, and we left to go our separate ways, feeling very pleased with the efforts of the afternoon.

'I'll ring you soon. Thanks for listening,' Lucy said, giving me a hug.

'Goodbye, nice to meet you, Anna.'

Her parents weren't as stuffy as first impressions suggested, and I warmed to them over our ice creams. A feeling I thought, and hoped, was mutual. I suspected they were just overprotective of Lucy, and a part of me envied her for having parents that cared so much. I was conscious of the lock of hair in my pocket and needed to find Herman as soon as possible. I was pretty sure from watching detective programmes on the television that DNA lasted forever, but I would feel happier once it was out of my possession.

Chapter 41

It was late afternoon by the time I reached the surgery; Herman wasn't there. I realised then that I didn't know where he lived, and the young girl puppy-sitting gave directions that were less than clear when I asked her. I racked my brain to see if I could remember him saying anything, but apart from knowing which direction he went in; I was none the wiser. I turned away, frustrated, and went to dial his number when the man with the overweight Labrador walked down the road.

'Afternoon, or is it evening?' he said. 'Just about cool enough for Toby's walk. A bit slimmer, don't you think?' he smoothed the dog's back and was rewarded by an enthusiastic wag and lick of the hand.

'He looks good. Did you enjoy your trip?' I asked.

He related the details of his journey home and then told me about the wedding. I started thinking of ways to extricate myself without appearing rude, when I remembered he was an estate agent and might know Herman's house.

'I don't suppose you know where Herman lives, do you? I need to give him something.'

'Certainly, I do. In fact, I sold it to him myself. Quite a tricky sale as I remember, but I pulled it off in the end.' he beamed with pride.

'Is it near to here?' I hoped he would not enter into a long description of his prowess as an estate agent.

'It's called the Net Loft, right round the harbour, next to the little museum. Lovely place, needed some work…'

'That's great. Many thanks. Must rush, see you again.' I cut him off midstream, which was probably rude, but I was itching to get to Herman. It was too hot to run, so I walked at quite a pace around the harbour; several times getting stuck behind meandering tourists out for a stroll.

The Net Loft was an old stone building. The ground floor was an open boat store, but on the upper floor there were three huge windows that opened on to a small wrought-iron balcony. Herman was sitting reading on the balcony. I shouted up to him and he pointed round the side to the back of the building to get in. There was a tiny, shady courtyard garden at the back with old, well-worn stone stairs leading up to the first floor. I skipped up the stairs and through the open door.

The room was vast, and quite dark after the bright light outside. I immediately noticed the windows and the stunning harbour view extending up to the old town. The inside felt cool and tranquil, and as my eyes adjusted to the dimness, I could make out wood panelling on the walls and tasteful, modern-traditional Greek furnishings. I wondered if Herman had furnished the room himself. There were books everywhere, and a guitar leant up against an enormous fireplace, which was taking up half of the back wall. An archway on the side led, I presumed, through to the other rooms.

'Anna, good to see you,' Herman stood silhouetted against the brilliant blue sea. He must have just washed his hair, or been for a swim, as it was still damp and for once he hadn't tied back. He ran his fingers through it, and it tumbled untidily round his face. I was distracted for a moment by how good he looked.

'Look,' I said, pulling, with care, the napkin out of my pocket. I unwrapped it and placed it on a small table. Herman peered at the lock of hair.

'It belongs to Christos,' I said, trying not to sound too smug.

'Wow! Well done. How did you manage to get that?'

I explained the events of the afternoon as he put the hair into a specimen bag he took from a drawer.

'That should be conclusive. Thank you, good work. Much better than a glass or cigarette stub,' he said.

'Do you play?' I asked, nodding towards the guitar.

'A bit. I was in a band at university.'

'What sort of music?'

'Sort of folky,' he said, picking up the guitar and started strumming and singing in German. 'Do you play?' He asked me.

'No, I learnt to play the recorder, not very well, and I used to sing when I was at school, nothing much since.'

'Sing me something.'

I was about to refuse, but pondered for a while, my mine blank, then I remembered the opening words to You've Got a Friend, cleared my throat and sang as best I could.

'Ah, Carole King, good choice. Good voice.'

I felt ridiculously pleased and a little embarrassed by his praise. Also, to my annoyance, I felt self-conscious and awkward.

'Well, I better get off. I'll see you at the surgery in a couple of days.'

'Do you need to rush?' he asked.

I nodded, feeling confused and started blushing like a schoolgirl.

'OK, see you soon.' He looked disappointed but amused. 'And Anna, thanks for your help with this.' He pointed to the specimen bag. 'I'll send it off tomorrow and then we just have to wait.'

I went back down the stone stairs, almost tripping over a small tabby cat that came bounding up the steps as though it knew it would be in for a warm welcome. As I walked under Herman's balcony, I could hear him strumming his guitar and humming to himself and wished I had stayed, but didn't feel I could go back.

Chapter 42

I hesitated once I reached the quayside. I had never been this far round before. So, I carried on and explored further. This side of the harbour was quieter, with no tourist shops and not on the route to the main beach. Outside a Kafenion sat three men, playing cards at a small table. They stopped talking and all three of them watched me as I approached and followed me with their eyes as I walked by.

'Yassou,' I said, and smiled.

'Yassou,' they responded in unison, grinning without, apparently, a full set of teeth between them.

Further along the harbour, an elderly lady was sitting on an old wooden chair outside her front door, with a younger woman sitting on the step beside her. The older woman appeared to be teaching her how to crochet or make lace. They were deep in concentration and didn't look up as I reached them. I peeped over the younger woman's head as I passed and glimpsed the dark interior of a small, sparsely furnished room. I could make out a big table and what I assumed to be a bed against the wall; it was in stark contrast to the whitewashed, airy tourist apartments that lined the other side of the harbour. I supposed locals occupied those apartments at one time and they were now converted to suit the needs and tastes of holidaymakers.

Right at the end of the harbour, with its entrance facing out towards the sea, was a tiny, whitewashed chapel. A priest, dressed in traditional black robes was sitting on a bench by the door, lost in either contemplation or prayer, as he gazed out at the view. I thought he must be so hot in his robes, as I felt a bead of sweat trickle down my neck, and I was only wearing a light cotton top and shorts.

I followed the path that wound in front of the chapel and carried on down towards the water. The coast here was rocky with no beach, but there were several large flat rocks that dipped towards the sea. A couple of these were occupied by sunbathers, but I walked on a bit further and climbed down to a secluded area, where I sat on a large rock and dangled my feet in the deliciously cool water. I gazed out at the endless blue to where the sea met the horizon and, in the haze, merged into one palate of shimmering colour.

The sea was deep here and a beautiful turquoise, turning to almost black in the depths just beyond where I was sitting. I suspected that if I jumped in here it would be a struggle to get back out, so I just swished my feet causing the seaweed, visible beneath the surface, to sway backwards and forwards as if dancing. A shoal of tiny fish darted away, alarmed by the disturbance.

I sat there for quite some time, musing on all the things that had happened over the past few weeks since arriving back in Greece. It felt like I was living someone else's life. I didn't deserve to be somewhere so idyllic, but after turning things over in my mind I decided I should just enjoy this time as a happy interlude until... until what? The thought of returning home made me feel anxious. What was there for me in the future? Where did I really belong? Every moment here felt blissful, but was it real? What about my house and my friends back home? The more I thought, the more uncertain I became. I could not or did not want to answer those questions, or at least not yet.

My train of thought moved on to Herman and his life. He was rather eccentric, but I enjoyed working with him and respected his skill as a vet, and now I felt we were becoming good friends. Living here seemed an unusual life for a young, single man, and I wondered what his story was. He had volunteered very little, and I didn't feel it was my place to ask. I wondered, but pushed the thought away, whether I was beginning to like him as more than just a friend. No, I would not allow myself to even contemplate that. He wasn't my type.

As I sat lost in thought, a wave, wash from an incoming large motor launch, swept across the bay and water splashed up over the rock where I was sitting, soaking my legs and shorts. I leapt up with a shriek of surprise and shook myself off; a cue to go I thought and, with soggy cotton clinging to my bottom, made my way back round the harbour. I looked up at Herman's balcony as I passed. The big glass windows were closed now, and I guessed he was back at the surgery. I wondered where he went and what he did when he wasn't working. Hard as I might try not to be curious, he fascinated me.

I carried on walking around the harbour, and when I reached the road up to the old town decided to take a taxi back to the bottom of the steps. I was looking forward to relating the events of the day to Alice and Ruth over a nice cold glass of wine, but to my disappointment, they were out when I reached the terrace. Feeling hungry, I made myself a sandwich and curled up on a comfy chair and tried to read my book, serenaded as always by the cicadas. In the end I gave up reading after my eyes travelled along the same sentence several times, and just sat daydreaming, enjoying the warmth of the evening. I smiled to myself, reliving the farce of this afternoon, and couldn't really believe that it would result in Herman finding his cousin; I certainly didn't have his conviction that Christos was his cousin.

Chapter 43

A week or so later, I arrived back from a walk, deep in thought about my dilemmas, and found Alice waiting impatiently for me on the terrace.

'Herman's here to see you, Anna. He seems a bit over excited about something,' she said, as I stepped through the arch. I could see Herman pacing backwards and forwards, deep in thought. He looked up when he realised I was there and rushed towards me and grabbed my hands.

'Anna, it's amazing. I've just heard from my friend. It's a match! Christos *is* Andreas.'

I'd never seen Herman so animated. He couldn't keep still and was hopping around the terrace like an excited child. 'After all these years, I can't believe it, and it's thanks to you and Lucy.'

'Wow, I can't believe it either. I'm stunned. I really didn't think it would be him,' I said, sinking into a chair.

Alice poured ice-cold water for us all.

'Thanks.' Herman knocked his drink back in one gulp and eventually sat down.

'So, what happens now?' I couldn't take it in. Christos was Herman's long-lost cousin. It seemed surreal. I'd been treating it all as a bit of a joke, but now it dawned on me. This news could disrupt the course of life for a of people. I wondered if after all this time it might be better to leave well alone.

'Well, I'm going to go to Germany for a couple of days. I need to speak to my uncle and aunt, tell them the news. I need to tell them in person, a phone call won't do, and then I suppose it's up to them.'

'Will the police need to be involved?' Alice asked, ever practical, and for the first time I realised we were talking about a major crime having been committed.

'I don't know, perhaps. They were at the beginning, of course. I think my uncle and aunt will have to make the decisions now. I must tell them, don't you think? Now I know. After all it's not my...' He trailed off, realising that this was going to be a tremendous shock for everyone.

'Will Christos's parents here get into trouble?' I asked. 'They seem such a close family. What if they... well, you know.'

'Oh, I don't know.' Herman, now looking red in the face, stood up and looked from one to the other of us, as though the full implications were also just dawning on him. 'I hope not. I think they are good people, but how did they come to have Andreas? I don't want there to be trouble.' He sat down again and ran his fingers through his hair.

'I think it is still right that my aunt and uncle should know. They have been in pain for many years. They must decide. Don't you think so?'

'Of course, and it is wonderful news for them. It's just going to change so many people's lives, but maybe for the better,' I said, trying to sound reassuring and upbeat, even though I echoed all his doubts.

'Good news, but it sounds like a can of worms to me,' Alice said, out of Herman's hearing.

'Yes, you are right, it is wonderful,' he said, smiling again.

'Perhaps we should have a celebratory drink.' Alice got up to get a bottle.

'No, I must go. I have things to do, things to arrange.' Herman jumped to his feet. 'Anna?'

'The surgery?'

'I'll close for a couple of days, but could you look after everything, particularly Mia and the puppies? I trust you, Anna.'

'Of course, I'll keep an eye on everything,' I said, and felt touched by his confidence in me.

'I'll see you tomorrow and we can go through it all. It will all be good, yes?'

'Yes,' we both chorused, and with a wave, he was gone.

'Well, what a day,' I said. 'I think I could do with that drink.'

'I do hope it all works out all right, for everyone,' Alice said. 'Come on, let's call Ruth and go and eat at the taverna. She'll be amazed when we tell her.'

Over our meal, after discussing every possible scenario for Christos and his family, I put forward an idea that I had been contemplating for a short time, that I should try to find a little place of my own. I was sure now that I was going to stay for a while, at least until the end of the summer, and much as I loved Ruth and Alice, I was used to my own space. I was sure they would understand and hoped they wouldn't take it personally.

'Well, as it happens,' Alice said, ignoring Ruth's protests and distraught look. 'I have a small apartment that I sometimes let out to tourists. I don't advertise or anything, it's just logged with the tourist office for ad hoc visitors.'

'Really? You're full of surprises.' Ruth raised her eyebrows.

Alice nodded. 'Yes, and it's available. The last visitors left a couple of days ago. I've been there today cleaning up. You could stay there.'

'Where is it?' Ruth asked.

'Just round there,' Alice pointed behind the taverna. 'You can see the edge of the balcony from our terrace. So, you won't be far away, and we can still spend most of our time together.'

I felt like leaping up and hugging Alice. She was amazing. 'That sounds perfect. I'll pay the going rate, of course.' I was so delighted; it was the best of both worlds.

'You will not,' said Alice. 'It's yours for as long as you want it. I don't rely on the income from it. So, I won't hear another word about money,' she said, correctly anticipating my intake of breath as the start of a protest.

The next morning, we all went to look at the apartment. It was ideal. One bedroom, a living area with a kitchen, a shower room, and a beautiful balcony with a built-in barbecue, table and chairs, and a large, thatched parasol. It was in pristine condition and equipped with everything I could ever need.

'You just need to be careful when it gets windy. The parasol has blown over a couple of times. Luke weighted it down so it should be OK now, and the phone signal's a bit hit and miss up here. I can provide all your linen and towels. So, what do you think?'

'It's perfect, a little gem.'

Alice glowed with pride and delight that I was so impressed and pleased.

'It'll be more convenient,' I said, more to Ruth, who was looking dubious. 'I won't be hogging the bathroom when you need it.'

Ruth laughed. 'OK, as long as we still see lots of you.'

'I'll cook us a barbecue later,' I said. 'My housewarming meal. So, once I've brought my case up, I'll go shopping.'

'Don't forget you need to see Herman before he leaves.' Alice reminded me.

I looked at my watch. 'I'll have to fly, but I'll still cook. See you later.' I ran back to Alice's place to get my bag.

'Take the car. The keys are on the table.' Alice called over the balcony.

Chapter 44

Herman had secured a ticket on the ferry to Athens, leaving the next morning, and he thought catching a flight to Germany should be easy. I expected him to be anxious or excited about breaking the news to his aunt and uncle, but outwardly at least, he appeared very calm.

He ran through all the essentials that needed to be carried out while he was away and showed me how to lock up and make sure everything was secure, even though I already knew. He agreed I could see and treat animals if it was a routine problem I could manage and no drugs were required, but he was going to put a message on the answerphone that the clinic was closed for a few days. It would only be open if someone turned up while I was there.

At last, he felt happy that I knew what to do. I felt confident that I could cope, but it was different being responsible for everything. My job at home gave me far more responsibility than the tasks Herman was expecting me to carry out, but it was different here, and I wanted to make sure I lived up to his expectations. At home, I was one of a team of six nurses and there were five vets, plus all the admin and reception staff. I could not remember ever being in the building alone. I was looking forward to it.

'Thank you, Anna, I shouldn't be more than a few days. Now perhaps I need to find some more German looking clothes, do you think?'

I laughed, surveying his combination of floral board shorts,

'No Problem' T-shirt, and flip-flops. He had scrunched his hair into a sort of topknot, on top of which he plonked a battered Panama hat,

'I think you might just look a little out of place in Berlin like that.'

'OK, thank you again. I'll keep in touch and see you as soon as I get back to let you know what is going to happen next.'

He gave me the keys and strode off down the street, looking back to wave before he turned round the corner. I watched him go and realised I would miss him, despite being excited about being in charge.

I spent every morning at the surgery and called in again every evening to feed the puppies, who were now eating solid food, as well as feeding from Mia. While I was there, I made use of my time by continuing to sort through cupboards and streamline the filing system. I enjoyed the autonomy and hoped Herman wouldn't feel I was interfering. Just in case, I made a mental note to tell him what I was up to when he next called. After a couple of days, I rang Lucy to suggest she brought Tommy to see the puppies. She was eager, and we arranged to meet at the surgery the next morning.

'Look, Tommy, doggies!' Lucy and Tommy sat on the floor next to the large whelping box where the four puppies of indeterminate breed were rolling around and playing with each other. They were five weeks old now and quite gorgeous, and were becoming very active. I lifted one out and put it down next to Tommy. He poked at it, and it rolled over; he squealed with delight. Mia watched nervously at first, but soon settled and seemed pleased to have a moment off from trying to keep them in order.

'No, stroke it like this, nice and gentle.' Lucy took Tommy's hand and guided him.

I watched Lucy interacting with Tommy. She appeared relaxed and natural with him, and I hoped her doubts about how she felt about him were fading. I wasn't into little children. I preferred them when they could hold a sensible conversation, but Tommy had a solemn air of cuteness about him. He was an attractive child with a mop of dark, unruly hair. I tried to remember from the news reports what his father looked like, but my memory was vague.

Lucy sensed me watching and looked up, smiling,

'My parents were delighted when I said I was bringing Tommy here. They were so enthusiastic it made me realise how much I've just left everything up to them, while I wallowed in self-pity. They said to invite you up to the villa to see them again soon?' she cocked her head questioningly.

'I'd love to. Do they know I'm an emotional wreck, as well as a giggling idiot?' I smiled, remembering how Lucy's father had not been amused when Lucy and I became almost helpless with laughter after we collected Christos' hair.

'You're very strong Anna, don't underestimate yourself. Anyway, my parents are so pleased I met you. Do you think Ruth and Alice would like to come as well?'

I nodded, certain that they would love the chance to see the villa and meet Lucy's parents.

Tommy, by now, was sitting in the whelping box, chuckling with glee, while puppies nuzzled all around him. Lucy lifted him out, much to his annoyance, while I retrieved the loose puppy from under the desk and popped him back in. Tommy climbed straight back in, and I stopped Lucy pulling him out again. He couldn't do much harm, providing he didn't sit on them.

'Does he know anything about his dad?' I asked.

Lucy sat back on the floor, where she could keep a close eye on Tommy.

'I tell him daddy won't be coming home anymore, but to be honest, I think he's too young to grasp the meaning. He says 'daddy gone' a lot, but I'm sure he doesn't know what it means. Apparently, according to some child psychologist, or someone who came to see us after it happened, it's important for him that I keep his dad's memory alive. It's difficult, when all I want to do is forget he ever existed. I can't see what difference it will make to Tommy now. I'm sure he doesn't remember him, and I can tell him everything when he's older. What do you think?'

I shrugged. 'I don't really know. I think you're supposed to be honest with children if they ask questions, but it's quite a difficult thing to tell him. I doubt he'll understand any of it for years.'

I looked at Lucy and could tell she was struggling to even think about her husband, and felt sure she needed better advice than mine.

'Maybe there's someone, another professional I mean, who could advise you?' I suggested.

She screwed up her nose. 'I've had enough of so-called professionals for a while.' I tried to imagine what sort of nightmare she must have been through, but knew my imaginings were nowhere near the reality. Her parents were right to whisk her away from everything for a while.

'I suppose we'll just have to take one step at a time,' she said.

I checked Mia, took her out into the yard to feed her and to give her a break from her demanding babies. She was a gentle dog. She had been grossly underweight when she arrived in labour a few weeks ago, but with good care and regular food, she was now beginning to thrive. I stroked her sandy coloured back; I could still see her ribs, but she was in much better condition than when I first saw her. Her tail wagged. She licked my hand, and her soft brown eyes looked into mine. I never failed to be touched by the bond between humans and dogs.

There were clouds scudding across the sky and I imagined that out of the shelter of the courtyard it must be getting quite windy. Perhaps there would be a storm later. I looked at Mia and hoped that she would be all right if thunder came. Of course she would, I told myself. She isn't a pampered pooch from England; being inside must feel scarier and alien for her. I stroked her ragged ears.

'You're a good girl.' Her tail wagged even more. I tidied up while Lucy and Tommy played with the puppies. I checked the messages and opened the post, most of which was in Greek, so I wasn't sure whether it was important and put it in a folder ready for Herman's return.

There was a brief message from Herman; saying he should be back on Thursday. He apologised for being away longer than planned, but he would tell me everything when he returned. He asked me to check a few other things, and to ring Ingrid to let her know he would visit next week rather than this week. I felt a surge of pleasure at the thought of his return and looked forward to finding out how his news had gone down in Berlin. After a final check of the desk, I returned to Lucy and Tommy. 'They're so adorable, aren't they?' Lucy held a puppy up under her chin and was nuzzling its head. 'What will happen to them?'

'Herman will try to find homes for them,' I said, clearing up their mess and preparing to bring Mia back in for the next round of feeding.

'I'd love one, but it's impractical, I suppose, at the moment.' She put the puppy back in the box, gave Mia a stroke and took Tommy's hand, ready to leave.

'Say bye-bye to the doggies,' she said, waving. Tommy looked unimpressed, and I was sure there would be tears and protests when Lucy took him away, but Lucy diverted the tantrum in time.

'How about a special ice cream?' she suggested.

'Yeh, ice cweam,' he said, and Lucy winked.

'Works every time. Will you join us?' she asked.

I nodded. 'Go on down. I'll catch you up in a few minutes.' I checked the puppies were all secure in the back room and closed the door. 'There are a couple of other things I need to do, but won't be long.'

Before leaving, I wanted to double check everything was as it should be, ready for Herman's return.

Chapter 45

Just as I was about to lock up, two men appeared round the side of the building and headed towards me. They didn't appear to have an animal, and I was unsure whether to open the door again or to lock it and walk away.

'Hey, you!' one of them said.

'Can I help you?' my hand was on the handle and the key was in the lock. I turned to get a good look at them and did not like what I saw. Before I could do anything, one of them grabbed my arm roughly, while the other pushed the door open. The one holding my arm shoved me inside, ahead of them.

'Where is he?'

'Who? No one's here.'

'The German, of course. Where is he?' The man who spoke was about forty or fifty. It was hard to tell. He had a swarthy complexion and was reasonably well dressed in dark trousers and a white shirt. He did not look or sound local and was not a tourist. He spoke English well, but I couldn't place his accent. I was certain it wasn't Greek. He spoke to the other younger man, who was eyeing up everything in the reception, in a language I didn't recognise. Their tone and manner were hostile, and I realised the older man had positioned himself in front of the door and my exit.

'Hey, you can't go in there.' I rushed to the door leading to the puppies to stop the younger man opening it. He looked at me with an expression to curdle cream, but remained silent.

There was an ugly tattoo of a lion about to pounce on his forearm; I wasn't a fan of tattoos. He wore jeans and a grey T-shirt that showed off his well-formed biceps. He shoved me hard out of the way, and anger took over from my anxiety. I was not having that! How dare he?

'Get out! Now!' I grappled in my bag for my phone, but the tattooed man banged it out of my hand, sending it spinning across the floor.

'No,' he shouted. 'Where's the German?'

He pushed me against the desk. His breath reeked of garlic, and there was an unpleasant aroma of body odour percolating from the damp circles under his armpits. It suddenly dawned on me that these men must be something to do with Christos. I could not imagine two thugs coming to discuss animal care and was certain all Herman's business affairs were straight and legitimate.

'He's not here. Get out!' I was shaking with rage and reached back onto the desk. My hand closed round the stapler, and I swung round and hit the younger man against the side of his head. He let out a stream of expletives in his native language; blood was trickling down his cheek. I regretted my actions at once. There was no way I could take on two men. I should run, but my instinct was to stay and fight, anyway my exit route was still blocked.

'Get out. Now!' I yelled. 'I'm calling the police,' I made a grab for the phone on the desk and as I did, I realised that I didn't know the Greek equivalent of 999.

The other man, who'd been trying to open the filing cabinet, leapt across the room and grabbed my shoulders, shaking me violently.

'Tell the German to keep his nose out or he will be sorry.' He flung me out of the way with such force I fell, hitting my head on the corner of the desk before banging it again with a sickening thud as I hit the floor.

The floor was cold against my cheek, and in the instant before it all went dark, I could smell the disinfectant floor cleaner that I had used to mop it earlier. I opened my eyes; I wasn't sure how long I had been lying there and was nervous about moving. All was quiet, and I assumed I was now alone. With caution, I concentrated on each part of my body. My eyes were functioning. I could see across the floor to the desk, which meant I was lying with my back against the filing cabinet. I could see my phone, screen cracked, a few feet away. Cautiously, I moved my legs and feet, followed by my hands, wiggling my fingers. I was reaching the conclusion that apart from my head, which was throbbing like the worst ever hangover, everything was intact.

A noise I recognised filtered into my consciousness, my phone ringing. I propped myself up on my elbow and crawled across the floor. Please don't ring off, I thought as I reached out for it.

'Hello,' I croaked.

'Anna. Where are you? What's happened? You sound funny?'

'Lucy, I'm hurt, get help.'

'Are you in the clinic?'

'Yes. The men…I'm hurt…' my voice trailed away.

'What men? Oh my God. Hang on. I'm on my way'

I must have sunk back onto the floor, possibly losing consciousness again, as the next thing I remember was the room full of people and noise, and someone carefully helping me to sit up. I could see Lucy, with Tommy hanging round her neck, Ruth and Alice, and a couple of Greek men. One turned out to be the doctor and the other a police officer. The doctor looked at the cut on my head. It wasn't too bad, and a couple of dressing strips were all that was needed.

'You'll have a headache,' he said, stating the obvious, as my head was now thumping even more.

'What time is it?' I asked and was amazed to find out it was only about thirty minutes since Lucy and Tommy left for ice cream; it felt like hours.

'Was she knocked out? Anna it's me.' Ruth was kneeling

on the floor next to the chair that I somehow was now sitting on. She took my hand but addressed the doctor.

'Very probably,' he replied.

'Do you think you were knocked out?' Ruth asked me.

I shrugged.

Concussed, and badly shaken, rather than badly injured, was the conclusion. The doctor spelt out to Ruth what danger signs she should look out for and stressed I should not be left alone for the next twenty-four hours. Ruth nodded, and the doctor gave her his card with his telephone number in case she was worried.

'Can I have some water?' My head was clearing. 'Those men?' I asked. 'Who are they? I can describe them.'

The police officer, who had now been joined by a colleague, was shouting into his phone. The colleague stood next to me and asked police type questions. He wrote down everything I said regarding their descriptions and became animated when I described the younger man's tattoo. I told them as much as I could about what they said, but as very little was in English, I doubted it could be much help. The other Police Officer now came over and nodded when he heard me trying to describe their language.

'Bulgarians, I think. The German police phoned.'

We all looked at the Police Officer, expecting him to go into more detail, but he was back on his phone talking and gesticulating.

'I don't suppose he deals with much crime around here,' said Lucy. 'Do you think these men are something to do with Herman's cousin being kidnapped?'

The Police Officer came back to us, and hearing what Lucy said, answered her query.

'Yes. To do with kidnapping and drugs. The German and Bulgarian police are after them.'

'Well, shouldn't someone be stopping them?' asked Alice. 'We don't want them getting away.'

'No ferry,' he said, as his phone rang again, and he was

relaying information to someone on the other end in a loud voice.

'What do you mean, no ferry? Why isn't there a ferry?' Lucy asked.

He pointed out of the window to a tree bending in the wind. 'Look at the weather. Bad weather, sea's too rough, so no ferry.'

I remembered it was looking stormy when I was with Mia earlier.

A knock on the door preceded a young man entering with a folder full of grainy photos that had been faxed from somewhere.

'Can you look at some photographs?' the Police Officer asked, taking the folder from the new man.

'She needs to rest.' The doctor intervened.

'It's OK, I'll take a look,' I said.

The Police Officer shot a triumphant look in the doctor's direction. This was his moment he wasn't going to let a medical matter thwart him. He passed me photos of men of various ages but all with the same dark hair and rugged, well-worn, unsmiling expressions on their faces.

'Him,' I said, and everyone craned their necks to see the photo. 'And there was an older man with him.'

A few more photos were examined, some clearer than others. 'That one. I think that's him, but I'm not certain.'

'Good, good.' The Police Officer was on his phone again, shouting instructions and what sounded like names, to no doubt an equally excited Police Officer somewhere else.

'I think someone has spotted them. I must go. We might need to see you again,' he said, and beckoning to his colleague rushed for the door, keen not to miss the action.

'Can we take Anna home now?' Ruth asked the man who had arrived with the photos, who was also something to do with the police.

'Yes, yes, you go. We'll come up if we need you. We have your address?'

'Yes,' Ruth and Alice both answered.

The storm was building in strength, and rain was beginning to fall in torrents.

'I expect we'll get a spectacular thunder and lightning show soon,' Alice said. 'We need to take Anna home before it starts'

'Do you feel all right?' the doctor stared into my eyes yet again.

I nodded, but soon stopped as the movement set up a pounding I preferred to avoid.

'Remember, call me if you are worried,' the doctor said, shaking Alice and Ruth by the hand.

'The puppies,' I suddenly remembered the man trying to open the door to their room.

'They're fine. I've checked,' Lucy said, and hoisted Tommy higher on her hip. 'I'll call tomorrow to see how you are.'

There was a flurry as everyone exchanged details, then Ruth and Alice steered me towards the car.

At the villa, Ruth and Alice fussed around me, making sure I felt comfortable, bringing me drinks and tempting nibbles to eat. Alice sat close, holding my hand and smiling warmly whenever she caught my eye. I would have enjoyed it if my head didn't hurt so much. Ruth insisted I stayed with them in Alice's villa that night, rather than walking up the hill to my own little retreat.

As expected, we were treated to a spectacular thunderstorm with lightning forking across the sky, lighting up the ink black sea. The rain was torrential, causing the steps and narrow alleyways to become rivers, but the temperature felt warm enough to sit outside under the cover of the canopy.

As instructed, Ruth and Alice took it in turns to wake me up overnight, to make sure my concussion did not return and send me into unconsciousness. I was fine, but we were all tired the next morning and dozed on the terrace, with little energy for anything else. Lucy rang during the morning to check on me and invited the three of us to a barbecue at her parents' villa later that week.

Chapter 46

We took a taxi to Villa Thea, the Davidson's villa at the top of the island. The journey took us up through olive groves where the old, gnarled trees were still productive despite the apparent poor quality of the soil. The taxi driver stopped, and we wondered if he was lost as he opened the window to speak to an elderly man who was leading a donkey along the road. The older man became quite animated, waving his arms and pointing back down the road. We looked at each other, wondering what was going on.

'My grandfather,' he said, driving away, beeping his horn and waving out of the window.

We needn't have worried he knew exactly where to go and after another mile turned off the main road onto a narrow track that wound down towards the sea. He turned again and slowed down as he drove through an arched gateway. The car stopped at the back of a large villa nestled into the hill with uninterrupted views out to sea. It was a large, double storied building, with an enormous, sheltered terrace running around three sides of the ground floor and a huge arched balcony facing the sea on the first floor. We climbed out of the car and gaped in awe.

'Wow, I thought my view was special, but this is amazing,' Alice said, taking it all in, when Lucy came down to welcome us. She ushered us around to the terrace; I was amazed that such a beautiful place could be so tucked away. Steps led down from the terrace to an infinity pool and gardens beyond.

I realised that Lucy's parents were standing up waiting for us, and dragged my attention away from the view.

Lucy introduced Ruth and Alice to her parents, and as soon as the formalities were over, Lucy's parents asked how I was, showing great concern about my injury. Lucy's father, who it turned out was a retired surgeon, insisted on examining my bump and declared that I would be OK, but that I was lucky I missed my eye when I fell. After everyone had settled on the terrace with a cool drink, we discussed at length the unlikely events that resulted in Herman finding his cousin.

'It's quite incredible after thirty-odd years that Herman just happened to be living on the same island as his kidnapped cousin. What are the chances of that? If it was a story, you'd think it was too far-fetched.' Mr Davidson's incredulity reflected what we all thought.

'He's back in a couple of days, so we'll be able to find out what's going to happen. It must have been such a shock for his aunt and uncle,' I said.

'That's probably an understatement,' he said. 'But it sounds, from what Lucy told us, that the police are on to the right gang and that those two who attacked you have been apprehended.' He paused nodding his head and looking at me with a grave expression on his face. 'You were very lucky, Anna. They must have believed you didn't know anything, or things could have been much worse. I wonder how many other missing children they're responsible for,' he said.

I shuddered, for both me and the other missing children. 'I don't think I want to think about the implications,' I said. Although, on the night of the attack I hardly slept for doing just that, but didn't want to think about it now.

'Hmm, Christos was one of the lucky ones. At least he went to a loving family and wasn't trafficked for, well something much worse,' he said.

'It doesn't bear thinking about,' Lucy's mum said.

'Well, hopefully, all will be well. We mustn't get too gloomy thinking about what could have been. Now, I must get the barbecue started, so you all relax and enjoy yourselves.' He walked away around the side of the villa. I flopped onto a lounger, while Lucy and Tommy tempted Ruth and Alice into the pool.

'It is so beautiful here, Mrs Davidson,' I said.

'Call me Pat, dear. Yes, very peaceful. I could stay here all the time, but Edward gets bored after a couple of weeks. He needs something to do.' She settled onto a lounger next to me. A small, not unattractive woman dressed in a green swimsuit with matching patterned sarong. She looked tired, but I got the impression she was a strong woman, and remembered her organising everything when they arrived on the quay. Her hair was dark like Lucy's, but it was clear Lucy inherited her looks from her father.

'Thank you dear,' Pat said. She patted my hand and smiled.

Feeling a bit confused, I just smiled back and said nothing. She continued.

'I knew I was right to insist we bring Lucy out here, get her away from everything. She's become more her old self, just in the few weeks we've been here. Although, I was worried when she told me about your attack in case she became over anxious again, but she was fine. Your friendship has been a real bonus. She's more like her old self,' she said again, looking across to the pool to where Lucy was laughing as she pulled Tommy around on a blow-up crocodile.

'Sometimes it helps to get away to have time to think,' I said, thinking about myself as well as Lucy.

'Yes, it does. Neither Edward nor Lucy was keen to come, but I just knew it would help.'

'How long are you planning to stay here this time?' I asked.

'I'm not sure. Another couple of weeks, I think. Edward thinks Lucy needs to get back into normal life. He thinks being here is a bit like being in a bubble and the longer she is out of touch with reality, the harder it will be to go back.'

I felt that she disagreed with her husband and would probably end up getting her way.

'I never really felt comfortable with Edwin,' she said. 'He was what my mother would have described as a wide boy. There was nothing I could put my finger on. He was flash with money and, to be honest, I could never get to grips with what he did for a job. He was a bit of a wheeler and dealer. Something in The City Lucy said, but she could see no wrong in him…' she paused. 'And he called me Patsy. No one calls me Patsy. Everyone except me thought it was funny. Lucy said he was just being friendly; I thought it was disrespectful.' She paused again. 'I know he was killed and so could be considered an innocent victim, but to me, he was never innocent. How could he be when he was cheating with that woman? And the effect of it all on Lucy was devastating. Don't get me wrong, I didn't wish him ill, particularly not to be killed, but my only concern was for Lucy, and I doubted she would ever return to even a shadow of her old self.'

'I can't imagine how traumatic it must have been. I suppose for Lucy it must be like recovering from a long illness,' I said.

Pat nodded. 'Yes, it's very much like an illness; her spirit and heart were broken, but I feel she is at last on the mend. She's stronger than I give her credit for, but my mother's instinct is to protect her, over protect her probably,' she smiled. We sat without speaking for a few minutes, just gazing out across the grounds to the sea, both lost in thought.

I thought about Carrie. I could no longer think of her as my mother. Her experience was nothing like Lucy's, but Dad's death was also traumatic and unexpected, and to a certain extent she was also coping with his betrayal. I couldn't remember her grieving; she must have done it privately or perhaps with Ruth. I guiltily couldn't remember ever taking her feelings into account but just wallowed in my distress of losing Dad.

'Lucy and Tommy are lucky to have you,' I said after a while, and turned to smile at Pat.

'Thank you dear, that's very kind. Now you must excuse me a moment. I had better go round to help Edward with the barbecue. You know men, they think they are the chief chef when it comes to barbecuing, but I'm expected to do all the preparation.' She laughed and set off into the villa.

Chapter 47

I lay back on the lounger and closed my eyes, listening to the laughter and splashing of Alice, Ruth, Lucy and Tommy in the pool. In the distance, I could hear the voices of Edward and Patricia as they discussed how to barbecue the fish Edward caught yesterday. A warm feeling washed over me, not just from the sun, but the warmth of feeling relaxed and part of a family in a way that I never remembered from when I was young. I mused over Pat's words that Edward thought being here wasn't reality. Maybe he was right, but it was a reality for Alice, who was making a good living here and for Herman, and certainly for the locals such as Christos. For them, it was very real. Was it real for me, I wondered, or was I using it as an escape? A very nice escape though, I thought as I drifted into a doze.

Lucy came and plonked herself beside me.
'I've got some exciting news,' she said, looking around to make sure no one else was within earshot.
I opened my eyes and propped myself up on the lounger to face her. She wore her hair in thin braids that fell to her shoulders, a tiny bead threaded onto the end of each one. Her face and body glowed with a gentle suntan, and she was grinning from ear to ear. She was an attractive woman and looked quite different from the person I first saw on the ferry several weeks ago.
'What is it?' I asked.

'An old colleague of mine is working as part of a team continuing the excavation of Akrotiri on Santorini. Have you been there? It's wonderful?'

I shook my head and waited for her to continue, not admitting that I had not been to Santorini, and had never heard of Akrotiri.

'She's asked if I would like to join her for a few days, or longer, if I can. But the best bit is, she has offered me a part-time job back in England.' She looked over her shoulder again. 'I haven't mentioned it to them yet.'

'What's the job back home?' I asked.

'Well, it's cataloguing archaeological finds, mainly bits of pottery and things like that from digs, doesn't sound very exciting, I know, but she also wants help to set up an exhibition. The best bit though, is that it would be in Manchester so I could move away from Surrey.' She beamed at me. 'Great, isn't it?'

'What about Tommy?' I asked.

'Well, fingers crossed my parents will look after him for a few days if I go to Santorini. It would be too good to miss as I'm in Greece already, and then back home he would have to go to nursery when I go to work. It was always my plan for him to go to nursery anyway, before…' She stopped, but I knew what she meant, before the murders changed her life.

'What do you think?' she asked, but I knew I couldn't say anything other than it sounded a great idea, and I thought it did. Although, I hoped she wouldn't be leaving too soon. I was about to ask her more when Pat reappeared and called us to the table for lunch.

'Say nothing about our conversation. I'll tell them later,' Lucy said, as we made our way round to the terrace.

We all gathered around a large, marble topped, garden table for a delicious meal of barbecued fish with wonderful salads. Lucy's parents were excellent hosts. I could see entertaining was their forte. Edward was convivial and appeared delighted when we all showed great enthusiasm for the fish.

He regaled us with his fishing exploits, which, on one occasion ended with him being pulled overboard by the size of the-one-that-got-away. For most of the meal Tommy sat happily in his highchair, stuffing bits of food into his mouth or throwing it on the floor, but after a while he started to grizzle.

'Bedtime, I think.' Patricia rose to take him inside.

'It's OK, mum, I'll take him up.' Lucy lifted him up. 'Now then, what about a bath and mummy read you a story?' Tommy put his arms around her neck and was happy to be taken away.

I noticed a quick glance, raised eyebrows and smile between Lucy's parents and assumed that this was a sign of more progress.

'Ruth, you are an artist! Come and give me some advice please. I need something for an empty wall.'

Ruth and Edward left the table and went into the villa. I followed, intrigued to see inside, and left Alice and Pat at the table discussing jewellery. The interior was very tasteful, large, open, airy spaces painted white, with quality but not ostentatious, furnishings. The view was the focal point of the room, which, overall exuded an air of wealth and tranquillity. I smiled when I thought of the contrast to our family holidays in a small caravan in Devon. Ruth came with us once or twice. I would have to remind her about it later.

'Now, I was thinking of something large to go just here,' Edward said, indicating a wide expanse of white wall to the left of a big wood-burning stove. Ruth stood surveying the wall and contemplating the room for a few moments.

'Well,' she said. 'To be honest, I don't think there's enough depth here for a big canvas. To get the best from a big picture, you need space to step back from it.'

'I wondered about that.' He nodded and stepped back beside Ruth, and they both stared at the wall.

'Now here, for instance.' Ruth pointed to another wall, 'would be perfect. You would get the full effect as you came through that archway. This wall,' she pointed back to the original space, 'would lend itself to a couple of smaller pieces or even being left blank.'

I wandered off, leaving them to discuss the type of art that would suit the location. Ruth was subtly steering Edward towards her own style, I was sure, and smiled to myself as I made my way into another room. This was an attractive, sunken sitting area, with doors leading onto yet another terrace. Lucy joined me while I stood there taking it all in.

'What an amazing place,' I said.

'It wasn't always like this. When my parents bought it, years ago, it was a bit of a wreck. It became dad's project; he designed most of the interior himself. Decided where the pool should go and how big the terrace should be. Mum just went along with most of it. We used to come here during all my school holidays when I was young, but I found it dull as a teenager. I wanted a bit more action. Mum would like to spend more time here now. Now it's all finished, but I think Dad gets restless. He needs more to occupy him.'

I nodded, comparing Lucy's story to the debates between Carrie and Dad, about whether they could afford to buy a static caravan when Rachel and I were young. They decided it was too expensive. We never went on a foreign holiday as a family. In fact, the first time I went abroad was when I went camping in France with Leila and her family, when I was about fifteen.

'You look miles away.' Lucy said and brought me back to the present day.

'Sorry, I was just thinking.' I smiled at her, but didn't elaborate.

'Let's go. I think we need another drink.'

Lucy led the way back out onto the terrace, where the others were already topping up glasses. The evening passed in wide-ranging conversations, plenty of laughter and alcohol. Possibly aided by the alcohol, it felt as though there was a genuine warmth of friendship in the air, despite all our different backgrounds.

Our taxi arrived all too soon to take us back to the old town, and we left with promises of meeting up again. Patricia made an appointment to visit Alice to discuss a commission for a necklace to match some earrings she already owned.

'I think Edward might be interested in seeing my work, with a view to me painting something for his wall,' Ruth said, settling back into the car.

'I thought you were steering him in that direction,' I said. 'Sounds like you two have had a productive day.'

'It's been a lovely day. What a beautiful place,' Alice yawned, and I think we were all asleep, rocked by the taxi, by the time we reached the steps at the bottom of the old town.

Chapter 48

I continued to go to the surgery twice a day, to look after Mia and her puppies, determined that the attack would not stop me from doing my job. It took me almost half a day to clear up. The men had caused quite a mess. They had opened the cupboards and drawers that I recently tidied, pulling everything out looking for who knows what, but they had caused no actual damage. I wasn't convinced they were looking for anything specific. They just wanted to make a point and flex their muscles when they realised Herman wasn't there.

A wave of fear swept over me at the thought of him being tracked down and hurt. I turned on the computer to see if there was an update from him and was relieved to see an email sent earlier that morning, saying he would be back at the weekend. He was delaying his return, as his aunt and uncle wanted to come back with him. I felt surprised, although I don't know why. It was completely natural that they would want to be reunited with their son as soon as possible. I couldn't help feeling a pang of anxiety for Christos and his family, who I guessed were all still in the dark about the changes to come. What a shock it was going to be.

It was late on Saturday evening when Herman rang, and I pushed the feeling of pleasure at hearing his voice again out of my mind, almost before it registered. He already knew about the attack on me and was concerned and apologetic for putting me in danger. We chatted for quite some time. He told me his aunt and uncle had already settled into one of the hotels near to his apartment. He asked if I would like to meet them the next day, and I jumped at the chance. We agreed to meet in the hotel foyer at ten o'clock the following morning.

The first sight of Herman's aunt and uncle was a complete surprise. I was expecting an elderly couple because, in my imagination, they were a small, archetypal, hunched up couple, hanging on to each other for moral and physical support.

'This is Elke and Hans,' said Herman, directing me across the sitting room of a discreet but expensive hotel suite. I hadn't realised such a posh hotel existed on the island.

'This is Anna,' he informed his relatives.

I held my hand out towards a tall, elegant lady, dressed in a loose white linen shirt and slim fitting white trousers. Her grey hair curled softly round her solemn face. I was certain Herman said she was seventy, but she would have passed for ten years younger. She shook my hand and smiled, but I noticed there was a sad weariness in her pale blue eyes.

'Anna,' she said. 'How nice to meet you. Are you Herman's young lady?'

Again, I was surprised by her perfect, almost accent free, English.

'I'm a friend and colleague,' I said. 'I work at his surgery sometimes.'

'Ah,' she said, raising a perfectly manicured eyebrow. 'Herman spoke of you often, and you obtained the vital information that identified Andreas, I understand?'

'Yes, well a friend and I helped Herman.'

She nodded, as if satisfied, and sat down on a small sofa, crossing her legs and looking expectantly towards Herman and her husband.

'Pleased to meet you, Anna.' Hans held out his hand and shook mine in a firm grip. He was a tall, grey-haired man who, although looking more his age than Elke, was still very good-looking. I could not help wondering what Herman's parents looked like, as he bore no sign of the elegance and style of his aunt and uncle. Hans, I understood to be Herman's uncle on his mother's side.

Hans took Herman by the arm and steered him across to the other side of the room, where they started an earnest discussion in German. Another smartly dressed man entered the room, inclined his head towards the door, and the three of them left.

I hesitated, feeling awkward and unsure what my role was in this situation, and yet I felt it would be rude to leave.

'Come and sit with me, my dear.' Elke patted the sofa next to her.

There was a jug of lemonade and several glasses on the table in front of her.

'Would you like a glass?' I lifted the jug and poured some into two glasses.

'Thank you,' she nodded.

'I imagine Herman has told you about our story?' she spoke in a quiet voice, and I leaned in a little closer.

'He's given me an outline,' I said.

'Andreas; I believe he's known as Christos now.'

I nodded, but didn't speak. I felt this dignified lady wanted to tell me her story herself, and I was an eager listener.

'He was sixteen months old, a beautiful baby, always smiling and laughing, and so good. Everyone told me I had been blessed with an angel.' She handed me an old, faded, colour photo of a smiling baby. She found it so readily in her bag and its worn state made me think it was never far from her reach. He was sitting on a rug surrounded by toys and holding a blue teddy or rabbit up towards the camera. He was waving at the photographer with his other hand.

'His hand didn't cause him any problem; he managed as well as any other baby with two perfect hands. I was upset when he was born. Of course, everyone wants their baby to be perfect, but the way he developed and managed made it seem almost irrelevant. You can see it didn't bother him. I thought after he went missing that being different would make him easier to find.'

'A little cherub,' I said, and handed the precious photo back to her.

She studied it, smoothed her thumb across the surface and then carefully replaced it in her bag.

'We live in a small town outside Berlin. I was born there and have lived there all my life. The war badly damaged it, but my parents thought it was their duty to stay and help breathe life back into the town. Anyway, after we married, Hans and I stayed on in the town. We live in a house with a big garden on the outskirts near to a lake. You wouldn't know now that the war had taken place unless you looked closely in some parts of the town. We employed a nanny to help with Andreas.

Hans worked in Berlin, and I was trying to write a history of our town, so needed a bit of time away from the baby. The nanny, Ruby, was American, a lovely girl. It was a fashionable thing to do in those days, to become a nanny in a foreign country, learn the language and have an adventure.' She raised her eyes to check I was still listening, and a faint smile touched her lips when she saw that my attention was undivided.

'That day, 16th July 1976, Ruby took Andreas out to the park; she did most days when the weather was good. I remember that day was hot, and I called to her to make sure he kept his hat on. I was working in my study and after about an hour she burst in completely hysterical. Someone had taken Andreas. It took me many minutes to calm her down enough to find out what had happened.' Elke paused; in her mind she was back in that terrible moment. She shook her head and carried on.

'I don't think the reality hit me straight away. All I remember is rushing to the park, Ruby sobbing behind me all the way. I was so certain I would find him, and it wasn't until I'd searched every inch and went home without him that panic set in. I called the police and called Hans to come home at once. Ever since, I have blamed myself for not calling the police straight away. It was the first thing Hans asked, why didn't I call them before rushing off? But it was my instinct to go to the park and look for him myself.

The police, Hans, neighbours, friends, everybody searched and searched, but of course the kidnappers were long gone. Andreas was gone. Ruby described them as middle-aged with dark hair and speaking a language she didn't recognise. Not much to go on. I said some dreadful things to her at the time, but of course it wasn't her fault. She was a good girl. Poor Ruby, she has never forgiven herself. We still hear from her, from America. She's married now with her own family. I think she feels guilty that she has children and Andreas is still missing.'

My heart went out to Ruby. Of course, it was dreadful, unbearable for Elke and Hans, but poor Ruby! Once, I had considered being a nanny; the travel and adventure appealed, but not the thought of being responsible for someone else's baby or child. Animals were much more up my street.

'What happened next?' I asked after a long pause.

'What happened next? Well, there were lots of police; lots of questions; lots of crying and then a numbness set in, which became my new reality. There was a spate of babies being kidnapped in Germany. My mother thought it was retribution for the war. I didn't really believe her. Although people seemed to universally hate Germans in the following few decades. Even now, in some countries like Greece, I feel that people only tolerate Germans for their tourist income. So, after a few weeks, the police went off to solve other crimes. Ruby went home to America, and Hans and I were left wondering and searching, everywhere we went.

Time went on, even Hans went back to work, but I was stuck in a time warp. I couldn't work; I couldn't sleep, and I wondered how the rest of the world could just carry on when my baby was missing. I tortured myself imagining what might have happened or be happening to him. Many times, I thought I saw Andreas with another woman and ran after them down the street to see if I could see his hand.

Even years later, I was still searching for my baby. I couldn't imagine him growing up without me. Hans appeared to move on, but my life was standing still. I don't think we understood each other anymore.' She paused again and twirled her gold wedding ring and another big diamond ring around her finger. I noticed how smooth her hands were with discreetly lacquered nails.

'I think men react differently, don't you?'

'Yes. Yes, I think you're right. He coped with his pain by working, but I'm certain, just like me, he never stopped hoping. He never talked to me about Andreas anymore. I never stopped looking. I knew in my heart he was still alive, but sometimes in my darkest times I wished they would find his body. Then we would know and could say goodbye, and maybe life would move on again. I'm sorry dear, I'm going on a bit, I know.' She half smiled at me and took a sip of lemonade.

'No, please don't apologise. Did you have other children?' I asked and then immediately wished I hadn't; the question seemed rather crass.

She raised her eyes to mine and held my gaze for what felt an eternity.

'Hans suggested it once, but you know when you lose a child in those circumstances, when they are taken, and you have no answers, a part of you dies. I felt to have another baby; to give my love to another would be a betrayal of Andreas. I daren't do anything that might distract me from my quest to find the truth.'

I nodded and remembered when I was a child having a cat called Jo-Jo. One day, he disappeared. I searched everywhere for him, but I never saw him again. I felt distraught and never stopped wondering what had happened to him. The passage of time forced me to accept that he must have died, but for Elke, the wondering and pain never stopped. I reached over and took Elke's hand in mine. My experience of losing a cat bore no comparison to her trauma, but in a miniscule way I think I recognised what she must have felt, and no doubt was still feeling. Having no news for over thirty years must have been pure torture.

'I can only try to imagine how awful that must feel,' I said.

'The pain never goes, but it's changed over the years, and it has become like a solid cube of ice in my core.' She touched her stomach momentarily. 'It's such a part of me now, I don't know who I'll be if it thaws. The Elke I was as a young woman all those years ago has long disappeared.'

'It must be a relief to know now,' I said.

'Knowing isn't everything. It closes one chapter of uncertainty and opens another.'

My heart went out to this quietly dignified woman; in one simple sentence, she seemed to also sum up my dilemma. Although, my own problems seemed petty in comparison. I really hoped that whatever came of this visit, she could find something positive to build on.

'I'm a little afraid,' she said. 'About meeting him again. Does that seem strange?'

'Not at all. It's a big step,' I said. Keeping everything crossed it would work out well.

'I've been searching for my baby, but of course, he's a grown man. Herman tells me he's married. There is so much I have missed; he might not want to know us. I don't know…' She couldn't bring herself to verbalise how she would feel if he rejected her.

Chapter 49

I don't know how long we sat together, lost in our own thoughts, before Herman and Hans returned. Hans appeared quite animated and was talking rapidly in German, with Herman interjecting to emphasise a point.

'Now then, let's please speak in English in front of Anna,' Elke said, raising a hand to stop them.

'My dear, I'm so sorry. How rude. Please forgive me.' Hans smiled in my direction. Herman looked quite surprised, but he smiled as well.

'No really, don't worry about me.'

'I think we should leave you to discuss things together. I will come again in the morning.' Herman leant over and kissed his aunt on the cheek and shook Hans by the hand.

'I look forward to seeing you again,' Elke said to me as I rose to leave.

'Yes, it was a pleasure to meet you.' I held out my hand, and she took it in both of hers.

'Thank you so much for listening.'

Herman held the door open for me, and we walked through the lobby of the hotel into the bright sunlight before either of us spoke.

'Do you fancy a drink, and I'll fill you in?'

'Yes, please.' I was eager to know who the other man was and what was going to happen next.

Over too many coffees, followed by ouzo, Herman explained that the other man was a German police officer who dealt with family matters, and that he was liaising with the Greek police. A double check of the DNA sample had confirmed that Christos was Andreas. Someone Herman described as a Greek liaison officer, a sort of social worker I assumed, had already visited Christos' family to discuss the findings with them and to offer support. More importantly, they would find out whether Christos would be prepared to meet Elke and Hans. It never occurred to me until Elke expressed a doubt that Christos might not want to meet his actual parents.

'They'll get back to us in a day or two. In a day or two! I ask you what are they waiting for? My aunt and uncle need to know now.' Herman's indignation was touching and a little amusing.

'I think after thirty years, another day won't matter.'

'That's so British.'

I laughed. 'I think Elke will understand.'

'I expect so,' he said. 'Anyway, do you want to know about your men?'

He continued to explain that the police already knew who the two men were. He said at the time of Andreas's abduction there was a criminal fraternity with networks across mainly Eastern Europe, who would traffic children and drugs to order.

'Stelios's father…'

'Who's Stelios?' I asked.

'Stelios is the man who adopted Christos, and Stelios's father, Dimitri, long since dead, had connections with the group through other acquaintances.'

He explained that Dimitri, concerned by the distress his son and daughter-in-law were going through, made enquiries about finding a baby boy for them to adopt. Dimitri told Stelios about a baby whose young parents had been killed in an accident. There were no other relatives able to take him in, so he would have to go into an orphanage. 'They probably didn't ask too many questions. Whether Dimitri knew the truth about where the baby came from is debatable, but highly likely. I'm certain Stelios did not know the truth'.

Most of the people involved were now either dead or very old, but there were still connections to organised crime, and the two men who came looking for Herman were part of this new faction, mainly based in Bulgaria.

'They didn't take kindly to me shaking the boat.'

'Rocking the boat.' I corrected automatically. Herman shrugged.

'Anyway, the police are after them for bigger things. So, our incident is going into their portfolio of evidence. Unless you want to take it further?' He asked.

'No, as long as they don't come back, and they get stopped from doing whatever it is they do,' I said.

'I don't think we'll hear from them again. Elke and Hans don't want to do anything to disrupt the bigger investigation, but they might one day have to give evidence. It's possible, but very unlikely, that you would be called to give evidence.'

'I'm not sure I'd be able to tell them much.'

'Don't worry, I think they have enough evidence from other sources. Are you sure you are all right? I could kill them myself for hurting you.'

I smiled, touched by Herman's concern. 'I'm fine. Tell me more about Christos, or should we call him Andreas now?'

'I'm not sure. The background to my childhood and growing up was always about Andreas being missing and now he's found. It seems strange,' Herman mused. 'Everywhere we went when I was young, we were always on the alert looking for Andreas. Aunt Elke told me once that if I ever saw a child with a bad hand, I must immediately tell my mother, as it might be Andreas. A boy in my class broke his finger and came to school with his hand bandaged. I ran home as fast as I could and told my mother I thought Frederic must really be Andreas. My mother explained properly about Andreas's hand and what happened to him. For weeks I left early for school to walk the long way, so I didn't have to cross the park.

Then in the summer my friends and I used to play hunt the kidnappers in the park.'

I smiled, and Herman continued. 'It's surprising how many people have missing fingers, for whatever reason, when you look, don't you think?'

I nodded, but in truth couldn't remember seeing anyone with a fused fingers before I saw Christos.

'Hans used to come to stay in the holidays and he, my father and me, used to go fishing, camping and climbing together. Boys' things my mother used to say. Elke was always in the background, quiet and sad. My mother used to spend time with her often. Mother said once that she thought Hans believed Andreas to be dead, but he never said so to Elke. Elke never gave up.'

'It's hard to imagine how they must be feeling now,' I said.

'Yes, elated and scared, I think. Will you come when we go to meet Christos?' Herman asked.

'Me? Well, I don't want to intrude.' I was desperate to go but didn't want to appear too eager. It would be fascinating to see how the meeting went.

'Elke would appreciate your presence, your support, I'm sure, but I'll ask her if you like. I would like you there as well, of course.'

'Yes, ask her, but I would be more than happy to come.'

'Good. Right, we should get back. I'll give you a lift to the old town.' Herman stood up to leave.

We drove along in silence until we reached the steps leading to the old town.

'Thank you, Anna,' he said, reaching for my hand as I prized myself out of his small car, which was full of boxes and supplies. I felt an unexpected frisson of excitement as our eyes met.

'That's OK,' I said, letting go of his hand. 'See you soon.' I shut the door and turned away. No, I couldn't, not Herman. Not anyone. I promised myself I wasn't going to get involved, not for a while, not after Dan, and anyway, Herman wasn't my type. I was tired and emotional from this afternoon, that was all.

I made my way up the cobbled streets and could see Ruth and Alice leaning over the balustrade. I waved, but they couldn't see me in the dark. As I approached, I could see they were holding glasses.

'To us,' I heard Alice say. 'To us,' Ruth replied. I watched them touch glasses and then exchange a look that lingered. I stopped in my tracks. The penny dropped, not just a penny, but a whole sack of coins. Why did I not realise before? Now everything fell into place. Snippets of conversations previously overheard between Ruth and Carrie and between Carrie and Dad came back. For the second time in a few hours, I felt very unobservant.

'Hi you two.' I called and ran up the steps to join them and bathe in their happiness. Neither said anything about what, unbeknown to them, I thought I had witnessed.

Chapter 50

'I've asked Elke, and she would very much like you to come when we go to meet Christos and his family.' Herman said this in passing, as we were clearing up after a busy surgery session.

'That's great, but are you sure?' I asked, feeling flattered and excited.

He smiled at me. 'Of course, she said you were very understanding, and she would like another woman to be with her.'

'When are you going?' I asked. I felt privileged and pleased that Elke should want me, someone she had only just met, to be with her at such a momentous time in her life.

'Can you be at their hotel at three this afternoon?' he looked at his watch. 'That's just over two hours, is that OK?'

'Sure. I'll just pop up the hill and get changed and be there at three.'

I dithered over what to wear, which I knew was irrelevant as I was going to be the last person in the limelight this afternoon, but somehow, I felt I should wear something appropriate for the occasion. Pale blue linen trousers and white top were my eventual choice.

'It's going to be quite something,' said Ruth, who was sitting on my bed watching me try on and discard several outfits. 'I can't imagine how his Greek parents will feel. It must be like a bombshell, or do you think they knew the truth all along?'

'Apparently, they didn't, but I don't know all the details. How do I look?'

'Lovely as ever. Will they need a translator, do you think?'

'Christos' parents? I mean Greek parents. I'm not sure. Elke and Hans speak perfect English, so does Christos, but I'm not sure about the others. I imagine they speak a bit of English. I'm sure Herman will have sorted it all out,' I said, picking up my bag and leaning over to give Ruth a peck on the cheek.

'I can't wait to hear all about it.' She came down the steps with me and waved me off.

I felt nervous as I entered the hotel and hoped it was as Herman said, and not that Elke had somehow been persuaded, against her better judgement, to let me join them.

Elke and Hans were waiting in the comfortable reception when I arrived. Again, the hotel surprised me. The elegant, understated style of the reception appeared light and airy with big arches leading onto a flower-filled terrace. Black and white marble, laid in large circular designs reminiscent of earlier times gave the floor a classic feel. The atmosphere was quiet and calm, not the sort of hotel for groups of boozy Brits, I thought.

'Herman has gone to collect the car,' Hans said, standing to shake my hand.

I sat next to Elke on a cream leather sofa. She touched my arm.

'Thank you for agreeing to come,' she said.

'It's my pleasure. Are you nervous?'

She nodded. 'Very,' she said. Sitting bolt upright on the comfortable furniture as if it were rock, she clasped and unclasped her hands in her lap. She wore a simple dove grey shirtdress and sandals and to anyone else she looked the picture of placid calm. I felt anxious for her and just wanted to hug her. She smiled, as if reading my thoughts, and I felt that deep down she must be a very strong woman.

'Anna, you're here, good. Right, the car is outside.' Herman appeared more nervous and agitated than anyone.

Hans and Herman sat in the front, and Elke and I sat in

the back. We completed our journey in almost complete silence, only broken by the occasional admiring comment when one of the many stunning views appeared round a bend in the road. I couldn't imagine how Elke and Hans, but Elke in particular, must be feeling as we drew closer. She could have become a Miss Haversham, stuck at that desperate moment in time, when her baby went missing, unable to move forward with her life. Somehow, even though the abduction of her baby son had dominated her life for over thirty years, she appeared well adjusted, but I remembered her comment about not knowing who she would be if the ice cube inside her thawed. She was about to find out. I looked at her, feeling scared on her behalf. She caught my glance and reached for my hand; her hand felt cold despite the heat inside the car.

The journey across the island seemed to take longer than normal, but eventually we arrived at the taverna. Herman parked around the back, and we made our way up an outside staircase to an open terrace. No one spoke. The taverna was bustling with clients and we could hear happy chatter and laughter rising to where we crossed the terrace and went up a stone external staircase.

Herman tapped on an open door before stepping across the threshold. We all followed. It took several moments for my eyes to become accustomed to the dark interior after the bright sunshine. We were in a large room, with a big table at one end and a couple of sofas and chairs nearest the door. There were cupboards and shelves around the edge, and two doors at the far end led off to other rooms. A bright rug was on the floor. It was a pleasant, welcoming room, and I caught glimpses of the beach and sea through the shutters. They were half closed. I presumed to keep the heat out, but I felt an urge to push them all open to let the sunlight flood in.

Christos and Maria, his wife, who was holding their young child, were standing in front of the table and Stelios and Katerina were sitting side by side on a sofa. On the other side of the room, to my surprise, was a priest dressed in traditional black robes and black hat, with his grey hair and beard bushing out around his face. It struck me as odd to invite a priest, but I realised that this was an equally momentous and stressful day for them, and they obviously felt the need for spiritual support.

I suddenly felt anxious on behalf of them all. I took a quick look across the room to gauge Elke's reaction, but as usual, she looked calm and serene. My admiration for her soared.

We all moved further into the room, and Stelios and Katerina stood up. Stelios placed a reassuring hand on Katerina's back. The priest didn't move.

Christos smiled broadly and went up to Elke.

'Mutter,' he said in German and hugged her, then turned to Katerina and drew her towards him. 'Mitéra,' he said in Greek, smiling at both women and hugged them close to him. For a moment, all three stood encircled by arms.

Elke took his deformed hand in hers.

'Mein Sohn,' she said, with tears streaming down her face.

I looked at Katerina and saw she was crying as well. Christos looked over the top of the women's heads.

'Vater,' he said, holding out his hand towards Hans.

'Patéras,' he beckoned for Stelios to come closer. Soon all five of them were hugging, with Christos in the middle.

I didn't think I had ever witnessed such a beautiful scene in my life and felt such warmth towards Christos for how he handled it. An enormous lump formed in my throat. Tears welled up and soon flowed over my eyelashes, cascading down my cheeks. I looked at Herman. He was brushing a tear from his cheek and when he noticed me looking, gave a smile of relief.

Christos disentangled himself from his plethora of parents and put his arm around Maria.

'This is my wife Maria, and baby Eleni.' He introduced them to Elke and Hans, and another round of hugs and tears began.

'Meine Enkelin,' said Elke, holding her arms out to Eleni, who obliged by smiling and reaching out for Elke to hold her.

Eventually, with all the hugging over everyone sat down, and Maria disappeared. She returned soon after with a tray full of Greek sweet treats and drinks. The conversation flowed without stopping and I need not have worried about translation. It seemed everyone was happy to converse in English, which was a bonus for me, as it meant I could sit just observing and listening. After a while, I noticed the priest was no longer in the room; he must have slipped out once he realised everything was going well.

Elke and Hans contrasted sharply with Stelios and Katerina. Stelios's thick hair was dark, but grey flecks were visible, and his moustache was already quite grey. He was a stocky man, dressed in dark grey trousers and a white shirt with the neck open and sleeves rolled up. His suntanned face was open with a ready smile. He looked older than Hans and lacked Hans' air of sophistication and wealth.

Katerina was small, quite plump, with a mass of dark curly hair and deep brown eyes. There were laughter lines around her eyes, but her skin was quite pale and unwrinkled. She didn't sunbathe like the many tourists she served in the taverna. She was wearing a deep blue cotton dress and cardigan despite the heat. A gold cross and chain hung around her neck.

Stelios said something in Greek to Christos, who lifted a large book from the bookcase and laid it on the table. Stelios invited Elke and Hans to sit at the table and placed the book in front of them. Katerina stood beside them and the rest of us craned our necks over their shoulders to see. It was a large photograph album, recording Christos' life from when he arrived to live with them as an orphaned baby, or so they genuinely thought.

There were photos of a smiling Christos in a young, delighted Katerina's arms. Photos of Christos as a toddler, a schoolboy, at Christmas, then later as he grew older on his bike and holding a windsurfer on the beach. A picture of him in military uniform, as of course there was still, at the time, conscription in Greece. Then wedding photos, and photos of him as a proud father. It was the record of a happy childhood in a loving family.

Once again, Elke couldn't keep the tears from streaming down her face viewing the photos of significant events, which, by rights, should have been hers to share.

She laid her hand on the album and looked at Katerina. 'Thank you for looking after him,' she said. Katerina, also again in tears, flung her arms around Elke. 'I'm sorry. We would never have taken him. I'm so sorry. Please believe me, we never knew.'

At that point, I wandered out onto the terrace. I needed to distance myself from the emotion before I started sobbing uncontrollably myself. Herman was leaning against the wall.

'I guess everyone is happy,' he said.

'I think you could say that.'

'I wonder what happens next.'

I looked at him. Neither of us had ever thought beyond this moment. 'I suppose they'll all stay in touch. Best to take one step at a time. At least this has been a success.'

'I'm finding all this emotion quite exhausting, aren't you?' he asked.

'I don't think I've ever been so touched by anything before in my life. It is draining, and I'm only an onlooker. How long are Elke and Hans planning to stay?'

'Do you mean here, or on the island? I don't know the answer to either. I can't imagine they will want to go back to Germany too soon.'

As we were talking, Hans came out and stood beside us.

'Thank you, Herman, thank you Anna. This has been a momentous day for Elke and me. I can't quite take it all in after all these years.' He leant on the railing and gazed out to sea, lost in thought for a few minutes.

'I think we should go back to the hotel soon; I think everyone needs some space to absorb the situation. We will come back tomorrow.'

With that, there was a rush of hugs, kisses and goodbyes and promises to meet again in the morning.

Elke and I sat in the back of the car again on the way back, and I couldn't help noticing how different she looked. Or was it just my imagination? No, I was sure she looked different. Her face looked rounder somehow, softer and there was a glow in her eyes that wasn't there before. Her hand felt warm when I squeezed it.

'I imagined this moment so many times, but the reality was indescribably better. I was always afraid he was unhappy, or worse, being abused, but well…' Words seemed to fail her. 'He has been happy and loved all this time.'

She showed no sign of resentment, but I couldn't help thinking of the contrast between Katerina's happy life and Elke's deep misery. Hans turned round and reached for his wife's hand. He looked drained, and I thought they must be desperate for some time alone. Herman dropped me off at the bottom of the hill, and I made my way up to Ruth and Alice, who were waiting to dissect every single detail that I could remember and recount to them.

Chapter 51

The two families continued to meet. Hans hired a car so that he and Elke could be independent.

'Anna! Hi, it's Herman. There's a party today at Christos' taverna. Can you come and bring Ruth and Alice?' Herman was shouting down the phone. I could hear a hubbub of noise behind him.

'Today?' I tried to remember what everyone was doing. Alice would be in the shop, and I wasn't sure about Ruth.

'Anna?'

'Yes, that sounds great. We'd love to. What time?'

'Oh, about three, well, anytime to suit you, it'll go on late, I expect, from what I can gather, and can you ask Lucy and her family as well?'

'I'll give them a ring.'

'Good, see you later,' he said, and was gone.

I put the phone down a bit surprised by the suddenness of it all, but thought the families had been planning a celebration, and now Herman wanted to invite everyone he knew as well. It would be a long, fun night, and I, for one, didn't want to miss out, regardless of what the others were doing.

I phoned Lucy, who was just as excited and said they would all be there. Then I went down to the shop to tell Alice. Ruth was there with her. The shop was busy with customers. Alice appeared to be about to make a substantial sale, and Ruth was discussing one of her paintings in minute detail with a man who sounded quite knowledgeable about her techniques. My news would have to wait until they'd finished. I could tell my agitated loitering was unsettling Alice, so I wandered across to Luke and Jorgy's shop. They were also busy, but I decided I needed a new dress for the party and began looking at their designs.

'Can I help you madam?' Luke whispered in my ear making me jump. He laughed. 'Are you just browsing or looking for something in particular?' He asked.

'I'm looking for a dress for a party.'

'Ooh, lucky you, going to a party; now then, with your tan, you need something light to show it off. How about this?' He pulled out a white silkscreen printed sundress. 'Try it on,' he said, taking it off the hanger and holding against me.

'It's not really me, I mean…'

'Try it on, you'll be surprised,' he said, handing me the hanger.

I was surprised. He was right. It was perfect. The dress had a scooped neckline, and thin, but not stringy shoulder straps. It had shape, but the loose fitting and light material meant it floated around my body as I twirled. Luke was right. It did show off my tan, and it made me feel good.

'Jorgy, what do you think of Anna?' Luke called to him, as Jorgy saw his customer out with a large bag and happy smile.

'Stunning. My compliments to the designer.' Both laughed, and I joined in, already feeling a bit tipsy with anticipation. They wanted to know all about the party. They already knew snippets of Christos' story, and I soon filled them in with the missing details.

'Well, would you believe it?' Luke said. 'It must be a one in a million chance. It should be a wonderful party. You're certain to be the belle of the ball.' he grinned and leant across and planted a kiss on my cheek.

Carrying my purchase, which Luke had wrapped with a bow, I skipped back across the street, to where Ruth was explaining to Alice how she had just sold three seascapes to the man she was talking to when I left.

'You're looking very pleased with yourself,' Alice said, as I walked through the door. I told them about the party and showed them my new dress, which sent them both into a flurry of indecision over what they should wear. The shops closure was never queried, and Alice was about to close when Luke appeared in the doorway and offered to watch the shop while we were away. Like three giggling schoolgirls, we rushed back to Alice's villa and sorted out what she and Ruth could wear.

A few hours later, we climbed out of a taxi next to the taverna, which was, I imagined, the first time in years it had been closed to the public. It was already busy with party guests. Herman spotted our arrival and came to meet us.

'Goodness, who are all these people?' I asked, scanning the taverna, amazed by its transformation. There was a long trestle table at one side on which three or four young girls were piling plates of food and vast bowls of salad. The usual tables had been arranged around the edge, leaving a big space in the middle, where people were mingling. Someone had strung lights all around the edge, and there were large bowls of local flowers and foliage on the tables. Luke was right, it was going to be a splendid party.

'Mostly Stelios and Katerina's family and friends, I think. Come and get a drink.' Herman steered us through the throng to a table where a young man was serving drinks.

'The punch is delicious,' Herman said, topping up his own glass. 'I need to be careful not to have too much.'

'Anna, I'm so pleased to see you.' Elke kissed me. I introduced her to Ruth and Alice and again noticed how different she looked, much younger and more relaxed. The effect of thirty years of not knowing falling away, I thought, and gave her a hug.

'Everyone is being so kind. I couldn't have hoped for more,' she said, but before I could say anything, someone whisked her away for a family photo. I watched with a lump in my throat as Christos posed with an arm around Katerina on one side and Elke on the other. Hans stood next to Katerina, and Stelios linked arms with Elke. It was like a wedding. The photographs with the parents and Christos included ones with Maria and baby Eleni, with Herman and the whole range of Greek relatives.

'Anna, Lucy, you must be in a photo. You are both key to this story.' Herman called us across. I hadn't yet spoken to Lucy or her family, but I was delighted they had already arrived.

I noticed Ingrid across the taverna and waved to her. She was with a tall blonde-haired man, but waited patiently for the photos to be taken before leaving his side to come across to me.

'Ingrid, how lovely to see you!' We hugged like old friends.

'I'm here with Berne,' she said and nodded in the tall man's direction. 'Erich stayed back to look after the animals. Just in case we miss the last ferry, and I think if this is how the party has started, we won't even try to make the ferry. I wanted Berne to meet you. It will do him good to let his hair down.' She grinned, and I was sure I noticed a quick wink.

'Ingrid, you're incorrigible,' I said, as she steered me across the floor to her tall, blonde, surprisingly handsome son.

'Berne, this is Anna. She works with Herman.'

'Hello Anna, nice to meet you,' he said, holding out his hand.

I took his hand and looked at him more closely. He was very good looking in a manicured sort of way, with well-groomed blonde hair and bright blue eyes, which lit up when he smiled. He looked very like Ingrid.

'It must be nice for you to have some time off to relax,' I said, feeling very self-conscious.

'I don't find relaxing easy. I have brought some work to Greece with me, but don't tell my mother,' Berne said in a stage whisper, looking at Ingrid.

'I'm sure she'll find a way of stopping that.'

'I certainly will. Books can be read for pleasure only,' she said.

'Anna.' I looked over to where Ruth was standing, talking to a couple I didn't recognise. She beckoned me over when she saw me look up.

'Sorry, it looks like I'm wanted. I'll catch you both later.' I made my way to Ruth's side to be introduced to another couple of Christos' relatives and help Ruth out with a complicated explanation she was involved in about where we lived in England.

Chapter 52

Later, as everyone mingled and chatted, I went and sat on the wall to take it all in. It was quite a gathering. Hoots of laughter drew my attention to a small group made up of Hans, Stelios, Edward, and a couple of other older men. It was as though they were old friends sharing reminiscences. Seated round another table, I could see Elke, Katerina, Pat, Alice and Ruth, and the conversation was flowing as easily as the wine. Lucy and Maria were sitting on the steps watching Tommy and Eleni play in the sand. Christos, Herman and another man were examining an old car parked outside the taverna with an intensity that, in my experience, only men can have about a car.

'Hi.' Maria slid onto the wall beside me. 'It's a good party, I think,' she said, watching the easy interaction of all the guests. 'It is nice for me not to be working.'

'It's very good,' I agreed. 'It must feel very strange for you all, particularly Christos. Such a shock for him.'

'Yes, but he's very excited meeting everyone.'

'Are his parents OK? I mean Katerina and Stelios, of course?' I asked.

'They are now, but they were confused and frightened at first. Now they are relieved and happy.'

We both smiled as we watched everyone. I thought it was probably the most emotional and happy party I had ever attended.

'How did you and Christos meet?' I asked.

She shrugged. 'We didn't really meet in the way you mean; we just always knew each other. My parents, that's them over there.' She pointed to a couple who were now amusing Eleni with a game. 'They have always been friends with Stelios and Katerina, so Christos and I were friends as well. It was obvious we would marry.'

I found it hard to imagine being brought up in such a tight community and marrying a childhood friend, but to Maria it appeared normal, and she seemed quite content.

'Have you travelled at all?' I asked.

'I have an uncle in Australia. I went there for three months after I left school, but I prefer it here.' she spread her arms to include the beach and sea and rest of the island beyond the taverna.

'I can understand why,' I said, surveying the scene. 'It's so beautiful here.'

'I went to London with my parents when I was younger, and Christos and I went to Switzerland for our honeymoon. I love seeing new places, but I love coming home more,' she said with a smile, and I envied her contentment.

'Do you remember the times when Herman and I, then Lucy and I, came to the taverna?'

She laughed. 'Of course, when Christos got hurt, and I remember you and Herman behaving a bit funny, but tourists are often doing funny things, so I didn't think too much about it.' She shrugged again, the shrug of someone who was used to foreigners behaving oddly and taking it in her stride. 'What were you doing when you were here with Herman? Was it to do with Christos?'

I explained about Herman's suspicion that Christos was his cousin after he noticed his hand and fair hair, and that we needed to obtain something that he'd touched to send away to test for his DNA. She expressed surprised when I told her about Lucy cutting a strand of his hair after the accident.

'I didn't notice, and Christos didn't say that Lucy cut his hair.'

'I don't suppose he realised. It was only a tiny strand, but it was enough to get a match.'

She sat, lost in thought for a moment, watching the scene in front of her.

'I wonder if things will be different now,' she said, and for the first time, I detected a note of anxiety. It would be strange if she wasn't concerned about her world being disrupted.

Eleni came running over to Maria and pulled at her hand for her to go and do something.

'I better go. I'll see you later. Enjoy yourself.' Maria hopped off the wall and followed her daughter.

I sat a while longer. I felt certain Maria and Christos' life would be different now that Elke and Hans were part of it, but hopefully different in a good way. I looked around at the ever-growing crowd and spotted Lucy sitting at a table, in deep conversation with Berne. Lucy was drawing some sort of diagram on a piece of paper and Berne was studying it intently and they both were becoming quite animated. A pang of loneliness swept over me, which seemed ridiculous in amongst such a happy, friendly throng of people.

I jumped off the wall and pulled out a chair at the table with Elke and the others and joined in their conversation.

'I'm trying to persuade Elke that she and Hans should buy a villa here,' said Patricia, as I sat down.

'Yes, wonderful,' said Katerina. 'It would be wonderful to have you near,' she said again, grasping Elke's hand to ensure she understood she was being genuine.

I was overjoyed for Elke; this must feel like a dream come true. I wouldn't have been surprised if Katerina and Stelios resented this invasion into their family, but Katerina wasn't showing signs of anything other than delight. Perhaps, deep down, she knew that Christos' adoption was unorthodox, to say the least, and now everything was out in the open she could finally relax. Who knew? I was thinking there was no such thing as a normal family.

'Well, maybe,' said Elke. 'I will talk to Hans later.' She

looked across to where Christos, now back from examining the car, was looking at an old photo album with Hans. The look on her face was one of pure love. She glowed with happiness, and everyone around her was drawn into her golden aura for a moment.

We all tucked into mounds of food, which smelt delicious and tasted even better. The punch, Greek wine, ouzo and Retsina, flowed freely, well into the warm evening. A couple of men started playing guitars and singing. Other people started clapping and Christos, Stelios, and several of the other Greek men, arms across each other's shoulders, started dancing. Before long, Hans, Herman and Edward were joining the line, and the clapping and singing reached a crescendo.

Once the men sat down, the non-Greeks gasping for breath, it was the turn of the women. Maria hauled Lucy and me onto the floor, along with Alice and Ruth. Katerina and Pat refused, on the grounds of needing to look after the grandchildren, but it soon became clear, as novices, we needed Katerina's expertise to guide us, so Hans and Edward scooped up the children. We danced slowly at first, dipping and twirling, then it became quite frenetic and ended with Alice in a heap on the floor to cheers and claps.

Herman picked up a guitar and started singing. He stopped. 'Anna, come and sing.'

Luckily, the punch and wine made me lose my inhibitions, and I was up beside him in a moment. We sang a couple of songs. Neither of us could remember all the words but no one cared, and we received rapturous applause. I felt ecstatic. As we sang, I could see Ruth and Alice, arms draped around each other's shoulders, sitting on the wall; Elke and Hans were dancing close together, looking into each other's eyes and smiling; Lucy was being twirled around by Berne, who now seemed quite able to relax and enjoy himself. I noticed Ingrid watching with a wide smile on her face.

All too soon, although very late, the party wound down

and taxis arrived to ferry people back home. Herman walked to the car with me,

'You look very beautiful tonight, Anna.'

'Thank you, Herman,' I said, feeling an involuntary thrill of pleasure. 'It's been a special day, a perfect party.'

'Goodnight, sleep well.' He closed the car door and waved us off.

Chapter 53

Ruth, Alice, and I were in high spirits all the way home and finished the night with a toast of Retsina on Alice's terrace. The day was dawning as I made my way to my own little villa. Golden rays punctuated the dark blue and pink sky. It was beautiful, and I wanted to rush back to Ruth to persuade her to start painting right away, but my need to lie down was too great, so I just drank in the scene before falling into bed. I slept soundly until the sounds of the day in full swing and sunshine streaming through the window, whose shutters I had forgotten to close, woke me. I got up feeling very heady and slightly sick. I drank a big glass of water, put on my biggest pair of sunglasses, and made my way down to Alice's terrace. Alice and Ruth were already there, also looking the worse for wear.

'Coffee?' Offered Alice as soon as I stepped onto the terrace.

'Please.' I flopped into a comfy chair. The coffee tasted as good as it smelt, and I realised I felt hungry. As if a mind reader, Ruth handed me a plate of honey buns, and I devoured one.

'I really should go and open up,' said Alice, getting to her feet and stretching her arms above her head.

'I'll come and help you,' I said, although I would much rather have stayed drinking coffee.

'Are you sure?'

I nodded. It was the least I could do, especially if Alice was feeling as weary as me.

Ruth looked up and said she would join us later, but as we left the terrace she was already curled up on the large sofa, looking as though she would be asleep within minutes.

For once the town was quiet, and I sat on the front step of the street dozing.

'So how was the party?' Jorgy bounded across the narrow street.

His bright voice sounded too loud, and I gave an involuntary groan then smiled weakly at him.

'I'll take that as it was very good.'

'It was excellent,' I replied.

'And how was the dress? Did it catch you a man?'

I laughed and shook my head, but an involuntary image of Herman's face popped into my mind. I shook my head again, partly to shake away the image and Jorgy took that as a no.

'Well, they must all be blind. You looked amazing.'

'I'm not looking for a man at the moment,' I said. 'I did get compliments about the dress, though.'

He nodded, satisfied.

The day passed by in a hangover blur, and all three of us went to bed early that night. I think I slept more soundly and peacefully than I could ever remember, and the next day, feeling back to normal, I went to work in the surgery with Herman.

We were unusually busy and there was little time to exchange views on how well the party had gone, which disappointed me. Herman told me that Christos and Maria were going to adopt one puppy, and he thought he had found families for two others. He wondered whether to keep Mia and the other puppy himself, if he couldn't find suitable homes for them. I would have loved one, but my situation was still uncertain, so I said nothing.

Herman rushed off to meet Hans at the end of surgery, leaving no time to chat. Feeling a little deflated, I made my way back to the old town later in the morning. To my delight, Lucy and her parents were in Alice's shop when I reached it.

Pat and Alice were busy in Alice's little workshop at the back of the shop, finalising a design for a necklace that Edward was going to buy for her to celebrate a wedding anniversary. Edward, himself, was discussing art with Ruth and showed great enthusiasm about the few pieces she was displaying in the shop. Lucy was trying hard to stop Tommy from grabbing the jewellery, which swung and glittered like baubles on the displays.

'Shall we go and get a coffee?' I suggested to Lucy.

'Good idea. I'll just let them know where we're going.' She went through to the back and after a few minutes, came back.

'Alice suggests going to Dimitri's and they'll all come and meet us for something to eat when they're ready.'

We walked up the steep cobbled steps, swinging Tommy between us, making him squeal with laughter.

'More, more,' he shouted whenever we stopped.

At the taverna, we found a large table in the shade of the big old olive tree and explained that we were waiting for several others to join us. Lucy pulled a book and toy car out of her bag and Tommy sat happily on the floor playing with them.

'Did you enjoy the party?' I asked, dying to know what she thought of Berne.

'It was the most fun I've had in months,' she said, and I was sure there was a slight pinkness to her cheeks that wasn't there before.

'And?' I said.

'And what?' She laughed. 'Oh, you mean Berne?'

I nodded.

'Well, he's interested in archaeology. Apparently, it was a subsidiary subject of his at university.'

'And?' I asked, grinning, as she blushed even more.

'He is rather good-looking and very charming, if a bit on the serious side. He's going to come across again before I go off to Santorini.'

'That's great, I'm pleased,' I said, but wondered whether

deep down I was really a bit jealous, not of Berne, I was sure he wasn't my type, but of having someone.

'Have you spoken to your parents yet about going to Santorini?' I asked, sipping my dark Greek coffee.

'Yes, they're pleased, but I think they're more pleased about me having a job and a plan for when I get back home.'

'When do you think you'll be going?' I asked.

'Next week, with any luck. I can get a ferry and then fly direct to Santorini. Janet sounded so pleased when I phoned to say I would go. I can't wait. It is such an interesting site. I know you haven't seen it, but do you know about it?'

I shook my head. 'No, not in any detail. Tell me about it.'

'It's a complete Minoan town that was buried by a volcanic eruption in 1450. The eruption affected Crete as well.'

I nodded. I had visited Crete as a student and knew about the destruction there, but I spent most of my holiday lazing on the beach.

'The major excavations happened in the sixties, but a roof covering the site collapsed a few years ago, so it's been closed to the public. It's nearly ready to reopen, but there's still some excavation work going on. It's a bit like Pompeii, only on a much smaller scale. I'm not sure what I'll be involved in, but I can't wait.' Lucy's enthusiasm was infectious.

'It sounds amazing. I'd love to see something like that,' I said. 'Maybe I can fit in a trip before I go home.'

'Are you planning to go back soon?' Lucy asked.

'I've got no plans as yet, but I guess I'll have to go back sometime.'

She nodded. 'This can be a hard place to leave.'

We carried on chatting until the others joined us. Everyone was in good spirits, particularly Ruth and Alice, who, it seemed, had both achieved good business deals with Pat and Edward. When our meal ended it was almost time for Alice to reopen her shop, and Tommy was beginning to get restless. We all made our way back down the street, saying our goodbyes at the shop and promising to meet again soon.

'I can't wait to hear about your trip,' I said to Lucy as we parted.

'I can't wait to tell you about it. I'll only be away a few days, so I'll give you a ring when I'm back.' She hurried after her parents, and a now sleeping Tommy in Edward's arms.

Chapter 54

It was a balmy evening, and Ruth was sitting on the terrace painting the view in front of her. She felt she would never tire of the beautiful scene. This evening dark clouds were gathering to the south, but the sun was still bright, creating some lovely contrasts of light and shade, and colour in the sky and over the sea. There was a gentle breeze, a blessing from the sultry heat of the day, and small waves were forming on the otherwise calm sea. She wondered if a storm was heading their way, half hoping it was so she could relish in the drama of it.

Ruth looked up and studied the sky, before mixing yet another shade of blue to dab on her canvas. She created a large range of hues, from almost navy blue through turquoise to deep green. The light here was an artist's dream, and the small number of artists working on the island surprised her. It was to her advantage that there weren't many. She had sold far more paintings here than she would in the equivalent time at home.

'Wow, that's lovely.' Alice peered over Ruth's shoulder.

'Thanks. I didn't hear you come in. Have you been busy?'

'Not bad, but lots of "just lookers" today. Looks like you've had a good day.'

'It's just so inspiring. I love it here.' Ruth put down her brush and turned to face Alice. 'What is it?' she asked, noticing a fleeting pained look cross Alice's face.

'Why don't you stay?' She looked questioningly at Ruth,

and Ruth realised she wasn't just talking about extending a holiday.

'D'you mean...' Ruth couldn't say the words in case she was wrong, but her stomach did a little flip, and now the thought had entered her head, she couldn't bear to think she had got the wrong end of the stick.

Alice reddened, turned and looked out to sea. 'I mean, I was wondering...'

Ruth pushed her chair back and went to stand behind Alice. She took the risk and slid her arms round Alice's waist and rested her head on her shoulder. 'I'm not certain what you're asking, but Alice, I can't think of anywhere or anyone I'd rather be with.'

'Oh, I am, I am asking that. Stay with me, Ruth. I can't bear the thought of losing you, now we've found each other again.' Alice turned round and stared into Ruth's eyes. 'What if I get ill, though? After Anna found out all that information, I realised I'm not clear yet. It could start anytime. I don't want you to...' Ruth raised her hand and put a finger against Alice's lips.

'Shh, don't say anymore. I love you, Alice. It doesn't matter. I would look after you if you became ill.'

'Oh, Ruth.' A tear trickled down Alice's cheek and Ruth wiped it away before gently kissing her.

After a few moments, they parted and looked at each other with such relief and love that they both started laughing. Ruth packed away her paints while Alice poured them both an ouzo. They sat on the terrace watching the dark clouds fade away into the distance, neither saying much, just overwhelmed by their own feelings of happiness and contentment.

'I've just remembered,' Alice said after a while. 'You know that little shop on the top square?'

Ruth nodded. She thought she knew the one Alice meant, rather out of keeping with the rest of the shops because it sold cheap souvenirs; but then she supposed there was a market for everything.

'Well, I was chatting to the couple who own it when I popped out this afternoon; nice, older Greek couple. They don't want to keep the shop going after this summer. It's not making much profit and they're ready to retire.' Alice swivelled to look at Ruth. 'It would make a great place for you to display and sell your art.'

Ruth sat up and paid more attention. 'Are they selling it?'

'Renting, I think, I'm not sure. How about we go out for something to eat and look at it on the way? What do you think?'

'Yes, it sounds interesting. Worth a look, at least.'

'You don't sound too sure.'

'I don't want to get my hopes up, but you are right, a place to sell my art would be a good idea. Let's see.'

A short time later, they were in the square, and Alice led the way into the little shop. It felt cluttered and dark, but Ruth could see the potential. The shop had plenty of wall space, and they could organise better lighting. She looked around while Alice explained to the owner, who looked older than Ruth expected, that they might be interested in the shop.

'Let me call my wife,' the old man put his hands round his mouth and shouted. An equally elderly lady joined them. The two of them engaged in a rapid conversation in Greek, none of which Ruth could understand, and when she glanced at Alice it was obvious she was only picking up a few words.

'I think they're interested,' Alice whispered.

The more Ruth looked around the shop, the more she wanted it.

'We don't want to sell,' the old man said eventually, speaking in English. 'But we would be happy to rent it to your friend.'

His wife nodded. 'Alice looks after her shop, so we would trust her and any friend of hers,' she said, smiling at Ruth.

'How much would the rent be?'

The couple looked at each other, had another quick conflab in Greek, then named a very reasonable figure.

'Per month?' Alice clarified.

'Yes, yes, we think that is fair. Do you think it's fair?' he looked anxiously from Ruth to Alice.

'Very fair, I think so, don't you, Ruth?' Alice was beaming.

Ruth agreed and felt in quite a daze. Her life seemed to have taken a completely new direction in a matter of hours. The old couple showed them around, squeezing past piles of boxes, that they assured Ruth they would clear away. As well as the actual shop where Ruth could display her paintings, there was a storeroom and a small kitchen and toilet. The real bonus was a tiny courtyard with a view looking across the island to the coast on the other side.

'It's perfect. I'd love to rent it. Thank you.'

'I'll never get you away from here.' Alice squeezed Ruth's arm.

The old couple said they must speak to their son who would know about contracts and everything that needed to be done to set up an agreement, but they didn't anticipate any problems. They agreed Ruth could decorate, add lighting, and change whatever was required to suit her needs, but stressed that the actual building could not be altered.

Ruth and Alice left to find a taverna to eat and talk. Ruth had so many ideas for the shop, and the pair of them got quite tipsy, toasting their good luck and their future. They agreed to return to England together in the winter, to sort out Ruth's flat. She thought she would rent it out before they returned to the island. There was so much to think about. They both felt intoxicated at the thought of their future lives together.

Chapter 55

'Anna, would you like to eat together tonight?' Herman said, as he locked the door after a relatively quiet session at the surgery.

'I'd love to,' I said, and meant it.

'Good. I'll come up at about eight, then. We can find a quiet taverna.'

I wasn't sure if he looked pleased or relieved, as he plonked his Panama on his head and with a grin and a wave set off towards the harbour. I watched him go. He wasn't traditionally good looking, but there was something attractive about him, and to my annoyance, although only mild annoyance, there were butterflies in my stomach thinking about the evening ahead.

After I washed my hair, I tied it up, then decided it looked better left loose, so just brushed it until it shone. I pulled several outfits out of the cupboard and agonised over what to wear. That evening, I took more care dressing than any other time since arriving in Greece, apart from for the party. I rejected a couple of outfits and plumped for a shortish white skirt that looked good with suntanned legs, and a green sleeveless top. Herman was punctual, as I expected, and we made our way up towards the castle to one of the tiny tavernas tucked into a small courtyard, surrounded with bougainvillea and strung with fairy lights. I had passed it before but not eaten in there. It was the perfect choice as a cool breeze was blowing, and the sheltered courtyard felt warm. People already occupied most of the tables, but the waiter showed us to a table in the corner, where we could see everything going on in the taverna and along the street, but it still felt private.

We spoke little until after we had chosen our food and there were two full glasses of wine in front of us, then we talked and talked. We talked about everything and nothing. I studied Herman, seeing him properly the first time, and was struck by his vivid blue eyes, very like his aunt's, and although his hair was fair with a reddish tint, his skin wasn't as pale as I expected, but glowed with a light suntan. He wore his hair loose, like it had been the day I visited his apartment, with the strand of Christo's hair; how long ago that felt.

At last, we exchanged thoughts about the party and all the momentous events that led up to it. Apparently, with Stelios and Katerina's blessing, Elke and Hans were going to buy a villa on the island so that they could spend more time together. It meant they could at least see their grandchildren grow up and share their childhood moments, a tiny compensation for those lost when Andreas went missing.

'Do they find it strange calling him Christos?' I asked.

'I asked them that, and they said it wasn't. To them, Andreas is still a baby, so Christos doesn't fit with their memories, but I don't think they care what he is called now.'

I thought I could understand what they meant.

'Do they recognise anything in him?'

'His hand, of course, and they think there is a family likeness. Several years ago, they asked an artist to draw a picture of what he might look like as an adult, but that picture bore little resemblance to Christos. Elke said they just know he is their son. She said there was a connection that only a mother would know.'

'It must be very strange for all of them,' I said.

'Yes, I think it is most strange for Christos, who now finds himself to be German. He told me Maria, and him and the baby are going to visit Elke and Hans in Berlin this winter.'

'That will be strange for him. I wonder how he really feels about it all,' I mused.

'Oh, by the way, before I forget, Elke would like to see you again before they go back home.'

'Of course, I'd love to see her again. She is such a lovely, dignified lady.'

Herman nodded and looked pleased.

'When are they leaving? Is it soon?' It felt as though everything was changing again, with Lucy going to Santorini and now Elke and Hans returning to Germany, all with plans, and I felt stuck. I had no idea what my future held.

'I expect it will be later this week, but they plan to come back again soon.'

Herman talked about growing up in Germany and how he always loved animals, but was never allowed more than a goldfish as a child. His father wanted him to be a doctor, but Herman only ever wanted to be a vet and, with a lot of effort, persuaded his father that being a vet was an equally prestigious profession.

'Are your parents still alive?' I asked.

'Yes both,' he said. 'They aren't that old yet, only in their late sixties.'

'No, of course,' I said, thinking how lucky he was. I had had three parents and lost them all. They would also still be quite young if they were alive.

'They would like to visit here with Elke and Hans sometime.'

Herman continued talking about his life in Germany. Girlfriends had come and gone but apparently no one was serious. It was while on an island-hopping holiday around Greece, with a previous girlfriend, that he decided he wanted to set up a practice here. The girlfriend, now just a friend, ended up going home on her own.

'My parents weren't over impressed with my decision and have never visited. So, when they do come, I'll have to impress them.' Again, he laughed, and I noticed how his whole face lit up when he smiled or laughed.

'I'm sure they'll be impressed; you've got a great practice here.'

'You don't know my parents,' he said. 'They are very hard to please.'

Our food that evening was delicious. We both chose dolmades to start, followed by fresh grilled fish cooked with aubergine, and a Greek salad. As we ate and drank more wine, quite a lot more wine, I told Herman how I came to be on the island with Ruth and Alice. I told him about my parents and Deborah, about Huntington's disease, and about how Carrie, my adoptive mother, abused me.

He listened, silent and attentive.

'She must have been a very unhappy woman, and it sounds like she died sad, bitter and unfulfilled.'

I looked at Herman, surprised that he was taking such a compassionate view of Carrie.

'She hated me.'

'She hated what you symbolised. Finding out her husband had a child, and that she was now expected to care for a it, must have been a nightmare for her. Few people could take on that without it having some adverse psychological effect. The way she treated you was wrong and cruel, but it wasn't you as a person she hated, it was what you constantly reminded her of.'

I wasn't sure he was right, although what he said made sense. I swallowed to conceal a sob, and guilt. A glimmer of sympathy for Carrie pushed its way into my mind but I soon quashed it.

'A friend of mine at university. His father had Huntington's Disease,' he said. 'My friend was worried that he might also have it, so he was tested while we were at university.'

'What was the result?'

'He was positive. After he found out he changed; he became withdrawn and started drinking. Drinking more than most students, that is, and eventually dropped out of university, he saw no point in carrying on.'

I listened quietly, trying to understand his friend's rationale.

'Are you still in touch?' I asked, hoping there was a positive ending to this story.

'No. I saw him a few times after he dropped out, but he had become difficult, angry at the world and still drinking too much. I hope he came to terms with it and made something of his life. Last time I was in Germany I tried to contact him, but I think he must have moved away.'

I said nothing for a few moments, absorbing what he had told me. 'It is a dilemma. Alice doesn't want to be tested; she says she prefers not to know. I thought I wanted to know. That was why I went back to England.'

'And did you find out?' he asked.

'They wouldn't do the test; the counsellor said I needed to think it through a bit more. Anyway, I think I've decided not to be tested.' The words came out of my mouth spontaneously; I surprised myself when I said them, as I hadn't made that decision before I spoke, but somehow now they sounded right. 'I think it's right for me; I'm just going to live my life for now and not worry about the future. At least for the time being.'

Herman sat, not speaking, just looking at me, for a few moments.

'I would very much like to live-for-now with you. Together as a couple, if you would like that?' he said, reaching across and tucking a strand of hair behind my ear.

It felt like a bolt of lightning had passed through me at his touch, and in that moment I knew that being with Herman was what I wanted, more than anything.

Chapter 56

We looked into each other's eyes. I could barely breathe but I could see my future alongside Herman as the most natural and perfect outcome for the rest of my life. A small black cloud momentarily blocked the surge of radiance that I felt. I had to tell him the truth.

'I'd like that very much, but first can I tell you something else?'

'Of course,' he smiled and took a sip of wine before giving me his undivided attention.

'I've told no one this before, not even Ruth, especially not Ruth. I decided to just try to bury it.'

'OK, go on.'

'You might change your mind about me when you hear what I've got to say.'

He inclined his head and squeezed my hand. I took my hand away. I didn't want to feel him snatch his hand away because of what he was about to hear.

'Well, that day, the day I saw my adoptive mother in the hospice.' I paused, not sure whether I should, or wanted to go on. Herman nodded in encouragement but remained silent.

'I killed her.' I didn't look at him. 'I tampered with her syringe driver.' I couldn't bring myself to say more.

He nodded, his eyes studying my face. 'How did you tamper with it?' His voice was soft and calm. Despite that, I couldn't raise my eyes to meet his.

'I pushed the button to let too much of the drug go

through.' My voice cracked and I could feel my cheeks burning and my heart thumping. This could be the end of a beautiful future even before it began.

'I doubt that killed her; besides, it would have been a mercy killing I think.'

'No, it wouldn't. I wanted to kill her. There would have been nothing merciful about it. I was so angry, so full of hate for her. Can you believe I hated someone on their deathbed?'

'She didn't deserve your love, and anyway, I think those machines are tamper-proof.' He reached across the table, but I didn't respond.

I looked at him at last. 'What are you going to do?'

'Do? I'm going to love you and protect you. You are a kind, caring woman, Anna, not a dangerous murderer. She was dying. Even if your actions hastened her end, which I think was unlikely, it would have only been by minutes. I'm a vet, remember, we put creatures out of their misery all the time.'

'I felt and still feel so confused. No one knows about this. I couldn't tell anyone before.'

He reached again for my hand and this time I lifted mine. He squeezed my fingers, leant across the table and gently kissed me on the lips.

'I love you, Anna. I want you always to be able to tell me anything.'

I nodded, closed my eyes momentarily, and knew I should tell him more. The blue flash of my scarf, pushed into Carrie's' mouth, rushed to the forefront of my mind. I forced it away, and a door slammed shut in my brain, never to be reopened. Only I would ever know what really went on in that room.

Herman was studying me. I knew I didn't deserve him, and I made a silent vow that I would try never to keep secrets from him again. A lump rose in my throat and as I swallowed, a tear spilled over my lashes and trickled down my cheek.

I smiled at him across the table. 'I love you, Herman,' I

said, and looked into his eyes, and realised that for the first time in my life, I really meant it.

'I love you, Anna, and just think if things had been different...' I realised he meant if Carrie hadn't told me about dad, and she hadn't died. 'You would never have come to Greece. I can't imagine what life would be like without you now.'

He leant across the table again and gently wiped my tears away before pulling me towards him and we kissed. When we parted, I felt quite giddy and took a big swig of wine to steady my emotions.

Ruth and Alice were walking arm in arm down the cobbled street, lost in their own personal glow of happiness. They were on their way down from the ruins of the castle wall, where the sunset had once again captivated them.

'Let's tell Anna our decision,' said Ruth, giggling like a love-struck teenager and squeezing Alice's arm.

'She's eating with Herman somewhere tonight. I'm sure they won't mind if we join them.'

'There they are.' Ruth pointed across the street to the small taverna and was about to cross over to join them.

'Wait.' Alice held Ruth back. 'I think they might not want to be disturbed.'

They both looked across and saw Herman lean across the table and kiss Anna.

'Oh, how lovely.' Ruth looked over and a smile spread across her face. 'If they... oh, that would be just perfect.'

'I think that when everything's considered, this has actually been a very good summer for us all, don't you?' Alice said and gently pulled Ruth away. They carried on down the street before Anna and Herman spotted them.

Chapter 57

The next morning, Ruth walked up to my villa and asked if I fancied a swim. It was one of those delightful Greek mornings where small puffy clouds, like cotton wool balls, dotted a clear blue sky. There was a gentle breeze, and I could think of nothing nicer than an early swim. Herman had stayed the night, but he was already up and on his way down to the surgery.

'That sounds perfect,' I said. 'Give me a minute to put my costume on and grab a towel.' I smiled at Ruth and was struck by how different she looked. Nothing specific, just a glow of contentment radiated from her.

We walked and scrambled down the path, using Luke's rope to swing the last few feet onto the already warm sand. No one else was in sight. Tourists rarely found 'our' little bay, and we felt quite possessive about it.

'Beat you to the rock.' Ruth had dropped her towel and was already running towards the water.

'Hey, that's not fair. You've got a head start.' I laughed and ran after her.

We soon reached the rock, which wasn't too far out, at about the same time, and hauled ourselves up, resting like two seals basking in the sun.

'You're looking very pleased with yourself today,' I said, once I had caught my breath.

Ruth smiled. No, she beamed at me. 'I've got something to tell you.'

I could guess what it was, but said nothing and pasted a quizzical look on my face.

'Oh yes, looks like it must be good news.'

She pulled up her legs and wrapped her arms around her knees. 'Oh, it is,' she said, sounding like an excited schoolgirl. 'It is wonderful news.'

'Come on then, don't keep me in suspense.'

'I'm going to stay here. Alice and I are going to live together. We've fallen in love. I can hardly believe it at my age.' She turned to look at me and, for the first time, a shadow of doubt flashed across her face. 'What do you think? Are you shocked? Do you think I'm a silly old fool?'

'Come here,' I said, and pulled her into my arms. Nearly tipping the pair of us back into the sea. 'I think it's wonderful. I'm so happy for you both. My two favourite aunts together!'

Ruth's delight was palpable.

'I've got some news as well,' I said, bursting to tell her. 'I'm staying here too, to be with Herman.'

'Oh, darling, I'm so happy for you. Alice and I saw you both in the taverna last night. We didn't want to disturb you. You both looked so serious. I thought there might be a problem, but it seems we need a double celebration.' She turned a delighted smile in my direction. 'Anna, are you OK?' Ruth looked at me and I realised tears were running down my cheeks. She put an arm around my shoulders. 'What is it? Don't feel pressurised into doing something that doesn't feel right. I'm sure Herman would understand.'

'It's not Herman. Everything's fine and I can't think of anything else I would rather do than stay with him. It's something else. I told him something last night, and he was so understanding.'

Herman had been understanding, and at the time I felt flooded with relief, but now all my bottled-up guilt and fear were subsuming my happiness.

'Was it about Huntington's?'

'No. Well, yes, I told him about that, but he was fine about it. It was something else.'

'Do you want to tell me?'

I turned to look at Ruth. How could I tell her I tried to kill her sister? I still didn't know if my actions that day killed her or not. Herman thought not, but how could he know? Ruth smiled encouragingly.

'You'll hate me if I tell you,' I said.

'I could never hate you, Anna. No matter what you might have done. I promise you.'

'I killed mother. Carrie, I mean.' I spoke in a voice barely above a whisper, half hoping she wouldn't hear my appalling words.

'No. You didn't,' she said, and reached for my hand. 'You didn't. I know you didn't.'

'But, how? I did something terrible. I was so angry with her. Angry with a dying woman, that's terrible on its own, but I interfered with her pump and stuffed...' I couldn't carry on. I started sobbing so hard I almost fell back into the water, and I wasn't sure I would have bothered to swim.

'Listen to me.' Ruth put her hands around my face and turned me to look at her. 'I know exactly what happened. Carrie told me.'

'What! I don't understand. I thought she never revived after I left?'

Ruth dropped her hands from my face and took hold of my hands instead. 'She did for a few moments. It was just me and her, before Rachel came back. I think Carrie knew exactly what she was doing. She wanted to provoke you.'

'But I...'

Ruth squeezed my hands, and I stopped speaking.

'First,' she said. 'The pump was turned off. Carrie asked the nurse to disconnect it before you arrived. She told her she wanted to be lucid to say her goodbyes.'

I was about to speak again, but just opened and shut my mouth. I didn't know what to say. I didn't know what to think.

'I think Carrie wanted you to be angry with her, to punish her for all the hurt she caused you. I'm not saying what you did was right, but in a way, it was understandable. She felt she deserved your anger and, in a way, your hatred. I've been furious with her myself over the years, over the way she's treated you compared to Rachel.'

We sat, with the gentle lapping of the sea against the rocks, the only sound. I didn't know what to think. Did it change anything?

'But I wanted to kill her. Isn't it the intent that counts? I think she laughed when I left the room. I thought she was going to tell someone. To report me.'

'Her parting gift to you, perhaps? She knew you would be wracked with guilt.'

'Was she that calculating?'

'I don't like to think she was, but finding out about you, when you were a baby and feeling she had to adopt you, warped her mind towards you.'

I shivered, although I wasn't cold.

'I don't know what to do,' I said. I felt confused. I knew whatever her motives towards me in those last few moments, I had wanted to kill her. I thought I had. Ruth turned my head towards her again and peered into my eyes, as though trying to read my mind.

'Carrie died naturally. Nothing you did changed that. That last confrontation with you seemed, in some strange way, to satisfy her. It's almost as though she felt vindicated. What you need to do now is live your life. You have a wonderful future with Herman. From what you've said, he understands. No one else needs to know.'

'But I still feel so guilty.'

'That, my darling Anna, is something only you can come to terms with.' We sat in silence for what felt a long time but was little more than a minute or two. 'Now race you back to the beach. We have a double celebration to organise.'

I watched as Ruth jumped off the rock and swam towards

the beach. Feeling unable to move, I stared into the crystal blue water until I felt dizzy. Did the information she had just told me make any difference? I wasn't to know the pump was turned off when I pressed the button. Carrie had told Ruth, but not, it seems, to get me into trouble. She wanted to relieve her own conscience by provoking me into doing something she knew I would regret. Why didn't Ruth tell me? Why didn't she quiz me about it at the time? I felt even more confused. In one way, none of it made sense, but in another, it made perfect sense, and Carrie had had the last laugh.

Ruth was now sitting on the beach, drinking from a water bottle. I slid into the water and swam towards the beach.

'Why didn't you say something at the time?' I said as soon as I reached her.

'Because I didn't know what to say and I didn't want to upset you, but mainly because Carrie asked me not to speak about it. I even wondered if she'd made it all up. If I'd realised you were carrying around so much guilt, I would have spoken about it before. Nothing you did hastened her death by a second. I want you to believe me.' She looked at me with such an expression of caring and kindness, I almost cried.

A tiny glow of relief warmed my stomach, but I knew nothing would ever change the fact that my actions were wrong.

'Now, promise me you will put this away into the past. Making yourself feel wretched won't change anything. The future is calling us both, and it's thanks to Carrie, finally, telling you about your mother that we're both here.'

'Thank you, Ruth, for everything. I owe all this to you.'

'Oh, stop it.' She gave me a playful shove. 'Come on now, we've both got new, exciting lives to lead.'

I laughed and scrambled to my feet. She was right. I replaced my hatred for Carrie with sympathy for someone whose life had been so bitter. There would always be a feeling of guilt over my actions, but I was going to shut that away in a dark recess of my mind, never to surface again. Ruth was right. No one else need ever know. My life and future were here with Herman.

Printed in Dunstable, United Kingdom